First published in Great Britain in 2008 by Comma Press
www.commapress.co.uk

First published in Amsterdam as *Amuse-Gueule* by Nijgh & Van Ditmar, 2001.

A CIP catalogue record of this book is available from the British Library.

ISBN   1905583176
ISBN-13   978 1905583171

With the support of the Culture Programme (2007-2013) of the European Union.

Education and Culture DG

Culture Programme

Culture

This project has been funded with support from the European Commission.
This publication reflects the views only of the author, and the Commission
cannot be held responsible for any use which may be made of the information
contained therein.

The publisher gratefully acknowledges assistance from the Arts Council England
North West.
Set in Bembo 11/13 by David Eckersall
Printed and bound in England by SRP Ltd, Exeter

AMUSE-BOUCHE

by
Arnon Grunberg

Translated by
Lisa Friedman and Ron de Klerk

'I have never described myself. I have only betrayed myself.'
– Max Frisch, *Montauk*

Contents

Miele's Mouth

My first contact with the actor couple Adrian and Patricia Miele was in the late summer of 1994. Adrian Miele called me one hot Sunday afternoon. After dropping his name he paused. My God, I thought, I have Adrian Miele on the phone.

During the months after my first book came out, all kinds of people approached me. But there wasn't anyone of Adrian Miele's stature among them.

Dear Mr Grunenberg,

On behalf of the television programme Forum, *I would like to invite you to appear on the programme of 19 September.* Forum *critically examines current events and our subject for September is the 50th anniversary of the Battle of Arnhem.*

Would it be convenient for one of our editors to visit your mother beforehand? We would like to discuss some general questions such as: What was your mother doing during the Battle of Arnhem?

We are looking forward to having your mother and yourself on the programme with us.

We hope to receive your affirmative response.

Sincerely, and on behalf of the programme presenter, Geert Stuif, as well, Marie-Louise Kistemaker

Dear Miss Kistemaker,

Many thanks for your invitation to appear on your television programme Forum.

Unfortunately, neither my mother nor I have anything useful to say about the Battle of Arnhem.

I regret that I cannot provide you with a more positive reply.
Best regards,
Arnon Grunberg

'Hello,' I said, playing for time. 'The connection isn't very good. Are you there?' That week's mail was staring at me from my desk.

Dear Mr Grunberg,

More than fifteen years ago, I attended the Vossius Gymnasium, just like yourself. I also grew up in Amsterdam South. I would very much enjoy exchanging experiences with you.

I can offer you anything except my body.

Please call me in the evenings after 8pm.
Fransje 't Hart
P.S. Your book is my bible.

Dear Miss 't Hart,

I am taking the liberty of writing to you rather than calling you after 8pm. You offer me everything except your body.

I'm afraid at this time I can accept neither.

Thank you very much for your kind letter.
Best regards,
Arnon Grunberg.

When Adrian Miele apparently thought the silence had lasted long enough he said, 'I would like to invite you over to our place. We could sit in the garden and talk. See what we can do together.'

'Talking is fine with me, Mr Miele,' I said with a slight lump in my throat. Adrian Miele, voted handsomest man of

1974 by readers of the women's magazine *Viva*, was now driving *me* crazy.

'Adrian,' he said offhandedly, 'just call me Adrian.' He informed me when and where I was expected, and hung up the phone.

Adrian Miele, the living legend, wants to see what we can do together, I thought. The same Adrian Miele who was once the sex god of the Dutch theatre world and who had caused a minor commotion by declaring that the male member was not something to be ashamed of. 'Vietnam is something to be ashamed of,' he had said. 'Korea, that's something to be ashamed of, but certainly not the male member.' And this blond faun now wanted to work with me. This was the first time I realised that my life had changed.

I took a taxi to Prinsengracht, where Adrian and Patricia Miele had their little *pied-à-terre*.

Patricia was waiting for me in the hallway. My footsteps sounded hollow on the marble. It was a long hallway and it took me a good three minutes to reach her outstretched hand. Her actual name was Patricia Zwaardvis. That's what it always said on the playbill: Adrian Miele and Patricia Zwaardvis. And then the rest of the actors in small print.

She was wearing jeans and a polka-dot shirt. A white sweater was loosely draped over her shoulders. 'I'm Patricia,' she said, 'come on in.' She didn't say her last name, which I thought made things easier.

She had on tennis shoes and ran ahead of me. We went down a flight of steps, through the kitchen and then into the living room.

'I'm afraid it's too cold to sit in the garden,' Patricia said.

Adrian, his back turned towards us, was facing the glass doors that opened to the garden. He was barking into a cordless phone. I thought it merely a coincidence that Adrian Miele was barking at someone just as I entered. Later I found out that he barked at everyone he happened to be talking with on the phone. I guess he couldn't help it. He sometimes even barked at people when he wasn't on the phone. Especially waitresses and cab drivers.

'Just throw your coat in a chair,' Patricia said. 'That's what Adrian Miele junior always does.'

At that moment Adrian Miele senior ended his phone conversation with a loud invective. He moved over to me. The bald spots on his head were carefully covered by strands of hair. In a couple of steps he was standing right in front of me. I shook his extended hand and, almost simultaneously, he pushed me down onto the leather couch with his other hand, saying, 'Make yourself comfortable.'

I now had a view of the fireplace; some forty pine cones were neatly arranged in front of it.

'Coffee?' Patricia asked. 'Espresso?'

'Delicious.'

'Wonderful,' Adrian Miele said. He was now sitting in a black-leather rocking chair. 'We're just waiting for Pieter Kortenhoef of Red Sea Productions. We recently started working with Red Sea Productions. Do you know Red Sea Productions? They do theatre, television, movies, you name it.'

I answered that I didn't know Red Sea Productions, but that this didn't mean much because I wasn't very familiar with that world.

Patricia brought me my espresso. Actually, it was just a drop of espresso clinging to the bottom of the cup, as if she had forgotten to do the dishes. Apparently Adrian Miele had noticed me staring into my cup, because he said, 'Yes, that's a double espresso. That's why there's just a little bit of it. We like that, double strength.' His voice and posture were those of a real leader.

Patricia handed me a spoon and said, 'Lovely.'

I didn't exactly know what to reply, so I simply echoed, 'Lovely.'

She presented me with a sugar bowl. It was filled with sugar packets from hotels, restaurants, and airline companies.

'We like young people,' she said, after I had picked out a packet.

'We do,' Adrian Miele said. 'The younger, the better.'

I took a sip. It was more like sugar with a little drop of coffee in it. 'Nice and strong, isn't it?' Adrian said.

I nodded. Just then, the doorbell rang.

'I'll get it,' Patricia called out. She put the sugar bowl down on the table and ran to the front door.

Adrian slammed his hand flat on a piece of paper on the table. 'Does this look familiar to you?' he asked. I leaned forward. It was an application letter that I myself had written when I was sixteen and that I had sent out to every theatre and production company in the Netherlands. Someone out there will surely be interested in having me as an actor, is what I'd thought. Mistakenly, as it turned out.

Miele grinned at me.

'You sent one of those to us,' he said. 'I've been keeping track of you ever since. Kept a little file on you.'

Voices sounded from the kitchen, followed by Patricia's cooing laughter.

I was wondering how many other people Adrian Miele had kept a little file on.

'We've been following you for all these years,' Adrian Miele said, 'and we'll be following you for the rest of your career.'

It sounded like a threat.

'Could I have some water, please?' I asked. My mouth was all sugary.

At that moment Pieter Kortenhoef entered the room. He was wearing a purple blazer. His hair was the colour of mild Gouda cheese. I rose to shake hands, which he did forcefully. Almost simultaneously he handed me a business card. 'This is me,' he said pointing at the business card. I looked at the business card.

Pieter Kortenhoef was still standing in front of me, an expectant look in his eyes, as if he was waiting for me to take out my own business card. I didn't know what to do, so I just said, 'This is me,' and pointed at my chest.

Adrian Miele had also risen from his seat. He slapped Kortenhoef amicably on the shoulder and then turned towards me. He was holding a shiny white business card. 'Let me just give you ours now,' he said. With his left hand he pushed me back down onto the couch.

I examined the two business cards. One was Kortenhoef's; the other was printed in elegant letters saying 'Helium Ltd'.

'Yes, that's us,' Adrian Miele said. 'Patricia and I have our own company. We used to do our own production work, but now we have Red Sea Productions. Because we're getting on a bit in life, aren't we Patrish?'

Patricia, now standing by the fireplace, nodded. She was holding five spoons and was still wearing the white sweater draped over her shoulders.

'Espresso, Pieter?' she asked.

'Tea,' Pieter whispered. 'My stomach.' He patted his belly while he said this, as if it had a baby inside that needed to be burped.

'Pieter was a little overworked,' Patricia said before disappearing into the kitchen.

'Right,' Adrian Miele muttered, holding the cordless phone, 'but he's his old self again.' Then he punched a number into the keypad of his phone.

Pieter Kortenhoef turned around in his chair. I felt overwhelming compassion for this man welling up, and I wondered if there could be any connection between his stomach problems and the fact that his hair was the colour of mild Gouda cheese.

Adrian Miele started barking at someone again and Pieter Kortenhoef opened his mouth, probably in an attempt to turn my attention away from Adrian Miele's barking. 'We read your book,' he shouted. 'Splendid!'

'Thank you.' I had to shout back to make myself heard because Adrian Miele had also started shouting. The whole house was booming now. We were downstairs, but it would not have surprised me if they could have followed the conversation word for word in the attic.

Patricia came racing out of the kitchen, balancing a cup of watery tea on a tray. When she put the cup down in front of Kortenhoef it splashed upwards. Most of it ended up on Kortenhoef's trousers. 'It's alright,' he offered, 'had to be washed anyway.' But Patricia pretended not to notice and was already racing the tray towards her husband.

'Mind your heart, Ade,' she shouted. 'Mind your heart.' Her voice boomed just like the others. She grabbed the phone from his hands and said quietly, 'This is Patricia Zwaardvis. We're in a meeting right now but we'll call you back later.'

Adrian Miele sank back into his rocking chair. He began rummaging through a stack of newspapers next to him, pulled out a magazine and shouted, 'Ah, there it is. Your interview in *Playboy*. You see, we read everything about you.'

Patricia sat down as well. But before she had settled she veered up and snatched the tea bag out of Pieter Kortenhoef's half-filled cup. He looked like a beaten dog. 'We always save these in the refrigerator,' Patricia said. 'We have everything we need, but it is a shame to waste money.'

My mother also used to keep tea bags in the refrigerator. There were periods in my life when my mother's refrigerator could best be described as 'the tearoom'. I was beginning to develop profound feelings of sympathy for Patricia Zwaardvis.

Finally we were all sitting down. Pieter Kortenhoef said, 'So we were thinking…' Adrian Miele raised his hand. 'I'll take this, Pieter.'

Adrian Miele was a bear. I only noticed it now, from the way he was sitting in his rocking chair. Somewhat like Rutger Hauer, but old and half bald. Nevertheless, it was still quite obvious why he had been voted handsomest man of 1974 by *Viva*.

'Would you like some more tea, Pieter?' Patricia asked.

'No thanks,' he whispered, 'I have my stomach to consider.' Again Pieter Kortenhoef patted his belly. It was a mysterious gesture. There was something remotely erotic about it.

'We were wondering,' Adrian Miele said, 'whether you would be interested in writing a play for us.'

I was about to open my mouth to say yes, but there was absolutely no need to do that.

'We knew you'd be interested,' he simply went on. 'Look, I don't know if you're familiar with drama at all. Patricia is fifty-five. There are hardly any roles for women of fifty-five. Of course she could easily play someone who's thirty-five, because she still looks quite good. But she's kind of through with that. Aren't you, Patrish?'

Patricia nodded, but there was no need for that either. Adrian Miele just kept going: 'So we were thinking of *Who's Afraid of Virginia Woolf?* You know that play? That kind of dark humour. I think you have that in you.'

He now moved to the edge of his rocking chair and said, 'We love dark humour.'

'We totally love it,' Patricia said, and Pieter Kortenhoef whispered, 'So do I.'

Only now did I realise the incredible size of Adrian Miele's face. It was three times the size of mine.

'We read all those interviews you gave and we've seen you on television, and we thought: That young man has dark humour.'

'We also read his book,' Patricia interrupted.

'Yes, we also read your book. Splendid. A lot of dark humour. We love that. So, what do you think? We need a part for a woman of about fifty-five. And for me of course. And for the rest, some young people, if at all possible.'

'Ade,' Patricia shouted, but there was no stopping him

now.

'Two chicks of twenty-five cost the same as an old dog, if you see what I mean?'

I said I knew exactly what he meant.

'Let Pieter handle these things,' Patricia shouted desperately.

'So, we have a woman of fifty-five, some fresh meat, and lots of dark humour. You got all that?' her husband continued, unperturbed.

I said one couldn't be professional enough when discussing writing and that I could deliver exactly according to his wishes. A woman of fifty-five, a man like Adrian. A Rutger Hauer type (right before his death). Of course I didn't mention that bit. Then some fresh meat. And all this drenched in dark humour.

'We should be opening a bottle of champagne now,' Adrian Miele said.

'But instead, we'll have another nice cup of espresso,' Patricia added.

For the fourth time that afternoon, Pieter Kortenhoef patted his belly, but this time he didn't make any comments. The man was making me so nervous that I started patting my belly as well.

Patricia piled up the cups on a tray. 'We bought these in Spain,' she said. 'We have a cottage there. This is very special porcelain from Seville.'

Pieter Kortenhoef and I leaned forward to examine the cups. I couldn't find anything special about them.

'Yes, we normally keep those in the cupboard,' Patricia said. 'We are quite frugal when we don't have guests.'

'So, you will do it?' Adrian Miele asked.

I was watching Patricia disappearing into the kitchen with the tray and I decided: for a woman like Patricia you must give it your all.

'Yes,' I said.

'Then we should discuss money matters,' Pieter

Kortenhoef began.

'Pieter, I'll handle it,' Miele said.

Kortenhoef sank even deeper into his chair.

'Of course we're looking at few grand for writing such a piece, but you see, I can't just pull that out of my back pocket.'

Patricia came in with fresh espressos. They contained even less than previously. 'Are we talking about money?' she asked. 'I don't want to hear anything about that.' And she pressed her palms against her ears.

'At our board meetings Patricia always starts knitting,' Adrian Miele said.

I was thinking what an enormous amount of knitwear Patricia Zwaardvis must have produced in her lifetime. Again, I noticed how much sympathy this woman inspired in me. For a moment I even thought she must be a saint. I had never in my life met a saint before, so I had no idea how to recognise one, but I could not rule out that Patricia Zwaardvis was a saint. She also had a tiny moustache. I thought that was quite becoming for a saint.

'I'm only telling this young man...'

'Arnon is his name, Ade,' Patricia said.

'I'm only telling Arnon that I can't simply pull six grand out of my back pocket.'

'No, nobody can pull that out of his back pocket,' I said. 'Not you, not me.'

'No,' Pieter Kortenhoef added, 'me neither.' And now he turned his body completely towards me. 'We do wonder, however, whether you're up to this. The pressure, I mean. It'll be a Large Audience Production, you see. And you're already writing so much. Can you take it down a step when you need to, or do you need help with that?' He seemed relieved. Maybe because finally, Adrian Miele had let him finish a whole sentence.

'No,' I said. 'I can easily take a step back if I need to. I don't require any help with that.'

He got up and retrieved his windbreaker from the kitchen. 'I'd better get going now,' he said, extending his hand. It was ice-cold. Like the hand of a dead person.

'It was nice talking to you,' he whispered.

'Yes, it was nice,' I said.

Before he walked off to the kitchen he patted his belly for the fifth time.

'We'll call each other,' Adrian shouted after him. An unintelligible sound emerged from Pieter Kortenhoef's mouth.

When we heard the front door close Adrian Miele said, 'They're very well-meaning you know, at Red Sea Productions.'

I looked at Adrian Miele. The way he was sitting in his leather rocking chair made me think of the film *Purple Window*. The film came out when I was born and got famous for its unveiled eroticism. No one less than Adrian Miele had starred in this movie. Whenever the film was mentioned people said – even though it had been almost twenty-three years ago – 'Oh, Adrian Miele was in that film. I can still picture him, the beast.' Adrian Miele played a beast in that film – figuratively that is – and his rod featured in several close-ups. After that, if I'm not mistaken, his rod didn't feature in any other films.

'I saw *Purple Window*,' I said. 'You were great.'

'Right,' Adrian Miele said. 'That was fun, but of course that didn't buy me this nice little canal house. I'm sure you understand that.'

I was about to say that I understood that very well, but Patricia Zwaardvis intervened.

'Ade,' she shouted.

'Now what?' Adrian Miele shouted.

'Don't just blurt things out!' Patricia said. She had moved to the edge of her seat. She had taken off her tennis shoes and was making rotating movements with her feet. When she noticed me watching her she said, 'When you have

11

rheumatic toes you have to pick up marbles with your feet. I do that every night, fifty marbles.' She gave me an encouraging nod as if to say I, too, should start picking up fifty marbles with my feet every night.

'Do you know who's living in our attic these days?' Adrian Miele asked.

I shook my head.

'André van Duin,' Adrian Miele said.

Silence fell. Miele and Zwaardvis looked up at the ceiling. For a moment it seemed as if they were commemorating André van Duin.

'He's no longer in Aruba,' Patricia said.

'No, he's in our attic now,' Adrian Miele added. 'If only you knew who we've had living in our attic.'

'Anne Frank?' I inquired.

Adrian Miele looked shocked. 'What? How do you mean? What are you trying to say?'

'That was a joke, Ade,' Patricia explained.

'I'm sorry,' I said. 'That was a poor joke.'

'All right, I see. Anne Frank,' Adrian Miele said solemnly.

Again they looked up at the ceiling. I had no idea who they were commemorating this time: André van Duin, Anne Frank, or both.

I just stared straight ahead, at the forty pine cones.

An hour later, they showed me out. Adrian Miele said, 'Just write us a little synopsis, so I can start applying for some grant money.'

I kissed Patricia Zwaardvis' hand.

'We'll definitely come see you in New York,' she whispered.

'Lots of dark humour,' Adrian Miele called out after me when I was nearly as far as the Rozengracht.

Exactly as Miele had requested, I wrote a synopsis. For Patricia, I came up with the part of Madame Moustache, the fifty-five-year-old owner of a brothel that no longer had any customers. Adrian Miele was to play Spatzki, wheeler-dealer, a kind of Rutger Hauer right before his death, and Madame Moustache's high-school sweetheart. All his money had been stolen by his son, Spatzki Junior. The entire play was set in Madame Moustache's bubble bath, where Adrian Miele tries in vain to get it on with Ophelia from Nieuw-Vennep. In the end, said Ophelia drowns a horrible death when Miele forces her to give him a blow job in the bubble bath. I was convinced this would please them enormously.

And it did. Three months after they received my synopsis Adrian Miele left a message on my answering machine. 'I've taken the liberty of applying for some grants,' Miele shouted without mentioning his name. But I could tell right away it was him from the barking. 'Keep up the good work,' he shouted. And before he hung up the phone he said, 'We'll be coming to New York.'

I couldn't help thinking of Patricia Zwaardvis. I secretly called her my little Zwaardvis and imagined how I would offer her a flower on the opening night. For me, this Patricia Zwaardvis was immortal even in her own lifetime.

In December of 1995 Patricia Zwaardvis and Adrian Miele came to New York. I had rented a stretch limousine. This was the first time in my life that I had rented one, but I thought it was the least I could do for Patricia Zwaardvis. They kept me waiting in the hotel lobby for forty-five minutes. They had taken up quarters in some Manhattan backstreet hotel for salesman types and the like.

'We just wanted to freshen up,' Patricia said when they finally came downstairs.

'It really gets to you, a long flight like that,' Miele boomed.

'Yes, we got a package deal we saw in the TV guide,' Patricia said, 'but fortunately they didn't make us check in with all the others. They immediately recognised who we were.'

'They recognised us from a distance,' Adrian Miele said. 'They started waving at us when we came through the revolving doors.'

'Well, of course we have very familiar faces, Ade,' Patricia said.

I showed them to the stretch limo.

'You're so crazy,' Patricia Zwaardvis shrieked as she grabbed my hand. Adrian Miele said, 'Yes, we were in one of these things once, remember Patrish?'

'Just drive around,' I told the driver. I opened the little fridge. Only Patricia didn't want whisky.

'To *The Cockroaches*,' Adrian Miele said, because that was the title of the play.

'Yes,' Patricia said, 'to *The Cockroaches*.'

The limo had three wide banquettes so we could each lie down on our own.

'We were wondering,' Miele said as he folded his hands behind his head, 'if we could have that bubble bath in the fourth act only. That would make it a sort of climax at the end, with a lot of smoke.'

'That won't be a problem at all,' I said.

'Isn't this just wonderful,' Patricia said, 'driving around New York in a limousine. We can even watch videos.'

'It is wonderful, but we've received this kind of treatment before, Patrish,' Miele said. He was panting non-stop. After half an hour, I asked him if he was alright.

Patricia said her husband had seen a heart specialist and that they hadn't found anything wrong, but that they couldn't guarantee anything either.

'And how about this Ophelia,' Miele said, 'did you have someone in mind for her yet?'

'Not yet,' I said.

'I guess that's up to us then,' Miele muttered. 'What kind of tits should she have, this Ophelia?'

'Tits, tits, Jesus,' I said, 'I haven't thought about that yet. I don't think it's all that important.'

'Like this, or more like this,' Miele asked, his hands indicating the different sizes I could choose from.

'Well, average, I guess,' I said.

'Average,' Miele said. He started to think.

'Frouke Braugarten,' he said after a while. 'Not too large, not too small, but nice and firm. Right, Patrish? Frouke Braugarten.'

Patricia Zwaardvis nodded.

'Yes,' Miele said. 'I'll give her a call. Frouke Braugarten.'

'Some people will walk out, I suppose,' Patricia Zwaardvis said, 'but I don't really mind that. They do that in the piece we're doing now as well.'

'Right,' Miele added. 'At the very beginning Patricia has to say "lick my ass". That's good enough to lose about eight people.'

'Indeed,' Patricia said, 'so now I just say "sticklebacks".'

'Sorry?' I asked.

'In stead of "lick my ass", I say, "sticklebacks",' Patricia said.

'Sticklebacks,' I said.

'Not a soul who notices,' Miele said. 'Not a soul.'

At nine o'clock I dropped them off at their hotel. They had to go to sleep right away.

'So we can expect the piece in a month?' Miele asked. I confirmed this.

'We have complete faith in you,' Patricia said and kissed me goodbye.

As I walked home I thought, I was right. Patricia Zwaardvis is a saint. She just doesn't realise it yet.'

One month later, I sent *The Cockroaches* to Adrian Miele. He called me two weeks later.

'We're quite upset,' he shouted through the phone. I didn't have time to ask what they were upset about; he simply continued his monologue. 'The synopsis said this young actress, you know, this Frouke Braugarten, was to give me a blow job. And now I see it's Patricia who gives me a blow job. I'm telling you, people out there in the hinterlands aren't ready for this.'

I still vividly recall how I was shaking the first time I had Adrian Miele on the phone.

'Listen,' I said, 'you can have it anyway you want. If you prefer Frouke Braugarten for that blow job…'

'No,' he bellowed. 'I don't want any blow jobs at all. If we start giving blow jobs in the Kampen playhouse they won't have us back for the next five years.'

'Mr Miele,' I said, 'once more, you can have it any way you want.'

'And those filthy words I have to say; I can't get these words out of my mouth. And then I have to walk across the stage naked. I can't do that either. We have to go out into the country a hundred times a year and I'm telling you: people out there are not ready for this.'

After these words, he hung up.

I wrote to them the very same day:

Dear Mr Miele and Ms Zwaardvis,

Everyone in the Netherlands who owns a VCR – and trust me, there are many who do – can admire Mr Miele's rod in close-up. So I can't quite understand all the outrage on your part. All I'm asking Mr Miele to do is shuffle across the stage naked in one particular scene. And with the lights dimmed, no less.

Might there be some medical reason that precludes Mr Miele from showing his rod in public? Discoloration perhaps, or some kind of atrophy? I'm merely guessing here.

Should this indeed be the case, then you can count on my discretion and cooperation.
As always,
Sincerely
With best regards,
Your faithful servant,
Arnon Grunberg

Miele called me the next day.

'What do *you* know about *my* rod?' he roared.

'Nothing,' I said. 'I only saw the film *Purple Window*. I'm a fan.'

'Leave my rod out of this,' he roared even louder. 'What kind of adolescent behaviour is this?'

'I'm merely trying to explain my point of view.'

'People will run out of the theatre screaming,' Miele yelled.

'How could I know that?' I said apologetically.

'And what happened to the dark humour? I read the whole piece four times and couldn't find any dark humour. Patricia and I love dark humour, but nothing. Not a trace of dark humour. The whole thing needs to be rewritten. Patricia thinks so too. Young man, I had wanted to bring you from the small stage to the big stage, but this is not right for a larger audience. Red Sea Productions' dramaturg, Pieter Kortenhoef, read it too: he can't understand it either. He also says: Normal people can't say this stuff, this filth. And as long as I can't get it out of my mouth, I'm gonna keep this six grand right here in my pocket. Do you hear what I'm saying? Dark humour is what we want. That's what people like, a bit of dark humour, a laugh now and then.' By now he was completely beside himself. 'They wanna laugh, the audience,' he screeched. 'They already get enough filth at home.'

'Ade,' I heard Patricia call out in the background, 'Ade, take it easy, Ade. Please, take it easy.' After that I was disconnected.

That same day I wrote:

Dear Mr Miele, dear Ms Zwaardvis,

I am very honoured and pleased that Mr Miele had wanted to bring me from the small stage to the big stage. Almost like Moses leading his people out of Egypt.

Perhaps Mr Miele is a tiny little bit grateful that I had wanted to get him out of the second-hand car business?

Hoping to hear from you very soon,
As always,
Your faithful servant,
Arnon Grunberg

I didn't hear anything for a week. Then I wrote:

Dear Mr Miele,
Just answer me, asshole.
As always,
Your faithful servant,
Arnon Grunberg

Two weeks later, I received a letter from Patricia Zwaardvis.

Dear Arnon,
I read your play three times and I was quite upset. I was so upset that I'm afraid we will need more time for revisions. We cannot perform those kinds of acts on stage, and we cannot get those kinds of words out of our mouths. I'm afraid no one can, in fact.

There's another thing that has kept me from writing to you: the hurtful tone of your faxes. We had such a good time in New York that I find it hard to believe. We gave you complete freedom to write whatever you wanted with only one condition: that it could be performed anywhere in the country.

I do hope we can find a way to get back together, we meaning you, Red Sea Productions, Adrian, and I.
Best regards,
Patricia Zwaardvis

I wrote back that same day:

Dear Patricia,
A sign of life, at last.

As far as my 'hurtful faxes' are concerned, you were probably thinking: That young man is a direct descendent of Jesus Christ; he'll turn the other cheek.

I am, in fact, a direct descendent of Jesus Christ. Patricia, my dear, last night God visited me in my dreams. He appeared in the form of your dear husband, Adrian, and he spoke to me and said: 'Arnon, wake up, you are the redeemer. Patricia Zwaardvis, actress, residing in Amsterdam, will crucify you in her home for the salvation of the world, and especially for the salvation of Red Sea Productions and the company Helium Ltd, of which I am the patron. This will occur in March of 1996.'

When God comes to you in a dream, even if this is in the appearance of Adrian Miele, you can hardly refuse Him a difficult request. So I ask you Patricia: crucify me.

According to God, who has taken the appearance of your dear husband, Adrian Miele, this is to take place in March. I said that before, but just like God, I tend to repeat myself.

This is a hard road to travel for us, Patricia. For you, because you are married to God. For me, because of having to be crucified by you for the salvation of the world in general; and for the general public in particular. We will have to prepare ourselves for this task in the next few weeks.

I will have to leave this world behind. And you, Patricia, you were chosen for this sacred act. You will drive the nails into my hands and feet. And this will all take place in your home in front of the fireplace. Do both of you understand that this makes your home holy ground?

Do the people of Amsterdam realise that Adrian Miele is God, my Lord?

Tell them, Patricia.

Patricia, God, who lives on through your dear husband, Adrian Miele, announced in my dreams that you are to cut off my circumcised

19

member for the salvation of the world, and to use a rusty kitchen knife that must sit in potting soil for twenty-four hours before the act.

Patricia, God, who lives on in your dear husband Adrian Miele, has commanded, through me, that you shall poke out my eyes with the very same needle that sewed your bridal dress.

Patricia, God, who lives on in your dear husband, Adrian Miele, has commanded, through me, that the prophet, Pieter Kortenhoef, shall receive the blood as it flows from where my member was once attached. This blood he shall take, and with it, he shall mark a cross on your wall.

Patricia, God, who lives on in your dear husband, Adrian Miele, has commanded me that my hair shall be cut off to be made into a wig for the half-bald God, Adrian Miele, your dear husband, our Lord.

After speaking these words, God, in the form of your dear husband, blessed me. He said, 'You, saviour, you who are my son, I wish to have Patricia Zwaardvis, actress, residing in Amsterdam, give me a blow job. And I want it this very season. Saviour, pack up your things, go forth to the Prinsengracht and spread my word, or I will strike you and your people with consumption and starvation. You shall be destroyed by your enemies and your temples shall be defiled by ass and cow, and by a stampede of horses driven by Joop van den Ende, and by me, God, named Joop.'

Then God, in the form of your dear husband, disappeared into a tobacco shop where he bought Himself a cigar.

Dear Patricia, I considered it best to inform you of this without delay.

Love,

Arnon

c.c. Red Sea Productions

Since then, I've heard nothing from Adrian Miele – nor from Patricia Zwaardvis. Several weeks later I did read an article in a Dutch newspaper indicating that Patricia Zwaardvis absolutely cannot stand rudeness for rudeness' sake.

Red Sea Productions invited me to dinner, because, as they said in their invitation, 'Believe it or not, we have faith in you and don't give up just like that.'

Sometimes, on a lazy afternoon, I think about Patricia Zwaardvis, and then I hope that there's someone watching over her.

The Days of Leopold Mangelmann

During the winter and spring of 1991, I was engaged, thanks to the efforts of Jan Ritsema, as a paid actor, a rarity that didn't last very long. I did, however, meet a female director, Matin van Veldhuijzen, who wanted to adopt me and to whom I owe my very first commission as a writer. She was on a sub-committee for the Amsterdam Foundation for the Arts. Having seen my self-published work, *The Machiavellian: A Justification in Seven Songs* (I apparently considered myself to be a Machiavellian as far back as that), the committee commissioned me to write a play. The fee was five thousand Dutch guilders. It was the first money I would ever make writing, not counting the typewriter I was given by the Amsterdam Theatre Company when I was fifteen, for my play *Queen Raspberry*.

During the same period I met Matin van Veldhuijzen, I also became acquainted with an actress, Johanna. We were in the same production, so we saw each other every day in the dressing room. She, too, had read *The Machiavellian*; I was handing out my self-published book for free to anyone who was interested.

After reading my book Johanna asked me to write something for her. A monologue. She wanted to sit on a black cube, naked, and wanted me to provide her with the text. I didn't mind doing that. I envisioned great things coming out of this.

I thought I could combine the assignment for Johanna and the one for the Amsterdam Foundation for the Arts. Unfortunately, the collaboration with Johanna came to a premature end.

The text that I eventually sent to the Amsterdam Foundation for the Arts was called *The Days of Leopold Mangelmann*.

I

LEOPOLD MANGELMANN: Are we celebrating something?

MRS MANGELMANN: Eating is always a celebration.

MR MANGELMANN: Not the way you eat. Just eat now. I'm eating, right?

LEOPOLD: So are we celebrating?

MRS MANGELMANN: We're celebrating the New Year. That's why the candles are lit. And that's why we're having honey, so the New Year may be a sweet year. Now eat, otherwise your food will get cold.

MR MANGELMANN: Could you be quiet for a moment, please? I can't hear a thing.

LEOPOLD: I can't swallow. It's stuck.

MRS MANGELMANN: Do you hear that? Your son is stuck again. You want to live, don't you? Then you have to eat. Drink some water.

LEOPOLD: It's stuck.

MR MANGELMANN: Quiet.

MRS MANGELMANN: If you won't eat, we'll have to take you to the hospital. They'll put a tube up your nose.

MR MANGELMANN: Quiet. This is important. There's a special broadcast on Schleyer.

MRS MANGELMANN: What do I care about Schleyer! Your son won't swallow his food. Ever since he was born, he won't eat. Just to bug us. Let that Schleyer go to hell. Just get your son to open up his mouth.

MR MANGELMANN: Your mother's acting a bit strange. It's because she was among the barbarians. She can't help it.

MRS MANGELMANN: You could at least eat the vegetables in the soup. I spent two days making that soup, took all the grease out of it, you know.

LEOPOLD: I know.

MRS MANGELMANN: So eat. I beg you. I pray you. When I had jaundice I was given an extra ration of jam. That saved my life. Now eat.

LEOPOLD: I don't have jaundice.

MRS MANGELMANN: You could catch all kinds of things if you don't eat.

MR MANGELMANN: I can't hear a word they're saying.

MRS MANGELMANN: Your father's stone deaf. And you'll be deaf too, when you grow up. Because you're just like your father.

LEOPOLD: When I grow up I don't wanna eat these vegetables.

MRS MANGELMANN: I don't care what you do when you grow up. Now I just want you to chew. Chew. Chew. Chew already.

LEOPOLD: I wanna be in the newspaper when I grow up.

MRS MANGELMANN: You unlucky soul. Only dead people end up in the newspaper. Or criminals and their dogs.

MR MANGELMANN: Dead people don't end up in the newspaper. They end up with their names on some mass memorial.

LEOPOLD: I don't want a mass memorial. I want my own memorial.

MRS MANGELMANN: Then you must swallow now. Oh God, please make him swallow.

LEOPOLD: It's stuck. I'm choking.

MR MANGELMANN: In America lots of people apparently choke on chicken bones. Be careful, I tell you. Be careful.

LEOPOLD: I have to spit it out.

MRS MANGELMANN: Just look at that. That's no longer human. And I have to wash all that. He's an animal, your son. Just like you.

MR MANGELMANN: You should keep your hand in front of your mouth.

LEOPOLD: I almost choked. Did you see that? I was almost done for.

MR MANGELMANN: Clear the table. For God's sake, clear the table. You can't do this when you're not at home, you know.

MRS MANGELMANN: We've got cake and pie for dessert.

LEOPOLD: Are we done celebrating now?

MRS MANGELMANN: You ungrateful swine. I was up baking all night.

MR MANGELMANN: We'll do our best. We'll do our best. We'll have a little more to eat.

MRS MANGELMANN: Now look at that. That tablecloth belonged to my mother. She embroidered it even. Do you have any idea what this tablecloth has been through? And now you puked all over it.

LEOPOLD: I didn't puke. I nearly choked. I'm stuck. I'm stalled.

MR MANGELMANN: This is psychosomatic, you know. We must have him checked out.

LEOPOLD: But that meat is raw.

MRS MANGELMANN: Now that's the limit. My meat raw? I'm gonna tell people how you harass your parents into their graves. This isn't done anywhere, not anywhere.

MR MANGELMANN: That's a good idea. You should also tell everyone he isn't toilet-trained yet. He poops on a potty next to the radiator.

MRS MANGELMANN: He can't use the toilet. He'll get sick. You know what your son is like, he gets sick everywhere.

LEOPOLD: I *am* sick.

MR MANGELMANN: No more pie for me. I can't face any more pie. I need to go to bed. I need to go to bed immediately.

MRS MANGELMANN: So now *I* have to eat the whole pie? How did I end up here? This absolute horror I ended up in.

MR MANGELMANN: I need some schnapps.

MRS MANGELMANN: Stop yelling. Mind the neighbours. We can't afford to have yelling.

MR MANGELMANN: You're the one who's yelling.

LEOPOLD: We're always yelling.

MR MANGELMANN: The kid is right.

MRS MANGELMANN: We haven't even said any prayers yet. Let's at least say a few prayers tonight, for God's sake. Or I'll never cook for you again.

MR MANGELMANN: You two say what you have to say, and say it fast.

MRS MANGELMANN: I should never have married that fellow.

MR MANGELMANN: Why don't you go live with your relatives in Scotland or Argentina or Jerusalem? Haven't your relatives spread out all over the world?

LEOPOLD: Next year in Jerusalem.

MRS MANGELMANN: We're not saying that tonight.

LEOPOLD: What do the people in Jerusalem actually say?

MR MANGELMANN: They say it anyway. Jerusalem is always next year.

LEOPOLD: Why next year? I can't wait that long. I'm choking.

MR MANGELMANN: We've been waiting for six thousand years now.

MRS MANGELMANN: If it weren't for people like your father, we would have been in Jerusalem already.

MR MANGELMANN: Could you at least start now?

MRS MANGELMANN: No, I'm not saying anything any more.

LEOPOLD: Why don't we leave, then?

MR MANGELMANN: It's very hot in Jerusalem. I don't do well in the heat. Besides, I'm a European.

MRS MANGELMANN: You're a monster.

LEOPOLD: Let's leave.

MR MANGELMANN: We can't just keep leaving. We're here now. We're staying a while.

MRS MANGELMANN: Why don't you eat something? Dear God, please let them eat some of my pie.

LEOPOLD: Jerusalem, the golden city.

MR MANGELMANN: Now let's not do anything foolish.

LEOPOLD: We don't have enough time.

MR MANGELMANN: We're certainly not going to rush things here.

LEOPOLD: I don't want to arrive in Jerusalem looking like a corpse.

MRS MANGELMANN: Then eat something.

LEOPOLD: If we go, we could sell our winter coats.

MR MANGELMANN: We're keeping our winter coats.

LEOPOLD: We'll be walking around in shorts.

MR MANGELMANN: Can we finally go to sleep now?

LEOPOLD: We'll be picking corn.

MR MANGELMANN: I'm not picking any corn.

LEOPOLD: We don't have enough time.

MR MANGELMANN: I want quiet. I want to have quiet *here*.

MRS MANGELMANN: The rabbis are saying that there's every indication the Messiah is coming.

MR MANGELMANN: Don't listen to any rabbis.

MRS MANGELMANN: Your father thinks that God is dead.

LEOPOLD: Is it true?

MR MANGELMANN: I don't want to talk about it.

LEOPOLD: We'll never get anywhere because of you two.

MR MANGELMANN: We hope we'll get somewhere.

LEOPOLD: Why are you always crying? Can't we ever have a meal without one of you crying? My whole life you've been crying.

MR MANGELMANN: At least we're happy not to be getting anywhere.

MRS MANGELMANN: If I have to eat all of that by myself, my stomach will keep me up all night.

LEOPOLD: Why is he crying?

MRS MANGELMANN: He's asking why you're crying.

MR MANGELMANN: Why, indeed. Why?

LEOPOLD: Well?

MR MANGELMANN: You'd have to live five thousand years to cry for everything worth crying for. Even for a girl who walked away across a large square that no longer exists, I'd like to sit down and cry for five years.

LEOPOLD: Five thousand years of crying. I'd rather die.

MRS MANGELMANN: Mind your words, you poor bastard.

LEOPOLD: I'm choking on your meat. I'm dying.

MRS MANGELMANN: This is the best meat I could find. How dare you not eat my meat? You have a whole long life in front of you. You're not getting out of it that easily.

MR MANGELMANN: Well, you don't know how to cook. He's right about that.

MRS MANGELMANN: Pigs you are, both of you. I wish you had never been born.

MR MANGELMANN: And we must put a stop to this spitting.

LEOPOLD: I'm choking. And I'm allowed to spit when I cry.

MR MANGELMANN: Close the door at least. There's a draught.

LEOPOLD: Why? I always forget to close the doors. I have other things on my mind.

MR MANGELMANN: I had the heat on for nothing.

MRS MANGELMANN: Let's just have some apples then.

LEOPOLD: I can't lift my spoon.

MR MANGELMANN: Why do you want so badly to be sick? You think it's fun not to be able to lift your spoon?

LEOPOLD: I *am* sick. Why do you like to cry so much?

MR MANGELMANN: I'm almost done, and then I'd like to go to bed.

LEOPOLD: I won't let you go to bed. I want you to finally stop this crying business.

MR MANGELMANN: You're terrorising the entire family. You're not the centre of the world, you know.

LEOPOLD: I *am* the centre of the world. And I'm choking.

MR MANGELMANN: You have to close the doors. There are other people out there.

LEOPOLD: I don't see any other people. Where are they then?

MRS MANGELMANN: You have to be aware of other people. They're out to get you. They want to wipe us out.

MR MANGELMANN: Don't go telling him any nonsense. Everyone is gonna be wiped out.

MRS MANGELMANN: But not by other people.

MR MANGELMANN: By who then? By that god of yours?

LEOPOLD: Five thousand years of crying, only to be wiped out.

MR MANGELMANN: Why have we never managed to complete a meal in this family?

MRS MANGELMANN: Because I regret every single day that I've been with you. You and that son of yours.

MR MANGELMANN: You're driving me crazy with your eternal pain.

LEOPOLD: *You* are the pain.

MRS MANGELMANN: We still have to welcome the bride.

MR MANGELMANN: It's much too late. It's been dark for hours.

LEOPOLD: Let's forget about that for tonight then.

MRS MANGELMANN: It's a special occasion.

LEOPOLD: Not for me. Always those tears in your eyes. It's repulsive. You're repulsive.

MR MANGELMANN: Every second you don't cry, you don't live.

MRS MANGELMANN: Finish your wine already.

LEOPOLD: He's spilling it on his trousers.

MR MANGELMANN: Quiet. I can't hear a thing.

LEOPOLD: We've been sitting here for hours now.

MRS MANGELMANN: It's dreadful being here; it's hell being around you.

MR MANGELMANN: It's hell wherever *you* are.

LEOPOLD: I'll be glad if we finally get to leave.

MRS MANGELMANN: I'll do something now. With or without you. I'm going to welcome the bride.

LEOPOLD: There is no bride. We're welcoming something that isn't there.

MRS MANGELMANN: The food I have to waste, that's a crying shame.

LEOPOLD: No, no.

MRS MANGELMANN: Do you hear that?

LEOPOLD: Look. He's spilling it all over his trousers. It's all in his lap.

MRS MANGELMANN: You too? Who in God's name am I making food for, then?

LEOPOLD: Anyone know any jokes?

MR MANGELMANN: There's this Negro reading the newspaper in the New York subway.

MRS MANGELMANN: *This* is a good joke.

LEOPOLD: Why do you need to ruin everything here? We were supposed to be celebrating.

MRS MANGELMANN: We're done celebrating.

MR MANGELMANN: Has anyone seen my fork?

MRS MANGELMANN: Your fork is on the floor, you poor bastard.

MR MANGELMANN: How could I possibly find my fork in this mess?

MRS MANGELMANN: Your father never wanted to throw anything out. He's a real museum piece himself.

LEOPOLD: What are you looking for now?

MRS MANGELMANN: I've been robbed by one of you.

LEOPOLD: What is it that you're missing, you fool?

MRS MANGELMANN: Everything, you wretch.

MR MANGELMANN: What, she's been robbed again?

MRS MANGELMANN: I'll sing the songs by myself then.

LEOPOLD: Does she really think that'll help?

MRS MANGELMANN: Anything's better than talking to you lot.

MR MANGELMANN: They've deemed us unfit for life; but that doesn't imply that we are, in fact, unfit for life.

LEOPOLD: I am.

MR MANGELMANN: What is that?

LEOPOLD: It's soup dribbling on the floor. Why are we still sitting here?

MR MANGELMANN: Your mother likes the rituals.

LEOPOLD: I don't even know what the bride feels like, or what she looks like.

MRS MANGELMANN: Take that food off his lap.

LEOPOLD: You do it.

MR MANGELMANN: Could someone get me a fork from the kitchen?

MRS MANGELMANN: I'm through getting things for you.

MR MANGELMANN: You can't possibly expect me to find anything in that kitchen. The place is like Westerbork.

LEOPOLD: So, there's this Negro in the New York subway.

MRS MANGELMANN: You're all butchers.

MR MANGELMANN: You're taking my food away!

MRS MANGELMANN: You're dropping your food on the floor, you pig.

MR MANGELMANN: Your mother misses the camp. It's the only place she can live.

MRS MANGELMANN: I was better off there than I am here with you.

LEOPOLD: Your lives are your punishment. But I'm not guilty.

MR MANGELMANN: I can't hear what they're saying on the radio.

MRS MANGELMANN: Just hold a spoon under your father's chin, will you. He's drooling.

MR MANGELMANN: Could one of you take out my teeth?

MR MANGELMANN: Not while we're having dinner.

MR MANGELMANN: They're bothering me.

MRS MANGELMANN: Like father like son.

MR MANGELMANN: Why don't you do something? Are you as crazy as your mother?

LEOPOLD: I don't have anything to do with it. I'm sick.

MRS MANGELMANN: You're both sick, rotten to the core.

MR MANGELMANN: As soon as your mother opens her mouth, she spits venom.

MRS MANGELMANN: Now, where's my prayer book?

LEOPOLD: I don't know.

MRS MANGELMANN: Your son will be the death of me.

MR MANGELMANN: Be quiet, the news is on.

MRS MANGELMANN: The news is on every hour, but not tonight.

MR MANGELMANN: Quiet.

MRS MANGELMANN: You'll be the death of me, too; the two of you will be the death of me.

LEOPOLD: I want to be your death alone.

MR MANGELMANN: Quiet, this is important.

MRS MANGELMANN: Hold a spoon under the guy's chin.

LEOPOLD: I'm sick, I can't do anything.

MRS MANGELMANN: I'll just sing alone.

LEOPOLD: So, there's this Negro in...

MRS MANGELMANN:
>Come in peace, crown of your husband
>Come o Bride; come o Bride
>Let's go, my friend, towards the bride.

MR MANGELMANN: ...the New York subway reading a Hebrew newspaper. A man sits down opposite him, watches him for a while, and says, 'Isn't it enough just being a Negro?' Can someone finally take my teeth out of my mouth?

LEOPOLD: Can you do something about his teeth?

MRS MANGELMANN: He has cake left to deal with. There will be no taking out of teeth here.

MR MANGELMANN: I want some beer.

MRS MANGELMANN: Look inside his mouth.

LEOPOLD: I don't see anything.

MR MANGELMANN: Get me some beer, fast.

MRS MANGELMANN: We don't have any beer. He still needs to finish his wine. Look inside his mouth.

LEOPOLD: I don't see anything. He swallowed them.

MRS MANGELMANN: Can't I leave you to do anything, you cripple.

LEOPOLD: Why don't you look?

MRS MANGELMANN: Slap him on the back.

LEOPOLD: I am.

MRS MANGELMANN: Slap him harder.

LEOPOLD: I might break his back.

MRS MANGELMANN: He's like a doll. You're like some doll. Go get the neighbours.

LEOPOLD: They're stomping on the floor. We must have woken them up.

MRS MANGELMANN: I hope they're awake. That'll teach them what it's like being awake.

LEOPOLD: Any sign of his teeth coming out?

MRS MANGELMANN: Nothing is coming out. This is what people in the gas chambers must've looked like.

LEOPOLD: But we're not in the gas chambers here.

MRS MANGELMANN: Everything leads us to the camp, and every camp is worse. Who's that screaming?

LEOPOLD: The neighbours woke up. Pour beer in his mouth, beer; we'll quench his thirst with lots of beer.

MRS MANGELMANN: He's gone insane. Do you see that? Your son has gone bonkers. Do you hear?

LEOPOLD: Why don't you say something? Why don't you sing?

MRS MANGELMANN: Dear Almighty, what in God's name is happening?

LEOPOLD: My body is enemy territory.

MRS MANGELMANN: And why can't we ever turn off the radio around here?

II

1.
LEOPOLD MANGELMANN:

I'm going outside. I have to.

My shoes are wet, but other people's shoes are wet, too. Sometimes their shoes are even wetter. They brace their umbrellas against the wind. They run to their cars. They step in puddles to splash their mothers' legs. They press their bellies against each other at the bottom of the stairs. They rearrange their hairbands.

After the purple bicycle lane I see the tram tracks and then the pavement. I see the sign and the chairs left outside even though they haven't been used in a while. I blow my nose, zip up my fly. I brush some spit from the corner of my mouth.

I could move on, I know that.

I don't need to be here; I could turn around and walk back.

I always enter in the same way. Quickly, leaning forward, I brush the hair off my forehead. I put down my coat on the chair opposite me, and spread out the newspaper.

A few minutes later I tilt my head up, cautiously. It's crowded. People are moving to and fro. They laugh and they talk. Now I can see a fat woman on a bar stool. She winks at me. I wave back and hear a voice: *Six can be seated now.* That's me, I know that.

I can hear their conversation.

'This tiramisu, is that a kind of pudding?' a woman asks.

'No,' she says, 'that's not pudding.'

'We want something like pudding.'

My chair is light blue, and so is my table. I have a red napkin in my lap; a wicker basket with four pieces of bread on the table. She has placed an empty ashtray in front of me.

There are many ways in which to imagine happiness, the doctor says. For instance, kissing a piece of bread that was in a wicker basket only moments ago. I let my tongue caress the grainy part, making it wet. Then I eat, in three, four bites. Raise my hand, ask for a new serving, kiss these as well, so the crumbs stick to my mouth.

The doctor says: Kiss people.

I did imagine, one time, kissing a belly or a face. But I don't like kissing anything that must die, or that has died. The doctor says that's no reason not to kiss someone. But he has never kissed me.

I used to want to be a hero. I still do sometimes. This is the right place for being a hero. If you become a regular, they give you a new name and your own table. They name you after your table, or after the dish you order most often. I've always wanted to have a new name.

I know the menu here by heart. I learn a lot of things by heart.

When I come in, they ask me, 'What would you like today?' And when they clear the table, they say, 'Was it all right?' I nod, it was all right. She says, 'Can I take this?'

Then they give me peppermints in all kinds of colours and the bill on a little tray.

She said, 'Would you like to come over to my place for

coffee?' Just ten minutes ago, when she brought me my wine.

I've been coming here for a long time and things have always gone fine.

The doctor says I'm the one who should be saying things like that, but what's the point if things are going fine?

Maybe I should go and see her.

I prefer to live in houses that don't have mail delivery. No mail for me.

Leaving is always the same as well. Very calmly after dinner. In passing the kitchen, I'm always friendly and say goodbye. I can see her reflected in the mirror behind rows of bottles.

'Would you like a stamp?' she asks.

Pardon.

'A stamp on your bill?'

My name is Leopold Mangelmann, but my mother always calls me little Mattel. Sometimes she calls me Leopold, when I've broken something. She says it's time I start doing something.

I already do a lot of things.

The doctor says so too. He says life is very short and it's time I made a start.

I don't want to make a start. I don't finish anything I start anyway. That's what my mother says.

I said goodbye to her. She has a ponytail; she has a red ponytail. I've crossed the threshold and I walk home cautiously. It's dark, there are cars and trams and bicycles.

In my hand I hold the slip of paper. It was written very quickly with a ballpoint. It gets warm in my hand. Soon everything will be different. I've heard the calling. I must tell my doctor that someone invited me.

2.

My neighbour's lights are on. Whenever I see his lights are on I go around the block, past the mailbox. I hoist up my trousers because they always sag. The hem is always dark with mud and rain. One has to be careful when wearing dirty trousers.

When I turned twenty-two the doctor told me it was time for me to start living on my own. That's why I'm living alone. I also have a kitchen, but I don't use it very often.

I always eat at my mother's and when she's not around I eat at a restaurant and sometimes I don't eat at all. The doctor says I should learn how to cook, that I should learn to take care of myself.

The doctor doesn't cook either. He has a wife who cooks for him. He says I should look for a wife too. I love looking at women. Sometimes I imagine that my pillow is a woman and then I push my nose into her until I nearly suffocate.

The door jams, my neighbour is standing at the top of the stairs.

'Hello neighbour,' he calls out.

I stand still and wave.

'Has the newspaper arrived yet?'

I walk to the mat.

Nothing.

'Pity.'

I think it's a pity too. When my neighbour isn't home I look at his newspaper. I do it very carefully so as not to make any folds. I love newspapers. I have a lot of them myself. I'm afraid to throw out newspapers; it's like throwing out a whole day.

I walk into my room. It was furnished by the doctor and my mother. It has all kinds of things in it. My neighbour also has chairs. I once went upstairs, to his room. People visit him sometimes and then they sit in those chairs. They're not afraid to talk loudly; I listen to their music. There's usually three or four of them. Sometimes only one, but then it's a woman. I sometimes have to open the door for a woman. The woman then asks where she has to go. Then I say, 'Upstairs.'

She comes back down and asks me where she can find the hot water. But I don't know where the hot water is upstairs.

When I first started living on my own the doctor gave me tablets. He said many people who live on their own take tablets. I said that I would rather not live on my own then, but he said my mother would mix the tablets in with my dinner.

So now I live alone. Everyone says I'm doing really well. I get dressed in the morning. At night I get undressed. But I would rather be in my pyjamas all day.

Once my neighbour invited me over. It was his birthday. First, I took a bath. It was fun. There were many people. I joined a little group of them. They were very nice. They made jokes about a dog and a lady. I also made jokes about a dog and a lady. The doctor said that was very good.

When it's my birthday I want money. The doctor and my mother visit often and they bring money. I used to get more money, but the doctor said I was using it for strange things and that this was not okay.

There used to be a grandma who came to my birthdays. But she wasn't a real grandma. We had adopted her, my mother said; she is very old and has no soul. She was very deaf and she was a vegetarian. She always took a large bottle from her bag and put it on the table. She then put her hand on the bottle and said, 'Cherry brandy, children.'

One day she got the flu. They wet her lips for a few days and then she was dead. But I didn't notice that until my birthday.

I don't like my birthdays. I do like sweet wine, and wine gums and those sweets that look like raspberries. My mother says I shouldn't eat only sweets. Because my teeth will fall out. Sometimes she's gone. Then she disappears into a building for a few weeks.

I can usually feel it when she's about to disappear. Then she paces up and down the house all day, just like me, and there's no dinner when I come home.

'Did you see anything strange?' she asks then.

I always see something strange.

She says: You should eat more and work, work, work at last. Then she goes upstairs.

She left a few days later. I'm not allowed to visit her. That's not good for me, the doctor says. After a few weeks she returns, she has a tan; she laughs and is friendly and very far away.

During the weeks when she's away a friend of hers often comes to bring me food. I don't like the food this friend brings. I throw it out. I don't tell that to the doctor. Once, I went to the doctor's home; we lit candles and we sang. I don't really like it when people sing.

The doctor said I should find an activity because sitting at home all day isn't good for me. Then I was sent to a lady who made things out of clay. I also had to make things out of clay. The lady was very good at this. I wasn't: my clay looked like sausages. She smoothed my hair and gave me cake.

I like reading and even better I like being read to. My mother won't read to me any more and the doctor doesn't either. He says I should ask my girlfriend to.

My mother talks to herself. She paces up and down the kitchen and throws her hands in the air. How I have sinned, Lord, and how you have punished me. It isn't fair, I'm no worse than other people.

She often argues with God.

Sometimes during dinner she grabs my head and presses it against her belly. At least I still have you, my little Mattel, she calls out. I don't mind lying against her belly, but I do mind it when I'm having dinner.

3.

You have to close, you have to close. But the rubbish bag won't close. I push the rubbish down, but it comes back up again. Grape seeds are stuck to my hand, and it's all scratched. I hide the rubbish bag.

This makes my mother sad and it makes the doctor sad. It'll be all right, he says, all right. But the rubbish bag won't close. Until a lady comes. She was sent by my mother. She says she wasn't, but I know precisely how it went. She closes the rubbish bag and waters the plants. There are plants here that are my mother's.

They are living beings, she says. Sometimes I remember and then I water them. But I haven't been allowed to do that for four weeks now. They say I drowned four of them.

When it gets dark, I draw the curtains. But there are many days when I don't because I haven't opened them.

The days are long, but so are the nights. I walk from the front to the back and from the back to the front. There are many sounds that frighten me.

When it's quiet, I look at myself in the mirror. I have nine birthmarks on my belly. They keep growing. The doctor says it only seems that way. Below my belly is my member.

My mother had trouble with her elbows. She massaged her elbows with an appliance that spun around. I tried the appliance on myself one day. It worked everywhere, but especially on my member. From then on, I used the appliance every day until one night it short-circuited. Then the appliance stopped working.

The doctor often talks about seminal discharge. I think discharge is a strange word. Like some invisible pond.

The doctor asked what I think about my body. I told him that there is a body but that I don't think anything about it. It moves below me and beside me and it is warm, but it isn't mine. It's all some sort of pet. I'm afraid of pets. I'm afraid of all animals. I used to have three fish. I poisoned them with lots of fish food.

When the weather is good I sometimes go to the park. There's a lady that I meet there. I don't know exactly what we do there. I think it's terrible to die alone; I would like to die together with a lady. That's what I told the doctor. I don't know if I'm afraid of that. I've never experienced anything like that. I've never escaped death, they say. I haven't escaped anything.

4.

I have a telephone; when it rings it's my mother. Now I also have a telephone number. A lady's telephone number. I put it next to my telephone. I often call the talking clock and the weather report to see if it's correct. There are many numbers written on lampposts. I memorise them all.

I would like to call her. The doctor would think that is very good.

My mother isn't here now, she's back inside the building and they're not allowed to use the telephone in there.

My neighbour has company. I used to listen in the hallway to what they were saying, but now they only say things they've said before.

The doctor says it's good I can remember so many things but I should try not to remember everything. He also says it didn't used to be like that.

He says some people saw this coming, and then he looks at me. My mother also says this a lot.

He asks me if I can remember things from the past.

I tell him I'm happy I don't have to make things out of clay anymore.

He says, No, from further back.

Further back I went to school. I was good at school, people said.

Right, the doctor says.

I walked down corridors.

Why are you walking down the corridors? You're supposed to be in class, a man says.

I can't sit in class; I must walk down corridors now.

That's not allowed.

When nobody is watching, I walk down corridors anyway. In the winter, the class windows become all frosted. I see people in the corridors. I met a man there who was with a woman.

'We'll show you something,' they said. The man took the woman's head and put his mouth to her mouth. Then they sucked their mouths together.

'This is my girlfriend,' he said.

I didn't think it was nice to suck your mouths together like that. I once had a girlfriend but we never sucked our mouths together like that. I had dinner with her in a restaurant, I visited The Hague with her, I kissed her on the cheek a few times.

Some people thought she looked like a folded umbrella but I told her I didn't think she looked like a folded umbrella.

'And what else?'

I used to walk in the streets. I walked there because I didn't feel like being anywhere else. I had cups of coffee in a café and counted the people who came in. My mother sucked tablets, my father chewed carrots, I did both. Eventually, I didn't even want to be in the streets any more, either.

I don't know any places where I would like to stay.

The doctor says I should look carefully.

There's always something missing wherever I go. And there are always faces with strange smiles and too many voices. Dirty glasses on the table that suddenly change position and turn clean.

I ask him if he's ever looked at the inside of his refrigerator. He shakes his head.

I have, one afternoon. Strange things happen in

refrigerators. I don't open them any more.

'And what else?'

People have left, I have left too. I've done everything I've seen other people do. There was nothing left I wanted to do. I hid myself, but they found me, of course.

The doctor nods approvingly, of course he knows all this.

'You need to go out more.'

When he has nothing left to say, he says I need to go out more. I find that difficult sometimes. I would like to become transparent. I want to have my body treated so it becomes transparent.

But I do go out. I go to the chemist's to buy wine gums or to the wine store. There are always a lot of people walking the streets. I walk the streets with bottles and paper bags.

I don't know what other people think. Maybe there are people who don't like me at all and who'll knock my evening dinner out of my hands.

That has never happened, has it? the doctor says. My mother says the same thing.

I know that. But he also says there are many things we don't understand that we have to come to terms with anyway.

I don't know why they would want to knock my evening dinner from my arms but I don't mind coming to terms with it. He doesn't understand that and says it is not something that is likely to happen. But I see many different things in the street, so much that it is difficult to remember it all.

At night, I twirl my hair by the window. My neighbour has gone out to a bar with his friends. It is quiet, but not quiet enough.

I feel good, nothing happens.

He says, Life just passes you by; it's a shame, a shame.

Life thunders on inside me.

Wouldn't you like to have a guinea pig or a turtle? the doctor asks.

I have said many times that I don't like pets. Some fish eat mosquito eggs. You can buy those in the shop. But there is no one who'll eat my seeds. The doctor told me to save everything; he looks at it and writes it down.

I like newspapers, they smell good and when they're fresh they give me black fingers. I sometimes fall asleep on the paper. The doctor and my mother say that this is dirty.

5.

I called her and wrote down her address; her name is Mieke. The doctor would be proud of me.

My mother is back in her building; she walks the garden, she doesn't see anyone. She is very quiet.

I've put a book in my coat pocket. A book about a fat man who can fly; it's my favourite book. I walked by Mieke's house. I walk by her house every day. The doctor says it's time I ring the doorbell. He doesn't know I can't do that; there are many things he knows nothing about.

There are good chairs and bad chairs. There are places that have no chairs at all. I think Mieke's chairs will be good chairs. But I won't be able to sit on them. I can't go in there and sit on the chairs and then leave again.

The doctor says I must learn to forget more, just like my mother is learning to do inside her building. But there are so many things I must forget, it's just too much.

He comes by every day, not for long, but every day.

The doctor says it's a big world and that I'm part of it too. The world is far away.

It gets dark early here, and then gradually later and then earlier again. I know all that.

I told him about Mieke, I told him everything I know. He says, You have to ring her doorbell, you have to do something.

I walk by her house, every day. Sometimes more than once.

Mieke is beautiful. That should be enough. I would like to tell her that but I don't know how.

Later I go to the chemist's and buy wine gums. There are many people inside. They could slap me in the face, that's how close I am.

Everybody needs other people, the doctor says. Like I don't know that.

If they can slap me in the face, they could also not do it. They could also say: You are Leopold Mangelmann. They could recognise me. There are many ways to be recognised. Mieke recognised me as well.

Fortunately, there are not many people left who recognise me. Except for my mother and the doctor there is no one I recognise either.

Mieke, for a moment, very quickly.

My mother lies inside the building, because she wants to be saved. Says the doctor. Everyone I know wants to be saved.

Mieke is pale, but she makes her lips red. In the morning before she goes out and again, later in the day. I can't describe what she looks like.

The doctor says I really should meet with her someplace. I don't know where, there are no places to meet.

Maybe she is roasting meat now, or maybe her boyfriend is sucking his mouth to hers, or maybe she's screaming.

The doctor has told me all about dread. Everybody screams in dread when they think nobody can hear them. I don't know where Mieke screams, but I would like to hear her.

He tells me she won't be beautiful forever, that her body will bend and sag. But now she is beautiful.

I hope she will want to save me. The doctor says I shouldn't rely on that, but he also says that nobody knows exactly what it is. So it's okay for me to have these thoughts when I walk down her street and afterwards, as well.

I've decided I will keep walking down her street every day until I can no longer walk. The doctor says this is completely useless. But I don't mind, I don't mind at all.

The doctor discusses everything with my mother. I know that. He also says: Your mother was in a war. That's why she walks through the garden without seeing you or me or anybody.

I wasn't in any war. I was in my mother. All around me are all kinds of things without a mother. They were taken here; they stay here for a little while. Last week I counted five chairs and two tables and three plants. Now I only see one table. I can't remember what the other table was feeling.

Still, I don't ring Mieke's doorbell. For I might fall off the world, and then I might die. I don't have propellers on my back, like that little round man in my book.

Ushi and Septembrius

The beach was like any beach on a day too hot for anyone to go out, a day on which you'd rather stretch out in a tub filled with ice-cold beer. But I knew that the man with the long legs and the short brown hair lounging in the deck chair didn't care about this: he was out here every day.

We had been here a whole week by then. Every corner of this coastal town smelled of food, and even the sea carried the smell of stale pizza marinara. My mother had gone into town to buy new shoes. She had been going into town to buy new shoes for three days in a row. And she would be going for the following days too, until every shop assistant in every shoe shop in town was raring to a the noose around her neck in person. My father was sitting to my right. My mother had put a white cap on his head; he hardly had any hair left and she was afraid his scalp might burn.

Just as there are people who are convinced they can fly, so my father was convinced he could walk. On the very first morning, he had tried to get up eight times and fallen down into the sand. My mother and I then had to pick him back up and put him back in his chair. But when he fell down for the eighth time that morning, my mother threw three little fried fish on the ground and shouted: 'You can't walk, old man, and you never will. And that's why you must stay put in your chair. Otherwise, we'll have to strap you in.'

My father was lying face down in the sand and cried, 'Of course I can walk, I'm not crazy, keep your hands off of me or I'll scream.'

Two elderly ladies with a dog paused to watch the scene.

'Ask whoever you want if you don't believe me,' my mother shouted. And then she walked over to a man further down and said, 'Please help me, my husband keeps thinking he can walk. Please tell him he can't walk, because he won't listen to me.'

He was still lying down in the sand; his cap had slid off of his head. 'Sure I can walk,' he called out to the two elderly ladies. 'If you'll just give me a hand, I'll show you I can do it.'

My mother returned with the man. Together they lifted my father and put him back in his chair. 'I'm supposed to tell you that you cannot walk,' he said. 'It's better if you stop trying.'

The cap was put back on my father's head and a newspaper spread out in his lap.

The man sat down next to me, and together we watched my mother walking off across the beach with a large bag. Immediately I realised what made her stand out among all those people: nobody walked across the beach with a bag like that.

'Are these your parents?' he asked.

'Yes,' I said.

'Would you like a beer?'

I nodded.

'Would your father like a beer as well?'

I walked over to him with a bottle of beer and pressed it into his hand. 'Here,' I said. 'Nice and cool.'

'How does that song go again?' he asked.

'No,' I said. 'I don't know.' Because he'd been asking me about that song for the entire week.

'I used to be a painter,' the man said. 'My parents didn't call me Septembrius. They called me Eric. But, you know, they had no idea I wanted to become a painter. Now I'm called Septembrius and I work at the casino. Don't ask me what I do there.' He pointed to one of the big hotels along the promenade.

'Don't forget your beer,' I called to my father; his cap had blown off again, but I didn't feel like looking for it.

'He saw a picture of President Bush in the paper yesterday,' I said. 'And then he said, "Look, that's my mother." I said, no, that's President Bush, that's not your mother. But he wouldn't believe me. He said, "Liar, this *is* my mother."'

Septembrius and I played backgammon that afternoon and my father fell out of his chair only once. The best score of the whole week.

At the end of the afternoon a girl came and sat down next to Septembrius. They apparently knew each other, for they started talking right away. This was in the period when I couldn't look at bare breasts without feeling guilty, so I tried to look only at her face. Of course that didn't work.

'Did he come?' Septembrius asked.

She shook her head.

'I'll give it until Tuesday. He said he needed more time to think. He said we'd met at the wrong moment.'

'When people meet, it's always at the wrong moment, it's the same old song,' Septembrius answered. 'Listen. There's a beautiful Russian song about a man who talks every night about how he got up that morning, saying to himself, *This will be a beautiful day. The weather is good, I don't have a headache and the war is over.* But then he went outside and wondered, *Why isn't Pushkin walking beside me?* And that's how he ended up in a bar. Would you like some fish?'

She shook her head and went for a swim.

To me, Septembrius said, 'When I was in secondary school, I was in love with Greta for six years. She was a minister's daughter, and we only talked to each other once a year, in May, at the annual table-tennis tournament. I don't know why I'm telling you this. Did you see that girl? She's in the same hotel as you. She's waiting for her fiancé. She told me all about him, which wasn't really necessary, because I've

53

been engaged twelve times now.'

My father had woken up. 'Let me get up,' he called out at me. 'Just let me get up now.' But I pretended not to hear him.

'Your father wants to get up,' Septembrius said.

'I heard. We're gonna be here for another week. A week, you see. Not so long ago, old Mrs Weinbaum passed away. So we had to go there. At the funeral he fell out of his chair and cried, *Leave me alone, I can walk*. So I just stayed put. She'd had the flu, Mrs Weinbaum. And then one night, that flu got her, because she was quite old. And sometimes the flu gets old people. All those stories about how old people die, they make me sick.'

'We spent a few days together,' he said. 'I only work at night. During the day I usually just lie down in my room. Yesterday Ushi said to me, "Septembrius, Hamburg is the ugliest city you can imagine. My parents are from Hamburg and they're as ugly as that city, and my brother's from Hamburg, too, and he looks just like my parents. All I want to do is leave there, but where am I to go? The rainforest? My fiancé is from Cologne. Cologne is ugly too, but not as ugly as Hamburg. If he isn't here in five days, I'll have to leave. I'll be out of money. And then I'll kill myself."'

'Then we went swimming, to that little island over there. She said, "Why don't you talk to me? What is there between us anyway?" But I was tired so I answered, "Let's just call it love."'

At that moment, my father shouted, 'For God's sake, how does that song go?'

'This gentleman doesn't know,' I called back, and I saw that he was down in the sand again.

He shook his fist at me as if it had been I who had knocked him out of his chair. I knew my mother would create a scene over the missing cap and that this scene would last until bed time. I saw Ushi's breasts approaching. She picked up my father and I was surprised; she didn't seem to mind his spit dribbling on her naked belly.

'How does it go, that song?' he asked her. '*Ich hatt' einen Kameraden, einen bessern findst du nit.* How does it continue?'

Ushi took a handkerchief out of my father's pocket and wiped his mouth. 'It goes: *Eine Kugel kam geflogen, gilt's mir oder gilt es dir?*'

'What's your name?' my father asked.

'Ushi,' she said and sat down in between us. I heard my father say, 'Ushi is sweet.' I shook my head. I thought he had said enough strange things for one day.

But Septembrius said, 'Ushi is a little whore from Hamburg.'

She walked down the beach to the tidemark, where children were playing.

'Now we have to leave her alone for a while,' Septembrius said. 'People who are crying don't want to be disturbed.'

And my father called, 'I'm just going to use the bathroom.' He got up, staggered, and fell down in the sand.

'Pick him up,' Septembrius said. But I was too tired and several people had stopped to watch.

'Please carry on,' I said. 'Just carry on. Everything is all right. He just forgot that he can't walk. We all forget something once in a while.'

It was too hot, and I had had too many beers. I was thinking of what they used to tell me about God. And that the world of pleasure is inexhaustible. But that in order to find this pleasure you should probably emigrate to another country, or another planet.

I felt Septembrius pulling my ear towards him as he whispered, 'You'll never be happier than you are now, young man, never.'

Letter to M

During the first half of 1991 and a large part of 1992, I was a frequent visitor of the Amsterdam restaurant Panini where I'd eat *penne alla pesto*, only because I desired a waitress there.

I sent some two hundred letters to that waitress, most by registered mail, and when this did not lead to a satisfactory outcome, I decided upon the ultimate gesture: I would write this waitress a lengthy letter and make it into a booklet.

And that's what I did. I had two hundred copies made because the printer had said, 'It makes no difference in price whether you want ten or two hundred copies.'

I sent the first copy to Panini and sold some to friends and acquaintances to cover the costs. The remainder I stored in my mother's garage.

The book was met with the same penetrating yet telling silence that had greeted my two hundred letters.

Only much later, in the summer of 1998, did I hear by accident that the Panini staff used to refer to me as the 'pimpled pesto eater'. Lovely alliteration. And strong argument for the power of language.

I call you M, because I can't spell your name, and I'm writing you a letter. I know nothing about you, except that you work at an Italian restaurant. You're as unknown to me as the great unknown that surrounds me.

Still, I don't want to fill in M. To fill her in would be an escape.

It is night, my hair is flattened by sleep, my hands are

small and young, but the skin at the ends of my fingers is red, rough and peeling. Someday, this night will become a single moment in bed where a mere glance will be superfluous. Your name will become a movement of my mouth that will speak no sound, because my brains refuse to send any more signals.

That is why I tell you this: here I sit; I've poured water in one glass and wine in another. Here, a coat hangs over a chair and magazines are scattered across the floor; sheets of paper are filled with unintelligible handwriting. Here is something that answers to my name and to your name and, later, to a thousand other names. Here, everything is a name, but too little a name, or a false name.

To conquer reality, what does that mean? No more escapes – escape could be survival.

The moments with M were scarce and lasted as short as a moment could last. Moments filled with promise are even more scarce. Every moment with M was filled with promise; that's why I write them down.

Last January I was walking through the city on my way to Central Station. It was snowing, and I decided to have a coffee somewhere. My feet were aching with cold and I think snow was seeping into my shoes.

When I paid for my coffee, M winked at me. I didn't wink back, because that looks like a neurological defect. Besides, I didn't know if M had a habit of winking at men.

One month later, I was cycling along Prinsengracht when someone called hello. It was M.

One Friday morning in July, I was walking through town with a woman. We had bought some paper. She said, 'Let's have a coffee here.' When we paid the bill, M winked at me again. I didn't respond; I'm not very good at body language.

The summer passed, slowly and heatedly.

In August I saw M in front of a copy shop. I was just

locking my bike and said hello. 'Hello,' M said. Then I went into the copy shop to make my copies.

In September I met with a chubby friend of mine. He wanted to eat Italian but not pizza. We walked around for a long time, hesitating.

About the dessert that night, M said, 'Doesn't it look beautiful?'

My chubby friend said, 'You'll get another Michelin star.' And I said, 'Wonderful, wonderful, it's like poetry.' There, the conversation flagged.

We walked back. 'Did you see that?' I asked, but he hadn't seen anything.

The following week I had dinner there again, by myself this time. As I was spooning up my pasta, I saw M go back and forth with plates, carafes of wine, desserts.

As I ordered my coffee, she said, 'You seem a little down today.'

'You think?'

'I've seen you in better spirits.'

'Confused,' I muttered. 'Confused as always.'

I was sitting at the table right near the kitchen. I later overheard her talking to the cook about a boat, but I couldn't quite make out what exactly had transpired on that boat.

I had dinner there many times after that. The pasta is delicious and the place is very comfortable. I had many people serving me, but I no longer saw M's face there.

When I felt like having a real evening meal – and I often did – I'd walk through the museum underpass to the restaurant at around eight o'clock. I'd take my usual table by the kitchen. The staff knew that I knew the whole menu by heart.

A lot had happened, I wasn't thinking about M anymore, wasn't expecting to see her again. I ate my dinner and wondered whether reality could be conquered and what that would be like. I was thinking about what would happen to hope if it was no longer fed by anything, dwelt on the conversations that took place behind me, or thought about the bread they forgot to bring me.

Last Thursday I was sitting here at my desk. I had read a newspaper and put it on a pile. I was trying to decide whether to buy French bread and mackerel or whether to go out for a hot meal. This took me half an hour; I decided on the latter, put some money in my pocket and embarked on my familiar route.

It's five steps down to the entrance of the kitchen and that's where my table is, near some other tables.

I saw M in the kitchen, chopping up lettuce – or something green anyway. How do you get reacquainted with someone you were never really acquainted with to begin with, someone you never really had to say goodbye to? Like there was never a time gap, like it was edited out. Like all my moments with M took place in a continuous sequence, somewhere, somewhere else.

Only in the voids between the afternoons and evenings had I occasionally thought of M.

I hung up my coat, blew my nose and thought how lucky I was that I hadn't chosen the mackerel that night. Now, eating my *penne alle pesto* and drinking my wine would be more than merely drinking and eating. I would have the paper in front of me without reading a word, a single minute would last ten minutes and ten minutes would last an eternity; I would be exhausting myself.

This was what the old, dead writer had meant by: '... but the truth is, I tell you, that one word is enough – one word can elevate the entire world.'

Seated behind me were a doctor and two nurses from Prinsengracht hospital. 'What does life do to you?' one of them asked. 'Life doesn't do anything to me,' the other answered. When they noticed I was listening in they whispered and giggled and I started imagining all kinds of wild things.

I said, 'I haven't seen you in a while.'

M said, 'No, I'm covering for someone. I usually work the day shift.' And as she walked away, she added, 'So you should come during the day.'

During the day. I should have come during the day.

I finished my pasta and ordered a French brandy. I do that sometimes.

I realised I had to say something. That I could never forgive myself if I remained silent again – but I couldn't think of anything. Everything I could think of saying seemed ridiculous to me. Whatever came to mind seemed clumsy and painful, laborious, and, most of all, not truthful. To play for time I asked for an espresso and another brandy.

'Double or single?'

'Single,' I said.

I was getting anxious and even my socks were wet. I really felt like running off somewhere. I was really scared. I get like that sometimes.

A light-blue chair and a light-blue table, a wicker basket with chunks of bread, a knife I haven't used, a napkin crumpled in my lap. Now and again the cook reads her Spanish newspaper. Something moves around, something red-haired, something clanking with silverware and glasses. Something that I tell myself I desire. And what does this red-haired something say? Nothing, she says nothing. Her mouth is made of plaster. And between me and this plaster mouth is neither a river nor a place to ford it.

What does stand between me and this something is a place where fear rules. And I know: when you enter the fordable place of fear, you've had enough, there's no turning back. You'll spend the rest of your days in a world without people.

On nights like that, I can see everything. And what I've seen keeps haunting me. It fills my days, until, after a while, something else comes round to fill up my days.

Once in a while something returns, much more intensely than the first time. It turns into ballast, becomes something that you wish would cease to exist. Then you know: desire, too, turns nothing into something. She, too, is part of a destructive, daily task. Is it at all possible to turn off this desire? Of course, you can turn it off on any day; at any second of the day you can decide to bury what little is alive in you in the coldness of the earth. That does not require any courage, it requires very little.

I desire M. That's what I'm saying. But can you say this without looking like an executioner? And can you say this without seeming desperate, because you know what you are saying: nothing, less than nothing.

So there I was, staying much longer than usual, pretending to read, thinking it was better not to move at all. Spirits rose at the table behind me.

What was the meaning of everything I had done and thought, if this was what it all came to? To speechlessness, to hope turning into fear instead of disappointment, to a you remaining formless.

You. Another horrifying word verging on nothing.

It has been said: He who says 'you' does not only say 'you', but also addresses the unknowable eternal, Thou.

If this were true, and if I believed this the moment it was true, then it would be M who tied me to this universe, and even more so to life itself.

If I spoke to her it would really be about everything. Like essentially it is always about everything, something I tend to forget, because what matters is what is true and what is not true. And I believed that M was true, that she was the comb that would comb out my reality.

This is what I was thinking while I finished my last sip of brandy, hurried to get my coat on and walked towards the entrance.

M said, 'I've always wanted curls like yours; you have nice curls.'

I looked at her face and the long row of bottles behind her. I don't have much to say about my own curls. As of five years ago, I've been putting a little red gel in my hair every morning so it doesn't fluff out. But that's really about it.

'Well, you have nice hair too,' I muttered. I paid the bill and took a peppermint from the bowl that anyone may grab from.

'It was nice seeing you again.'

She smiled, I think, and asked me if I wanted to take the bill home and whether it should say anything on the bill.

'What's your name?'

I hadn't done that in a long time, asked for somebody's name. It's an act of blind recklessness to just tell someone your real name, I find. It means that even years later, that very person could recognise you and call out your name across the street. The mere recognition is an accusation.

But it was obvious she wanted to tell me her name. And I, too, wanted to tell everything, finally tell everything.

The kitchen was about to close, people were wiping their mouths, putting out their cigarettes, ordering another Amaretto, and there she stood. She was speaking the same language I also speak and think in. In a single word she said who she was and asked for my name.

I have one name that's Russian, one French, one Hebrew, and a German one. My parents wanted to give me a boundary-less name so I'd feel at home anywhere, so I'd be from everywhere.

Of course she didn't catch my name. She served me from her till with dry hands and I survived it all.

Then I dashed outside and wanted to tell everyone what I had seen.

I don't know much about the things that really matter. I spend much of my time working out escapes.

I know I could long for – and I think that maybe I do

– hearing her say about the cassata ice cream: 'Doesn't it look beautiful?' And to see her, the way she looked that evening. And to hear everything M said afterwards once more.

This letter has been going on for three days by now.

They're ringing the church bells today and next door they're making bacon and eggs. They consider me a bit of a twit in this place because I sit here every day in the same position, at the same time of day. Because I still don't have the nerve to do what they all consider so obvious.

I was just rereading to see what I wrote to you. That I've seen you and things like that.

I suspect. Suspect to see you, and even more to write about that. You could take it seriously and run the risk of making a fool out of yourself. Or you could not and deny what you considered relevant. But it remains suspect. Here. What's alive. What can live. But one word only: suspect.

When writing about something so insignificant – what it might be, later, not now – causes suspicion, such suspicion, so much suspicion that it nearly can't be real, and shouldn't be real, then language, too, will have left us. At least the language I speak. The language that returned and can no longer find a place in this world.

She says, 'It hurts to breathe. And when I speak I don't live, I die, I destroy myself over and over again.'

I don't know what I'm doing. What I should be telling you is that I'm just as desperate about my life as a fifteen-year-old. And that at night I engage in conversations with forty-year-old men who tell me they are pigs and that I, too, am on my way to becoming a pig.

And yet this is exactly what I continue to do: try to postpone hopelessness. I continue being helpless. I continue thinking about hope. But not the kind of hope that makes you walk through fire. The kind of hope that says: 'Good afternoon ladies and gentlemen, you now have arrived at a place where there is no more hope. In this place, hope and death are words for the same thing.'

They say that language is a punishment. But even if it is a punishment – which I do not believe – then still I will continue to search for words for something like you for a while.

Today, at the herring stall I was waiting for my two fish cakes. I'd been standing there listening to dirty jokes for a while, but it was taking too long and I was starting to think about hell. Last night I had heard a man say to a woman who was crying: 'This is the little hell, dear, and later there'll be the big hell.' I imagine her like this: a fence around her, signs saying: 'Should have stayed home, no need to have come, go away, turn back.' A man knocking at the gate. 'Why are you here?' a vexed little satan asks. And then the man says, 'I so much want to meet a human being, I so much want to meet M.'

To find words for something like you. I mean finding something beautiful and knowing the stories about what goes on in the world. And having seen for yourself what goes on. And of course your own horniness can drive you mad, but that's not what I'm talking about. I mean having these emotions without understanding why. And not being able to describe these emotions, which you can do when you've read a wonderful book. You can't do this until you've turned her into a book as well.

And I wanted to tell you that looking for words lasts only a day and a night. And that I don't know what it feels like to have your feet touching the sand.

There are people who say I should finally start writing about my mother's nightmares and about what life at home was like in those days. But I have my whole life left to write about that. And I will most certainly not be writing about your hair anymore in a few years. In a few years from now, I will have done things I thought I'd never do. I'm already doing things that I considered disgusting only a few years ago, when I thought myself to be a better human being. But I can tell you there's nothing I dislike more than people who consider themselves to be better human beings and who think they've chosen the right side.

I had a friend who wrote to me that the most important thing in life was: *sei a Mensch*. I told him I'd rather breathe than be a *Mensch* and that I had to leave him alone with this idea. And even if he were to succeed in giving meaning to this phrase and I were to admire him and find him hopeful, I still would have to leave him alone with that idea. When I'm thirty I will have done most everything you're not supposed to do and then I can still die in a hospital bed on wheels.

After that, he didn't want to see me anymore, nor write to me.

I keep wanting to hear the same things, also what you said about the ice cream. Because it's so completely pointless. Because maybe someday, when most memories have faded, I'll remember that one sentence about a night with tri-coloured ice cream and the pitiful gooseberries on top.

The morning following that Thursday I woke up early. At ten o'clock I was walking in the direction of Panini. First I stopped by several cafés in that neighbourhood where I had a glass of wine or mineral water.

Finally, at half-past two, I entered. It was crowded and I didn't see M. I was seated opposite a lady who had already started her lunch. I must admit I was embarrassed, although I don't know why.

Afterwards, I went home. I was so tired that I lay down on the couch and fell asleep right away. A lady I met on the way thought I looked haggard and asked me what had happened.

Now, it's another day later, the afternoon, almost the evening. I just went out for a walk and got myself some Indonesian take-out.

I don't want to stop talking just because I have nothing new to say. I also don't want to keep quiet just because you can say more by being silent; people are silent so often already, and for so long.

There are many lips that are coloured red every morning, and there is even more red hair. And how many letters have been written that say, *I can't forget your face.*

I wish I could write that.

I can and will forget your face and your lips, your red hair and even everything you've said. In fact I may remember nothing at all while leafing through an old diary one day, happening upon the mysterious message, *Wrote letter to M.*

I just went there again. I read the newspaper but didn't see anything. In a nearby bookshop I had a discussion about freedom with a bookseller and felt bored.

When you first hear a name, you should start getting used to forgetting it. I haven't heard M's full name yet. I want to hear it a few more times before I start forgetting it. I especially want to hear it from M's mouth a few times and try to remember what it's like when she says her name.

To hear M's voice that has left her body and will therefore never end up in the coldness of the earth. So I can wonder where it has gone, where all voices have gone.

I love you.

I thought such a thing could never be spoken again. Not because it didn't have any meaning. But because a word should have consequences for the words that follow. Because I could be saying anything.

Our nights are filled with dreams and night it is. And in one of those dreams you, M, walk around, and in another dream you stand on a bridge and I pull your hair real hard, so hard it cuts my hands.

Liars tell us that in fact we don't know anything. We know everything.

Dreaming through the night, this is like setting fire to what you know. And remembering is not something from before because you just burnt that really well – it is desire. Desire, that is the time before dying and saying 'I love you', it is pretending to have gone mad in your final hour.

'What is this flying around?'

'Those are my brains that I tried to grill, but they're lighter than fire.'

Maybe we could at last go to the cinema now, because everything you know could drive you crazy. I would like to write to you that to know is a punishment and also that to know only a little bit about you is a punishment, that to know each other is a punishment and extremely dangerous, too. And still, I long to know you better. As if that would help, as if that has ever helped, as if there are still places where our love doesn't make us want to puke.

To live in the time in which you dream, M. Time that remains young, unscarred. Time in which I love you, time in which I can say everything and have you say everything. In that time it's like you're standing on a bridge, hands on the railing as if you're being photographed and me pulling your hair with all my might. Not a hair remains on your head.

I spent the rest of the afternoon here. I opened my mail and read the newspaper. Then I wanted to put on my shoes to buy sugar and coffee. I had to use scissors to cut open the lace of my right shoe because it had a knot in it that I couldn't loosen. I haven't had sharp nails for fifteen years, as you know.

Now, nearly at the end of this letter, I have to tell you: I haven't refuted anything. I'm still here, but in fact already there. While I desire you, you have by now forgotten me.

People say: 'This was a bad day.' And they hope that what is absent will become present and the other way round.

I'd been standing by the open doors for a while. At about quarter to five I heard this:

'Look, a bumblebee.'

'Are you afraid of bumblebees?'

'Are *you* afraid of bumblebees?'

'I'm a little bit afraid of bumblebees and I'm not afraid of bumblebees.'

'I'm not at all afraid of bumblebees.'

'Is Stephanie afraid of bumblebees?'

'Let's go and sit on the balcony.'

'Yes, let's go and sit on the balcony.'

I'm interested in people because I'm afraid of them and I'm most afraid of you.

Fear doesn't understand jokes, it's like cheese with holes, it doesn't understand my humour either and I wouldn't recommend taking a boat trip across it.

I find the sound that my coffee machine makes when it's nearly done quite unique and I like to listen to it, but it isn't enough for me. If it were enough for me I'd go and sit under a tree and wait for the rain to come, and the dry clarity afterwards.

The people I was connected to, the people I loved, they were all dead. I'm not sure now if they were completely dead, but they were definitely not alive.

You're alive, I'm sure of that. And I'd like to connect to you one way or another. I don't know of any way to do this, I only know terrible ways.

I think you have to do embarrassing things by yourself. That's why I live a secluded life and that's why I'd like to prove that it's possible to meet someone without starting to pillage and destroy right away. I have failed at this every single day. I can't think of a sensible argument for this.

I believe in fear. Without fear, you lose everything. If I'm afraid of you and you're afraid of me, that makes us afraid together.

I see your thin white legs sticking out from underneath a dress and I see my own thin white legs sticking out from a pair of trousers. Underneath us, I see rocks, and on our shoes I see the dust from our trip. I try to look at us, but all I can see are our thin white legs.

You say, 'Let's eat here.'

And I say, 'We've almost reached the place where I can no longer say your name, where I can no longer look at you without endangering myself. Where I will finally understand what it means, what it must mean to hear your voice. To be face-to-face with the words that come alive in the middle of the night. It's the place where letters are made up of thousands of creatures. Dozens of voices are hidden even in the dot on the letter "i".'

And you say, 'You'd better stop now or you'll go insane. Then they might as well come and pick you up in a van.'

Reluctantly, I stopped talking and the following day I saw you. I must have stopped talking for you. But you say, 'I brought all kinds of nice things to eat; I can't carry it all anymore.'

'I'm afraid we'd be sitting on an ant's nest,' I say. 'I just saw a tiny black ant walk across your leg.'

I have to shove it off.

'What happened to the hair on your legs?' I ask.

'I remove it in summer.'

'Incredible, the hairs on your legs are seasonal workers. And your leg is so light, so light, I've never seen a leg so light, I can't do any heavy lifting.'

'You're not lifting anything; I'm moving my own leg.'

Something is following us, it's our thoughts and the voices of others, hand-in-hand, who have opened the hunt for us. They think.

Where life collides with life, there is too much life.

There, life must be destroyed.

I can't see the desire to be with someone in any other way than as a life-long plea to be removed from this life. From this reality where I've lived through the attainable, from this language I no longer wish to learn.

It's dark in here. Not in a figurative way, but concretely. I don't know any other word for dark than this. And when there is light, then something is on fire along the way. And when we come closer there is a man on fire, or a woman, or their daughter. A little further, and we hold a match to our hair.

Maybe you can still grab someone who isn't black on top yet and embrace that person for the time being.

I fall asleep in the middle of the day, then I make sounds with rubber bands or I listen to the sound of the coffee maker. Hearing that makes me think of an old, balding man on the toilet.

Nothing drives me more insane than the sounds people make; still, I can't do without.

I also twirl my hair and climb a ladder to water the plants hanging from strings, but I'm afraid of heights. So I do it when nobody can see me.

I had wanted to see M again, but I stayed here by the bumblebees.

When you look at someone else, you can already see his spirit dancing on a nameless grave.

I believe that when people open their mouths to talk to someone else, they're initiating a murder. And when they don't speak to someone else, they're thinking up a plan to cut through his body parts.

For the rest, I think you're beautiful and I want to love you.

A single word alone, a single minute, makes everything I've said here ridiculous.

Fear is insane hope.

For the rest, I washed three cups this afternoon and played with a piece of shoe lace.

Finally I wondered whether I only allow you to live in language, like so many things, or whether I could also endure you as life around me. Or if you must remain absent in order for me to endure you, to exist for me at all.

For me, words are not merely a means of saying something, but a means of escape. Language *is* escape. If, despite everything, you speak in a language, you attempt to escape from a place from where no escape is possible.

Where I come from, they were unable to talk to each other. They talked all day long and, sometimes, even until the middle of the night. They didn't just talk to people but to objects. They talked to everything you could possibly talk to; it could drive you crazy. Yesterday, a man was playing a flute on a bridge in my neighbourhood. I gave him some money because it was so cold, and he said, 'It's gonna be some night for me, kid, it's gonna be some night.' And a woman standing next to him said, 'Well, I'm glad you'll have some night for a change.' Things like that really cheer me up.

I wanted to write to you about what really occupies my mind. That I saw a girl somewhere that I dream about, day and night. A girl I want to dream about.

I want to dream about you. Dream only about you, for the rest of time. Because other dreams puke at me, and other words puke at me, and death makes me puke – and all the places that death has touched make me puke. That should not be a crime. That should not be impossible.

(Besides, in my latest dream about you, you were trying to explain the recipe for Black Forest gateau. And in the dream before that you were also working on a Black Forest gateau. What kind of dreams are these? What kind of preoccupation is this? I don't even like Black Forest gateau.)

I love all words that are about you. That are insignificant, that should be cleaned. Rinse the poison from their skins, try to keep them alive, as long as we want to live. In words, this is what I want.

I want to get up at half past eight. I want to have breakfast at 't Haantje (French bread with Emmenthal, double espresso). I want to buy the newspaper. I want to read the newspaper. I want to listen to the stories from the tall man who comes to 't Haantje every morning and who says, every morning: 'I just washed myself again, but again it didn't help.' And: 'Whoever invented the bed, they should crown him.' I want to walk back home. I want to be nervous about going to see you in a little while. I want to be so excited and nervous that I stop for a little wine everywhere. I want to see you at work. I want to go back home. I want to write you a letter. I want to meet with you somewhere at the end of the afternoon. I want to buy you chewing gum. I want to ride the tram to Zoutkeetsgracht with you. And back. Or to Plantage Parklaan. It doesn't really matter where. I want to look in the windows of the bookshops. I want them to put more pepper on their mozzarella sticks at 't Haantje, without having to ask for it all the time. I also want them to wash their hands more often. I want to buy wine and ask the shop owner to help me carry the bottles. I want to drink wine. I want to clip articles out of the newspaper, lose them in this mess, find them again a year later and read them as if I've never read them before. I want to think about that, even to the point where it becomes painful and awkward. On a beautiful afternoon I want to walk with you to Amstel Station and then take the number 12 tram back. I want to walk and sit and whisper about what I see and what I hear and read. I want to think about you. I want to put salt on wine stains. I want to touch your hair. I want to sit down on the platform and watch the trains. I want to listen to what people are saying to each other, and I want to remember that. I want to hold your head. I also want to go to those bakeries that have seating in the back so you can eat your biscuits and cake right there. I don't want to go swimming. I don't want to go to Nepal, nor to the rain forest or wild-water rivers. I want to sit here and talk softly to myself and in an hour I want to think: *I'll go out and find myself something to eat.* I want to kiss you. I don't mind going to another city, if that's what you'd like. But I won't carry a backpack, I'm not hitch-hiking, I don't visit discotheques and I don't smoke joints. I want to sit down at street cafés there and drink coffee and watch you. I want you to call the waiter because he won't notice me anyway. Besides, you have longer arms. I want to count your freckles. I want to avoid noisy people. I want to write booklets nobody'll ever read. I want to finally be able to spell your name. I want Jan Ritsema to come after me with a carpet-beater. Chase me through town. I want to think about thinking about you. I want to know how tall you are. I don't want to dance. I want to pace up and down the room for an hour because I don't know whether to go out for an espresso or not. I want to do it anyway and look at you again. I don't want to buy new shoes. I want to tell you: 'My life is a succession of visions and so far, you're my best vision.' I want to ask you if I may undress you a little, or if you'd prefer to do that yourself, and where, exactly, and when. I want to put my glasses down on top of a cupboard so they don't get crushed. I want to walk around the neighbourhood so I can see how people eat. And breathe in the smell. And think about that. Talk about that with you. I want to suddenly stop and ask you: 'Suppose the opposite of a miracle were to happen and suddenly I couldn't walk anymore. Would you carry me?' And then you say: 'I've never tried that before; I'd probably drop you a few times, I guess, but I don't mind carrying you.'

Why wouldn't I want to conquer the whole world, actually?

(On my way home from the restaurant, I ask:

'That rosé I bought last week, do you still have it?'

'I put the last two bottles aside for you,' he says. 'Shall I give you a box of d'Aqui?'

'Give me another box of d'Aqui.'

He smiles.

I smile.

It can be great, a day.

Neighbours are eating outside. Flies are gathering around empty bottles, a bird shat on my trousers.

I caught you.

In the dark shame of my dreams it is too cold for doing water ballet.

Let's become the rain disappearing into the ground. Or even better: cheap Italian wine.)

But first have dinner with M.

I want to eat whatever she eats, except bacon. But if it's on my plate, I'll also eat bacon.

Maybe she'll say: 'I want you to buy me an umbrella.'

We go into a shop.

'Do you know a shop where they sell umbrellas?' I ask.

'No,' the lady says. 'We're a fish shop.'

'Maybe you'd like some fish?' I ask her.

She would.

It's incredible, the things she can eat, but it's wonderful to watch.

All of a sudden, she says, 'I want to fondle your curls.'

'No,' I say. 'Please, we're in a fish shop, what will people think of us? Besides, you have mayonnaise all over your fingers, I'll have dollops of it in my hair and people will think I'm a slob. I'm totally embarrassed.'

But she pays no attention and fondles anyway.

The Accordion

February 22nd was my birthday. A couple of people had called me that day to see if they could come over for a drink in the evening. I'd said that was fine. A little later, some more people called and asked me if I was having a party. 'No,' I said, 'I'm just having a few people over for drinks.'

I woke up in the middle of the night. At least that's what I thought: it was early in the morning. I felt a large plaster on my elbow and remembered that I had fallen down in the garden while showing a girl the garden house, and that I had said: 'It's already freezing again.'

My next recollections are from the 23rd of February, early in the morning. Somebody's knocking at my door. It's Pauline, my guest.

'There's someone to see you downstairs,' she says.

'What time is it?' I ask.

'Eight o'clock,' she says.

I go downstairs. In the hallway there's a man with short, brown hair whom I don't know.

'I was at your party yesterday,' he says. 'It was very nice.' I look at him.

'Yes,' he says, 'you may not remember, but I came with Michaël.'

I vaguely remember that Michaël had indeed brought someone along.

'The thing is,' the man continues, 'that I left something here, a drill in a white plastic bag. And I need that drill for my work, you see, so that's why I dropped by.'

Yes, I can see that.

And is it alright for him to have a look around? It is.

I open the door. Bottles everywhere, overflowing ashtrays, glasses, and throughout the room – on the floor, on the carpet, on the chairs, on the table, on the books – lychees. And lychee peel and lychee seeds. I had bought fifteen pounds of lychees. The greengrocer thought it was a bit much. But I didn't think it was all that much. Maybe Hanne was going to be there.

I sit down. I have to. The man walks around; every now and then I can tell from the crunching sound that he's stepping on a lychee. Then he sits down as well.

'I can't find it,' he says. 'And I'm sure that I left that drill at your place. And without that drill, I can't work, you see. I'm looking for my drill.'

I'm sitting there in my underpants and my red T-shirt; I'm rather cold and I don't feel particularly well, either. The table is cluttered with empty bottles of Naonis. Naonis, that's Italian champagne. I had bought twenty bottles. I thought Hanne was going to be there.

I'd written her many, many letters that said: 'When will we drink Naonis again and eat lychees?'

But I can assure everybody that I've had enough Naonis to drink and lychees to eat for the rest of my life.

'A lot of lychees here,' the man says.

They're everywhere, literally everywhere, and the floor is all sticky with lychee juice.

Suddenly I remember the start of the great lychee fight. People in the sitting room started throwing lychees at people in the dining room. And then people in the dining room started throwing lychees at people in the sitting room. Someone tried: 'You shouldn't throw food around.' But someone else called, 'Lychees are alright, they have a hard shell.' And Michaël said, 'They're a very sensual fruit.' And then the great lychee fight really erupted. A woman started screaming: 'Hit me with lychees, hit me with lychees.' But that woman was drunk and fortunately didn't stay very long.

'I'm really a musician,' the man next to me says. 'But once in a while I do some work on the side, and I really need the drill for that. Are you sure that nobody took my drill home with them?'

I'm not sure of that.

It's ten past eight. I feel that I'm getting worse by the minute.

'By the way, let me introduce myself,' the man says. 'I'm Ginger Cobi.'

'Excuse me?' I say.

'Jacob in fact,' he says. 'And then Red Jacob because of my hair, but my friends call me Ginger Cobi. You can call me Ginger.'

'Ginger,' I say.

'I don't want to seem rude, but would you have something to drink for me?' Ginger Cobi asks.

I feel too miserable and weak to say no. I suggest a glass of water.

'Maybe a drop of beer?' he says. 'I just got out of bed, and after a night like last night, a beer sometimes helps.'

He doesn't really look like someone who just got out of bed. He looks more like someone who last got out of bed twenty-four hours ago. I haven't seen myself in the mirror yet but I'm sure I look about the same.

There are three unopened bottles of beer left on the table. I shove them over to Ginger Cobi. There is actually nothing but bottles on the table. I don't recall buying so many bottles. I do recall Hanne calling to say she had the flu and that she was in bed with a fever.

'Yes, I'm a musician now, you see,' Ginger Cobi says while he's drinking my beer. 'About three years now. I play at parties, weddings, and art openings.'

I'm debating whether to have a beer as well, but I'm afraid it will make me throw up.

'The accordion,' Ginger Cobi says. 'You know the

accordion?'

I say I know the accordion.

'In my car, you see,' he continues, 'I have the accordion, because I'm playing again tonight, but first I have a job on the Elandsgracht, and that's what I need the drill for.'

I look at the label of a half-empty whisky bottle.

'What are you thinking about?' he asks.

'Hanne,' I say. Sometimes, you feel too sick to be anything but straightforward.

'Hanne,' Ginger Cobi says. 'I've known two Hannes in my life, you know. The first one was the wife of the owner of my local cigar shop and the second I don't really remember. I've known so many people, and many of them are dead, you see, 'cause that's how these things go. I've also worked in a bar, but, you know, a greengrocer eating too many of his own apples, that's not a problem.'

'Right, that's not a problem,' I say. I try not to think about lychees.

'And then, three years ago, this friend of mine says: "Ginger, you're so good on the accordion, you could make that your living." You see, I studied philosophy, but that doesn't even earn you peanuts. Now things aren't so bad. Some months are better than others. But then I just take on some extra work on the side.' He opens a second bottle.

Ginger Cobi, is what I'd like to say, I don't care if you drink all the beer in the world, but could you please leave me alone now, will you? But I can't get the words out of my mouth.

'So now they're waiting for me there,' Ginger Cobi says. 'On the Elandsgracht. I was supposed to start at eight. Do the bathroom. But do you think Ginger Cobi doesn't know what it's like to wait, hmm, do you?'

I tell him that for the moment I'm not thinking anything at all.

'Everybody's waiting for somebody, but Ginger Cobi waits for no one.' He slams his fist on the table. An empty bottle crashes to the floor. It's a miracle only one bottle falls. 'Cheers,' says Ginger Cobi. 'Shall I show you my accordion?'

All of sudden I've had enough. Enough of that man, enough of his accordion and of his drill, enough of empty bottles. And just as you can have a lucid moment between two delirious ones, I make a decision, there in my underpants in the early morning, sitting next to Ginger Cobi who just keeps rambling on. And I say, 'I've had it. I'm leaving every empty bottle just where it is. I'm not going to the recycling bin. Not anymore. Not before. Before she's come, she, who reads to me quietly. This is a sacred decision, made on Tuesday morning, February 23rd.'

He answers, 'Everybody's waiting for somebody, but Ginger Cobi waits for no one. It's a song. Actually, I should get my accordion out so I can sing it for you. It's my best song, if I do say so myself.'

'My house will be a museum of empty bottles,' I say. 'The first empty-bottle museum in the Netherlands.'

'That's great,' Ginger Cobi says. 'Then I'll come and play the accordion. Liven things up a little in that empty-bottle museum of yours.' He puts his arm around my shoulder and says, 'You're a friend, you're Ginger Cobi's friend.'

He empties the second bottle.

Ginger Cobi had a third bottle of beer and then went home. At least, that was his intention. At the door he said, 'Let's see where I left my little car; it's not gonna work out today, a red Suzuki.'

For the record, I want to mention that I did throw up after all – at about a quarter past twelve, in my bathtub. It was the lobster soup I'd had at the Film Museum the night before.

I cleaned the bathtub with a lot of Jif, and while I was cleaning, I kept having this strange thought: I should be washed at ninety degrees Celsius, the stains won't come out otherwise.

Because the idea kept rattling around my head, I wrote a letter to Hanne that same afternoon, in which I said I indeed wanted to be washed at ninety degrees Celsius.

Mandelstam wrote: Forgive me for what I'm saying. Read it... softly, softly.

Johanna, The Book

The first book I ever made for a woman was *Johanna, The Book*. The woman in question was Johanna, the actress for whom I was to write a monologue.

The gift did not receive a warm welcome, however.

When I handed her the book, she took my hand. I pulled back because my hands were all sweaty. I didn't think that would be such a good start for an erotic relationship.

Later, she wanted to burn every single copy of the book: she wanted to prevent it from falling into the wrong hands.

Thanks to Johanna, I learned about desire turning into book–burning.

Even a woman you haven't conquered can enrich your life.

What I really want to ask you is: could you let me become one of your memories, then I'll let you become one of mine?

But 'letting' is not the issue here. They surround me, like uninvited guests, like annoying children.

So now urinating, too, is becoming a hardship. Some people talk to their dogs, their plants, or their refrigerators. I now do it automatically, here and in the bathroom. I talk and talk; don't remember all that much.

What's there to tell about a day like today? That I'm sitting at the table, with my coat on because it's cold, reading poetry by Fried and eating too many cherries? My guest cancelled on account of the flu. I walk to the kitchen, pour myself a glass of mineral water, open the doors to the garden, sit at my desk. I haven't done anything for days.

I've tried my best to bribe the day at sunrise; but it showed no interest at all. I've tried to placate my hands and my thoughts, tried to mollify them with a little singing, but they, too, didn't answer. Like some strange occupying force they still decide who – or what – becomes a spectre, a phantom. I've cursed her because she renounces, finagles, and distorts. And yet, aside from her, there is the idea, the memory, a memory turned inside out; the expectation only, nothing viable. And certainly not the here and the ever-insufficient now. I'm an arrogant fool, a liar, and I'll be defeated because I oppose that which enlightened spirits praise so highly: The Moment.

The moment. It is the pacing back and forth from living room to dining room and from dining room to kitchen, from kitchen to bathroom, and from bathroom back to living room. It's the hesitation – to open the wine now or to wait another hour. It's going down the decaying steps to reach the wet grass and then return to the starting point. The moment is staring at a few dozen gnats that always buzz around the same branch of the same tree, at the same time. (The only thing I'm not sure of is whether they're always the same gnats). And finally, it's the nervously feeding on grapes or some other fruit; the drinking of wine, the waiting for the evening to come when this is no longer necessary. Then there is the nervous scratching of the back of your head, even though the last louse there was exterminated more than a decade ago. I'm a dangerous dreamer, people say, or worse, because I want to turn even a shrivelled leaf into a tree, a bare bone into a lamb, a droplet of wine into grapes, sand and dust into gold, our casual meetings into a story, you into a book, life into life, death into life.

From nothing or nothing-but... I want to evoke grandeur. I will turn you into a book.

A book, so I can always pull you out of a drawer or off

a shelf by your spine; so I can open you unabashedly. A book, so I can carry you around to the post office, into a café, or to the newsstand. A book, so I can drool over you while you're lying in front of me at dinner. A book, so I can press you to my chest, let my tongue wander across the pages wherever and whenever I want to. A book, so that you can get all moist, and the glue in your binding will come loose, your paper will turn translucent, the ink will dissolve. So you can get warm, so your pages curl up and turn black, decompose.

A book that I can keep lying around my room, rip out pages from in a blind rage. A book, so I can bury you to silence your cries, and dig you up again to silence my cries. A book to keep under the pillow in some hotel or other, or to leave behind accidentally when visiting ladies who don't even fancy me.

A book, so your talk doesn't turn into endless cackling, so the whiteness of your skin doesn't peel off like cheap paint, and so our meetings won't turn out to be mere listless conversation.

A book to blow my nose in, or to wipe my tears with or my cum. You will become a book so that I can escape everything.

And see, no alchemist has ever succeeded in this, turning a cow into a book, my Johanna Frederika; unfortunately the registry number is unknown.

I tap on the table six times, walk to the kitchen in six strides to take six swigs of wine, because our meetings numbered six. Let no one believe that they were especially spiritual or even unique. Six times four fleeting hours: a defence against oblivion that is almost bound to fail. From the very beginning in fact, because here, while I'm leaning on the doorknob, holding a glass of wine, scepticism, disbelief, and ambiguity clearly have the upper hand, and all eventualities are covered.

I can still hear you say: 'Johanna Frederika, just like a cow.' You were a cow, and a cow is what you wanted to be, but I considered myself to be among the vermin that crawls on this earth. This is how I used to walk down the street: as a monster, inhumanity incarnate. With nothing but the unspeakable request on my lips: here I am, the scum of the scum, evil itself; have mercy on me.

Six more swigs of wine.

This is what remains: how can I possibly have seen you without having seen myself, without running off like some frightened animal? How could I ever weigh you – fear is beyond measure. For those who poke around in ashes and cinders to discover anything worthwhile. And yet, only from that can possession be secured, memory be branded.

This is what I thought it was, not what I found.

Scheltema, February 26, 1991, seven o'clock in the evening

First
JF   Have you had dinner? I've had soup.
AY   No, not yet.
JF   Would you like something to drink?
                I'm having a double espresso.
AY   Glass of wine, red.
                Didn't know you cooked.
JF   I do. But always the same thing, the same
                soup.

Later
JF   He wanted to see me home, even though he
                had to go to the other side of town. So we
                took a taxi together, and, before we got in,
                he asked me to marry him. But he was all
                saggy, his skin translucent. I said: No, I do
                love you, but still, no. He cried out: '*je suis
                malade, Jo'anne.*' His name was Philippe.
AY   Yes.

Later

WAITER   He used to come here with this oversized friend of his. Like a comedy team, they looked.

[*Addressing two tourists*] no sleeping here, this is not a hotel.

How's your friend?

AY   Fine, yeah. He's very busy. He has a girlfriend now.

JF   [*Laughing*] Well, let me have another espresso.

Outside

JF   Then I had a fling with a rugby player, but I'll tell you about that some other time. Was it useful to you, this evening?

AY   Absolutely, I have all your men in my head now.

Rechov Ha'avoda, Wednesday, March 27, six o'clock in the evening

AY   I found her in the kitchen, poking some chicken or lamb.

JF   Aha, was it easy to find?

AY   It was all right; for a moment I thought I had ended up in some stranger's house.

JF   So yes, here it is. I was thinking how strange it is for you to be here, right?

AY   Yes, very strange.

JF   There he is.

HIJ   No curry, sold out in every shop. Hey.

At dinner

AY   It's so lovely to be here, although I was a touch anxious about the first few minutes.

	But it all went so smoothly.
HIJ	After this war, I said, I want to enjoy every minute of my life.
AY	Yes? You see, I think – you go to the market, you see beautiful tomatoes, you buy them. And when you're home, the tomatoes are rotten, mouldy, full of worms. And life is worse, there are no tomatoes.
HIJ	You don't know what happiness is.
AY	I know, I know it very well, but it's not to my taste.
JF	Shall we go to Jaffo, have a drink?
AY	We had anisette cocktails. I don't really like anisette.

Keijzer Brasserie, Wednesday May 8, one o'clock in the afternoon

AY	Did you have a good time?
JF	Wonderful. I also went to grandma's funeral.
	Awful. Afterwards, we had to pay the rabbi right away.
AY	Awful, awful.

Later

JF	So, this is where you work?
AY	Yes, I have strawberries, sparkling wine.
JF	Lovely.
	I went to Rome in the meantime.
AY	Really?
JF	I was asked for a part. They're adapting Oberski. Do you know that book? I may be playing the girlfriend. It's really great. There's this wonderful scene, they've just been freed, and she's in the bathtub with this little boy. I imagine it'll make quite a splash.

AY	Splash?
JF	A party.
AY	Right, I don't know, but I guess if they've just been freed, they might have other things on their mind besides partying.

Rapenburg, Wednesday, May 15, one o'clock in the afternoon

JF	Could it be any more like Amsterdam?
AY	No.
JF	Some soup?
AY	Yes, sounds good.
JF	This is my thesis, it was; well, why don't you read it. I thought that was a good plan for the afternoon.
AY	*Zeig deine Wunde, Beuys?*
JF	I want to break myself open, that's what I love about this.
AY	Yes, I understand that.
JF	This Johan, my first boyfriend, I met in camp. Met him again later in a nightclub, when I was twenty-six. In my hometown.

I asked him: 'Are you happy?' 'How do you mean?' he said. 'Well, you know,' I said. 'Nobody's ever asked me that,' he said. We danced all night long; he simply didn't want to go home. He said, 'When I'm in bed with my wife, she just stares at the ceiling.'

My father has one of those large station wagons and we went for a ride. We found a quiet spot and made love for two hours. At some point, it was four o'clock by then, I really had to go home. I wanted to take him home, but he said, 'No, I can't go home. My wife will smell it anyway.'

Before we said goodbye he said, 'You've

	made a dream come true: I've been kidnapped by a woman.'
AY	Yes, that's a beautiful story. But I'm not sure if it is my greatest dream. To get kidnapped I mean.
JF	I always wonder what he would have thought, seeing my name in the paper.

Vertigo Café, Tuesday, May 21, half-past eight in the evening

JF	What a totally shameful film that was. I'm glad I turned down that part.
AY	Shameful, terribly shameful.
JF	Great food, indeed. So, I don't know. I've told you so much already. Tell me about your experiences.
AY	Oh, I just sit with the French windows open, and I....
JF	No, I don't think I could live on desire alone. I need human contact. But you see, tonight for instance, I have another appointment and I so much regret that. Then I have to watch my words all night long. I've really had enough of it. You know what I'll do, I'll just move it forward by two hours, that'll only leave two hours to go.
AY	Two hours?

1B, Tuesday, May 28, six o'clock in the evening

JF	I've been talking all afternoon. I'm not talking anymore, I can't talk anymore. Maybe this is a crazy idea, but would you like to go to Paris with me tomorrow?
AY	Yes, I guess I would.
JF	They're showing that French film I was telling you about.
AY	Yes, that'll be fun.

JF	I have a feeling that there's this odd kind of friendship developing between us. Can you confirm that?
AY	Yes, I can confirm that.
JF	Then I'll see you tomorrow at seven.

Later, train

JF	To a beautiful day.
AY	Absolutely.
JF	This guy, you know, I was totally green back then, he gave me this advice: never eat zwieback before kissing.

Later, Gare du Nord

| AY | Thanks. Goodbye and don't eat too much zwieback. |
| JF | No, you don't either. |

Later

The train back was so packed I had to sit in the dining car. I ordered a cheese platter but I suppose the man didn't quite catch what I said because I was served rabbit and two bottles of Beaujolais. I arrived back in Amsterdam with that sour kind of taste in my mouth. I didn't have enough money left for a cab so I had to walk home. I kept thinking: That rugby player, she never told me about that rugby player.

Later

I woke up the next morning with my head on my desk, on a sheet of paper nearly consumed by red wine. I could still decipher:

You, unknowable one
unteasable one

I have only these words left to impart:

91

'looking at each other, each expecting
the other to declare a willingness
to do what both desire, though do not dare'

what was fermenting with you before me
standing non-mouthing, non-knowing,
non-striving, non-holding

what has been long forgotten, by God
holds your unknowable self, which wrings itself out
atop the heads of those who have counted it all
    before,
who have all been counted before

that, too, allows itself to be eaten, to be implored
to be tricked into wanting to become or to be

to want to speak, reverent as if before your grave
non-star of mine, escape, they said, un-save me.

I decided to put it away in the folder, with numerous little ideas that I had written down.

It's been a long time now. I once again spend my afternoons with the French doors swung open, enjoying a good glass of wine. But that rugby player, I still can't get him out of my mind.

Jola the Dancer

Her name was Jola. She was a dancer and had a yellow Beetle and a son my age. Her husband was a philosophy student and her lover sold roses – between the two of them, they had financed the car. Her husband knew about the man with the roses, but the man with the roses didn't know about the husband. The man with the roses called himself Sem and he'd come early in the morning after finishing work. He'd wear a green hat and baseball shoes and he had an old black bicycle that he rode like a precious horse. He'd laugh, no matter what you said to him, he'd simply laugh without ever replying. Sometimes, he'd take a deck of cards from his coat pocket. 'Pick a card, any card,' he'd say. Then you had to take a card, memorise it, and put it back into the deck so that he could say, 'Was it the eight of hearts?' And then you'd nod, 'Yes, the eight of hearts.' Once he'd started off on the cards there was no stopping him. He'd keep harassing you until you'd given him all your spare change. If the roses weren't selling well he'd take on cleaning cafés and bars, but he really loved the cards. You could tell by the way he'd hold them and how he'd quickly caress them, almost unnoticeably. Jola said he used to play for money. That he was one of the best players in Europe at the time. That he'd been on a winning streak for two months, got overconfident, and lost everything in five days. He never mentioned it himself. Whenever you asked him anything he'd just say, 'Pick a card.' And he'd show you a new trick that was always very clever, but couldn't really impress anyone. It may have been because of his posture or the extinguished cigar dangling from his mouth.

Jola's husband's name was Sytse. They'd been married for eighteen years and for eighteen years, he'd been trying to become a good Catholic. When their son was two years old, Sytse said he could no longer live under the same roof as his wife. He rented a room from a blind lady on Valeriusstraat for whom he did the grocery shopping and filled out the tax returns. He did the same for some other people just to make a living. Once a month he'd visit his son and inquire if they needed anything. Seated in his own chair and drinking from his own cups he'd look, according to Jola, like a priest on those occasions. He was a tall man who wore glasses, and the couple of times I actually saw him he never reminded me much of a priest but rather of Monsieur Hulot. Jola was from Warsaw. Her father sold umbrellas and the kind of trinkets men buy their prospective wives. She never said anything about her mother other than that she'd died. Jola also said she'd bought her mother two pounds of tomatoes on that day. The more her mother declined, the more she started fancying tomatoes. In those days in Warsaw, tomatoes apparently were a rarity, and by the time she'd found them it was too late. Sytse had gone to Warsaw because he admired the Polish and their church, and he considered it necessary for his studies to learn Polish. He arrived during the summer, and a few months later he happened upon Jola's father's shop and bought an umbrella and a second-hand raincoat that wasn't really for sale. After the deal was struck, they came to talk about the church and about Poland. When Jola came home that night, her father said, 'We have a guest. He's in the living room. Don't mention the dance academy, don't mention your brother, and better not mention your mother, either.' Jola's brother worked in the Gdansk harbour and had been busted several times for public drunkenness; Jola's mother was dead and it wasn't just the neighbours who said she'd died of sorrow. Her relatives said that they, too, would choose death over living with a man like Jola's father.

That night, like almost any other night, they ate 'doves'. Doves are cabbage leaves stuffed with ground meat. Sytse didn't speak much, Jola didn't speak at all; that's why her father spoke, so much and with such animation that he didn't notice the food clinging to his moustache. Even when he was silent, as he usually was, he didn't notice this. By the end of the evening, over a glass of vodka, Sytse praised the food, and complimented Jola's father on his beautiful daughter, and the Poles on their beautiful church, and Jola on her beautiful hair. That's when the father took out his best bottle of vodka and said that the Communists and God made it rain in Warsaw all the time. This made everybody laugh, except for Jola, who had heard him say this at least a hundred times before, and who knew he'd go on saying it until the day he died. She said, 'Dad, your moustache.' 'What,' he said, annoyed, because he was someone who didn't like being interrupted when he was speaking. 'Your moustache,' she said, 'there's some of the dove left in your moustache.' Her father wiped his moustache and said that having a daughter was a wonderful thing, but that having a son was a wonderful thing too, and that he missed having a son like a farmer missed having his land. He didn't mention Jola's brother, whose only signs of life were telegrams asking for money. At the end of the evening he said, 'My daughter wants to become a dancer, but, by God, I did some stupid things too when I was young.' In a soft voice he added, 'I had five sisters. They all ended up as mothers and good wives to their husbands. Don't ask me how, but they ended up being mothers and forgetting all about their foolishness.'

Two months later, Jola and Sytse got married. Three months later, they left for Holland. She took her clothes and her framed degree from the dance academy. They moved into an attic in the Jordaan neighbourhood of Amsterdam and that's where she gave birth to a child. Sytse focussed on his studies and at night filled out other people's tax returns; Jola taught students and elderly gentlemen who wanted to work on their bodies. She was attractive, and people who could tell said she was very talented. This is what Jola told me during the Sunday afternoons I spent in her attic just after she got up to teach me to move like a man.

I have a picture of her from the time when she had just arrived in Amsterdam. I don't know why she gave it to me and I never asked her. She's standing on a tour boat holding a child. She has long hair.

Her son was seven months old the first time she didn't come home at night. Sytse considered imperturbability a virtue, so he didn't say anything when he met her on the doorstep the following morning. He was on his way to church; it was Sunday. When she went upstairs she saw that all of her son's toys had been smashed. On the nights when she didn't come home, her perfume bottles were trampled and her stockings slit open. That's how she developed the habit of carrying all her valuables and breakables with her in a large bag that gradually started to look like a house. It even began to smell like a house.

The thing Sytse loved even more than his imperturbability was silence. In her absence, he smashed everything except the furniture. But even that he didn't do, I imagine, in a fit of anger, but rather like a worker executing his duties somewhat resentfully, but nonetheless with great precision. Sytse left her on Easter Monday. He took a small suitcase with him and found a room the same night at the blind lady's; he told her he was unmarried and planned to remain unmarried for the rest of his life.

'It wasn't really a question of leaving,' Jola told me, 'he merely left in the way you show out a guest who has stayed too long.' With Sytse no longer at home, she stayed out even more frequently because she didn't like empty houses. In fact, she didn't like houses at all. She brought her son along to the dance studio and the cafés where he was passed around like a mascot, and when he was a little older, he got to put the coins in the jukebox.

Jola's next-door neighbour was a plumber who had a

son and four racing bicycles and his next-door neighbour was a woman from Krakow. Her name was Ewa and all she knew about her parents was their surname. She made clay sculptures. Jola often dropped by to make a phone call when her own phone service was disconnected. She asked for food when her own refrigerator was empty and went there to speak Polish when she had a hangover. Ewa always welcomed Jola's visits. Because a person who spends day and night by herself doesn't torture herself wondering about the reason behind any unannounced visits. One spring day, Jola asked Ewa if she could mind her son while she went out to get some groceries. She returned two weeks later and told Ewa that she'd been in New York, where gentlemen treated her to fur coats the way children here are treated to candy. Ewa never believed any of Jola's stories. Not because they were so hard to believe, but because, for some people, lying is merely a basic need. It would be a crime to try and untangle their lies. Like destroying a spider's web. And besides, it's extremely hard to do, because these people are so clever at lying that they'd never admit to a lie and only make up new lies to cover up the old ones. Jola's son spent more and more time at Ewa's. When he began to talk he started calling her Auntie, and even when he didn't sleep over, Ewa cooked for him and they ate together. He was the most recent and the youngest man in Ewa's life: the previous three had either died or been locked up in the nuthouse.

I met Jola when I signed up for dance classes. The only remaining obstacle to my acting career was my poor motor skills. Dance classes would take care of the problem in no time, so people had told me. I didn't own a ballet outfit, but I was allowed to wear shorts and a T-shirt. Jola inspired awe in me from the very first moment I saw her: her short blonde hair combed back, her red ballet outfit, the fervour with which she grabbed my ankle right during the first lesson while whispering in my ear, 'You have strong legs but an extremely weak back.' I didn't have any contact with the other students. I found people in general scary, and particularly didn't trust people who danced. But after classes, Jola would take me out to cafés where she'd borrow ten guilders off me and whisper in my ear, 'I know you don't have any money either.' I quickly got used to her accent, yet her sudden touching still surprised me sometimes. This annoyed me because I was an actor, and actors shouldn't be so easily unsettled by the hands of a dancer, no matter where these hands wandered. Often, in the middle of the night, out there in the cafés, she'd make me demonstrate the waltz she'd just taught me that evening. And so I did. There weren't many things I wouldn't have done for her in those days.

One night she told me, 'You look quite sexy with those smudgy glasses.' If there was anybody in the world who could teach me about women, it was Jola – I knew that right from the start. I told her I wanted to become an actor so she started doing speech-coaching sessions with me and gave me extra movement exercises in her attic. First she'd made me stop by the all-night deli to buy her cigarettes. Then I had to make her coffee and she'd tell me stories that I only understood half of, because they had neither a beginning nor an end and were interspersed with Polish words. From the stories I got to know all her lovers, whom I couldn't tell apart even after two Sunday sessions. I also met Sem in her attic. He came upstairs with his bicycle and a plastic bag full of roses. He greeted me as if I had been coming there for years and then he fell asleep on the couch. 'My fiancé,' Jola said. She spoke softly and mysteriously. 'Aha', I said, and glanced at the man lying asleep with his hat covering his face.

Jola could have joined the National Ballet as a dancer. She had already signed the contract, but on the day that she was scheduled to show up for the rehearsals she went to Poland, only to return two months later. That didn't surprise me in the least. She was a difficult person to make appointments with. Her speciality was staying away from places where she was supposed to appear.

Her attic smelled of stale perfume, and once in a while of fish, in which case I had to ferret out the source of the smell. Usually I'd find a plastic tub filled with shrimp meant to be cooked a week ago, but for some unknown reason they were never cooked at all. I'd show them to Jola. 'Oh, I remember that night,' she'd say and start off on a story that lasted an hour and ended in some quiet backstreet in Warsaw twenty years ago. I don't know if Jola collected men. I mean, I don't know if she did it intentionally, whether she had decided upon it. But if all of her ex-lovers were to visit, her house wouldn't have been big enough. Even four houses wouldn't have been big enough. Her passion only came alive late at night. In the mornings and afternoons she was chilly and grumpy, and she complained about money and banks that wouldn't give her any more cheques. A stack of cheques and a small personal loan were the only things missing to make her happy, she once told me. She was obsessed with money in general and personal loans in particular. But there wasn't a bank left in Holland willing to lend her even a penny. I've seen her dance on tables at night, or squeeze the crotches of complete strangers. Some had beards, others were bald and wore necklaces. Sometimes they were ancient, other times merely school kids. She didn't seem to have any particular preference. When there was nobody else she'd squeeze my crotch.

At my fifth Sunday session, I got to meet Ewa, and the plumber, and Ewa's dog, Tromka, which I think is Polish for trumpet. That's when the four of us started spending the evenings at Ewa's studio. The women instructed me on how to become an actor, and how to approach a girl, and how to dress. It actually came down to telling me that I should buy new clothes, that the trousers that were sagging from my scrawny butt looked like a shroud draped on a dead man. So I bought a new pair the very next day, even though it meant I had to steal the money for them off my father. They told me to grow my hair and change my posture so I wouldn't look like an old grandpa in his eighties. They said I should go abroad, see the world and be among my own generation instead of hanging out with two old Polish women.

The plumber told me that some people thought it strange that he should share his bed with his son. But his house was so cramped he'd nearly had to put his racing bikes in bed as well. 'Besides,' he added, 'it keeps the heating costs down.' He then resumed his musings for several hours, and only seemed to revive just before he left, saying, 'I shared a bed with my father too.'

Later in the evenings, other Polish immigrants would drop in. There was Jossi, who had come to Holland to be a deep-sea diver. And Jaszek with his red beard. And Ursula, who wanted to start a school for positive thinking one day, and a magic salon the next, because back in the Ukraine she knew at least a hundred fortune-tellers. And there was Bruno, the muscle man who'd lost an eye and helped people move their stuff for seven guilders an hour. As the night progressed, I could no longer follow the conversation because it became more and more Polish. I sat there thinking about my mother who, by the time she was my age, had left for Buenos Aires on a freighter. First, she'd fallen in love with the captain, later with the entire crew. She used to tell me there was never anyone who'd cooked her better food than the cook on that boat. Still, when they docked in Buenos Aires, she refused to promise any one of them that they'd see her again. Eighteen months later, she took another freighter back to Europe. My father stood waiting for her on the dock as her ship came in.

The mere idea of having to be vaccinated was enough to keep me from any long trip abroad. I also ignored Jola's advice to study abroad, even though I gave her a polite nod each time she brought it up. It wouldn't be long before my great break as an actor. 'You're irresistibly funny,' I'd tell myself while walking through the drizzle from Jola's house to the all-night deli on a Sunday afternoon. 'You're a real comedian,'

I'd whisper as I bounced a coin from my shoulder into my hand and from my hand back to my shoulder while I was waiting for the Moroccan man to find the cigarettes beneath the counter. Eventually the word comedian started sounding so hopelessly outdated that it made me sad. I'd watch the smoke pour from Jola's mouth, her fiancé asleep on the couch, the plastic bag of roses and the incredible amount of lipstick she had lying around the house. I thought about the gentlemen treating her to fur coats as if they were candy, and I decided it was time for me to start giving out fur coats like candy myself.

When summer came, the dancing classes stopped. Jola wanted to leave for Poland with her fiancé and she invited me to come along. I had to grab this opportunity to see the world, so she said, and to experience the smell of her father's shop so I'd know what it was like to be alive.

I accepted the invitation. We would take the Beetle. It was the only possession she actually took care of. She got completely plastered the night before we left. That wasn't a problem; her fiancé was driving. Around Braunschweig, the car gave out. We spent the night at a *Gasthaus*. At night, Jola danced for the guests and Sem slept in my bed, because we'd been given the only room left. Sem had lived in fourteen countries and was now on his way to his fifteenth without it fazing him at all. We stayed at the *Gasthaus* for four days, just a little outside of Braunschweig. We slept in the mornings, sat in our room in the afternoons, and spent the rest of the day at the bar waiting for the rain to stop so Sem and Jola could fix the car. They thought that having it fixed would cost them a thousand marks, and they figured they could do it themselves if only the rain would stop. On the fourth day, they got into an argument. I don't know what it was about – I was downstairs at the time. When I came back upstairs, Sem had packed all his stuff. He said there were likely to be other places to sleep in Braunschweig. 'And what about my Beetle?' Jola screeched. 'Who's gonna fix my Beetle?' But Sem went.

Jola was shouting after him that she had met a lot of dogs in her life, but that he was by far the worst. It didn't seem to impress him in the least. That evening, Jola spent the last of her money on a single fare to Warsaw. I didn't go along. I hesitated right up to the platform. Jola was looking around, hoping to find Sem there, but there was no sign of him. I told her that under the circumstances, it was better for me to go back. So I never got to meet the people I would have met, never went to the cafés I would have gone to, and never experienced the smell of the old umbrella shop so that I'd know what it was like to be alive – that I would have if I had gone along with Jola. As for the car keys, I gave them to the owner of the *Gasthaus*.

I saw Jola again in Amsterdam a few months later. One night, at Ewa's, everyone was there again. Bruno, Jaszek, Jossi, the plumber, and Ursula, who now was thinking of starting an export business in first-class eggs. Ewa said I should travel along on the egg truck so I could finally see the world. Bruno answered that I would see a lot more of the world if I helped him move people. And Jossi was saying that Bruno's mother had complained to the headmaster that her son's only pastime was beating the shit out of people, and that she thought that wasn't the healthiest attitude for a smart fourteen-year-old. He was about to tell us a whole lot more about Bruno when Jola walked in. She was accompanied by a large, bald black man and a woman. 'This is my mother-in-law,' she said, 'and this is my fiancé.'

Everyone was looking at the black man and his mother. A cloyingly sweet smell clung to the mother and her son smelled of tobacco. The three of them were living together in Jola's house. Jola said that she was very happy, but still waiting for that damned personal loan. We asked Jola where she'd been the whole time. She told us she had been dancing for tourists in wooden shoes, broken her leg, and escaped from the hospital. Her stories could no longer be called lies. It was mist. Her head was an empty beer keg spouting nothing but sludge. Ursula said the eggs were gonna make her a millionaire; she shook hands with Jola's new fiancé and said, in English, 'I'm a businesswoman, we're all businessmen and businesswomen.' Bruno started laughing and said, 'There's another businessman.' He pointed to the window. We saw the green hat and Sem's unlit cigar. He had been back from Braunschweig for a couple of weeks and often dropped in at Ewa's for a hot meal. But why should he show up now? Especially today, why had he picked this very evening? He, who had cleaned cafés in fourteen countries and called himself King of the Can? He, who made so much money one night that his parents could have lived off it for a whole year. We expected him to throw himself at Jola, if only because of the money that she owed him. Bruno was already on his feet. He could pick a fight the way some women pick up a man. But Sem entered the room just as he always did: like a dog that wanted to be left alone. When he saw Jola he paused and said, 'Give key, bike still upstairs.' She handed him the key and he simply left. 'Who's that?' the black man's mother wanted to know. 'A friend,' we all replied. Except for Ewa who said, 'A florist.' He returned ten minutes later. Without the bike, for Jola had sold it. He gave the key to Jola, gave Bruno a friendly tap on the shoulder, and left without saying a word.

Before Jola and I had a chance to set a time to resume my dance classes, her fiancé and his mother pulled her away. 'Jola is swelling up,' Bruno said. When we looked, we could see that he was right. Especially her head. But Jola pretended she hadn't heard anything and called out from the doorway, 'We must plan a trip to Poland. Nothing ever happens here, but there, life is really fast. It's the right kind of country for you, a country for men what are coming.'

'We're all businessmen and businesswomen,' Ursula said once more, but Jola was already gone.

After that day, I didn't see Jola for a long time; I merely heard stories about her: that she wasn't teaching anymore; that she was dancing in wooden shoes for the tourists; that she had broken her leg and had escaped from the hospital. That she had given a male nurse a black eye and that I should call her so she could show me the world.

When someone came calling at my door a few weeks ago, I immediately recognised Jola's accent. 'Are you a rich man yet?' she called. 'Then you should come dance with me again. You have strong legs, but a very weak back. You need a strong back. You must come dance with me. Are you rich yet? They say that you're rich now. Come dance with me. This evening. Tonight.'

I never opened the door. Just half an hour before Ewa had called me and said, 'Jola's on her way to your place. Don't open the door.'

We Learn English by Talking to Each Other

On January 15, 1995, I moved from Amsterdam to New York, bringing with me three suitcases, a woman, a laptop, and a portable Canon printer. The plan was for us to stay in New York for about a year. That plan failed. I still live in New York.

Between February and June 1995, I took English classes in a Manhattan hotel: five days a week, two hours a day.

I had also taken English lessons at my high school, the Vossius Gymnasium in Amsterdam. My teacher was Mrs Baljé. She had a habit of throwing wet sponges at me, and because I was under the impression that this would entertain my fellow students, I always threw the sponges back. That's how I became proficient at wet-sponge throwing.

In New York, Mrs Baljé has never been far from my thoughts. I even imagine walking into her classroom again, saying, 'Mrs Baljé, shall we start our sponge fight right away, or should we give it another fifteen minutes?'

The walls of the room were painted green and the door was pink. It had a window that looked out on an office building, eighteen chairs, and an old wooden desk with a clock hanging above it. A girl in the corner was writing.

'Is this room 405?' I asked her. She nodded without looking up. I sat down on the chair next to the door. It was two o'clock. Outside, snow was falling. One by one they came in: the people that I would be seeing in this room every week from two to four for the next ten weeks. I saw two girls that looked Latin-American to me, eight Asians – one of them a very pregnant woman. There was a black man, a guy with a baseball cap, and two people of indeterminate origin. Nobody was talking. Some wrote in their notebooks, others simply sat staring.

At ten past two Mrs Hodgson entered. She had a small brown bag in her hand that gave off the smell of hamburger. Her face was friendly, but she had left everything that could possibly be sexy about her at home. Strands of hair hung down her face. They had clearly been blonde at one time, but she had mixed something in, and now they were the colour of rose-hip tea. 'Are you the new one?' she asked. I got up to hand her my registration form. She gave it a quick glance, cleared her throat and said solemnly: 'Welcome, Mr Greenberg. Friends, this is Mr Greenberg.' And so I was no longer Mr Meanwork.

The ad in the subway had said: 'New Americans, learn English. Call 1-800-English.' I had called a few days later. Kristina answered the phone. She congratulated me for having decided to learn English and told me that the language institute was located in the Hotel Pennsylvania. I went there the next day. Hotel rooms had been turned into classrooms; the reception desk was in a former kitchen. 'What is your name and where are you from?' Kristina asked.

'Greenberg from Amsterdam,' I said.

'All right Mr Meanwork, would you like to have classes in the morning, the afternoon, or in the evening?'

'In the afternoon,' I said, 'But my name is Greenberg.'

'Will you be paying the whole sum at once or rather in instalments?'

A ten-week course was three hundred and thirty dollars. That wasn't too bad.

'We will give you a small test first, Mr Meanwork.

Someone will be with you in a moment.'

'Greenberg!' I called after her, but she had already started dealing with the next candidate. A few minutes later a short man with a moustache came into the hall, calling out: 'Meanwork, Mr Meanwork, please follow me.' I followed him. We sat down at a desk. He asked me where I was from, what I had done yesterday, and what kind of work I did.

'I've written a book,' I said. He shook his head. I would have made a more credible impression if I had told him my name was Ernest Hemingway.

'What is your profession?' he said.

'I'm not allowed to work here because I don't have a Social Security number.'

'So you are...' He was waving his left hand in circles.

'Unemployed,' I added, relieved that I had understood him. He wanted to see if I had working knowledge of the word 'unemployed'.

'The test is over,' he said. 'Thank you.'

'But I've hardly been tested.'

'Mr Meanwork, the test is over. End of discussion.'

I hoped that I hadn't ended up in some shady language school: I'd just laid out three hundred and thirty dollars. A little later I was told they had assigned me to the most advanced group. I was surprised. Maybe it is true that in Amsterdam more people speak reasonable English than people in some New York neighbourhoods.

'Who would like to ask Mr Greenberg a question?' Mrs Hodgson said. 'We will learn English by talking to each other.' She looked at us. Everybody was staring straight ahead; the girl sitting next to me was drawing flowers in her pocket dictionary.

'Angela from Brazil,' she said, 'Ask Mr Greenberg a question.'

She was sitting opposite me. I guess she was about thirty. We looked at each other for a moment and then stared ahead again. 'Are you married?' she asked finally.

'I'm not married,' I answered.

'Very good,' the woman with the rose-hip hair said. 'Friends, we didn't come here to learn Korean. Mustafa, you ask a question.'

The guy with the baseball cap said: 'What work do you do?'

'I work in a copy shop,' I answered. Mrs Hodgson wrote it on the blackboard: 'Mr Greenberg works in a copy shop.' I noticed two students copying it down in their notebooks.

'We will now read a story by Marjorie Kellogg,' she said, '*Tell Me That You Love Me, Junie Moon.*'

I had to read from my neighbour's copy. He was from Mali. We read that Kellogg had been a social worker and that she had written stories about people with serious mental and physical problems. This was followed by three questions. One of them was: 'Do you know anybody with a serious illness? Describe something about these people.' A young woman from Colombia had to answer the question. She had brown eyes and her mouth was painted as red as she could possibly make it. When she spoke it looked like a little floundering fish. She told us about her friend who had had an accident and had no legs left. 'Very good,' Mrs Hodgson said, 'Ask Mrs Melendez a question about her friend.' She pointed to a Korean. Of all of us, he was the least able to speak English. It took about two minutes before he asked: 'Is he happy?'

'He is happier than he used to be, because now life means much more to him.'

We went on to the next question: 'Why do think many people would prefer not to live near a centre for drug addicts or AIDS patients?' She picked another Korean.

'The AIDS patients can run outside and bite my children,' he said slowly.

'No,' Mrs Hodgson replied in a friendly voice, 'AIDS patients are not dogs. Who *does* know what AIDS patients are?' Everyone just stared again, with the exception of the girl next to me; she was still drawing in her dictionary. Her right cheek was covered with little red bloody spots. They didn't look like picked-at pimples to me. Rather, it looked like someone had mistaken her cheek for an ashtray.

★

The Koreans had been decimated.

They practically disappeared from one day to the next. Louis was the last one to go. He was the oldest Korean. Whenever he came in, he'd put on his reading glasses; when he left, he'd take them off again. When he first joined us, he'd told us he was in the construction business, and that he had a twenty-year-old son who was also in the construction business. For a whole week he sat with us silently. Then Mrs Hodgson asked him to kindly form the past participle of the verb 'to eat.' There was quite a long silence, but finally Louis answered that there were few things he found as annoying as people asking him questions all the time. 'It's not a particularly indiscreet question,' Mrs Hodgson offered, but Louis was relentless and we never saw him again after the incident. The next day Mrs Hodgson said, 'The last of the Koreans has fallen.'

I usually sit between Rita and Babacar. Rita is from the Georgian Republic. At least twice an hour during class she powders her face with white stuff. It makes her look like someone's rubbed her with Jif. She wants to become a heart specialist and her hobby is reading books about human health. She's the exception: when Mrs Hodgson asked us whether we wanted to change careers or what we'd wanted to be in the first place, all the men answered, 'businessman' and all the women said, 'businesswoman.'

'So, you're all businessmen and businesswomen,' Mrs Hodgson exclaimed enthusiastically. And we all cheered, 'Yes!'

Babacar is from Senegal. It's odd. Babacar is a right-minded man. It's fascinating to hear him talk about Pascal and Voltaire – and still he's genuinely convinced that only Jesus can bring salvation. Seated next to Babacar is Dzjeva. I don't know how to spell her name, so I'm using the phonetic version. She is twenty, from Yugoslavia, has two healthy children and a husband. Her hobby is watching television. Yesterday she asked me if I could spell 'insurance company'.

'Why do you want to know?' I asked. We had just started tackling the sentence, 'By Christmas time we will have shot three little rabbits.'

'My husband had a cleaning job,' she said. 'But he was fired because he only has one eye. They told him people with one eye miss a lot of dust.'

'That does make some sense,' I said, 'you have to admit.'

'He served in the CAF.'

'What's the CAF?'

'Croatian Armed Forces,' Dzjeva said.

'I see,' I said, and spelled 'insurance company' for her.

After giving us homework, Mrs Hodgson opens the window and sings softly, 'We had it all, just like Bogey and Bacall.' That seems to be her favourite song. At least she sings it every day.

When class is over I go to Andrew's, at the corner of 35th and seventh. The bar is shaped like a squiggle so it can seat as many people as possible. There's a lamp hanging above each stool so your food's well-lit. They close at six, and by the time I arrive there are always the same people. There's the black woman who only drinks coffee, smokes, and puts her hands on her head and meditates. A balding man sits next to her. He works in the garment district around the corner. When he comes in, the woman behind the bar says, 'How was your day?' And he answers, 'Medium, just like your hamburgers.'

At my end of the bar there's a woman and a little boy of

about seven. They always bring a wheelchair. During the day, the woman sits in the wheelchair and begs for money, but at night she climbs out and has a hamburger at Andrew's. The little boy helps her beg. When he's finished eating, he puts his hood on and falls asleep.

The barmaid is from Egypt. She calls me Mr Bagel Lox, because that's what I always order.

We're pleasant company. We mind our own business. We watch the Egyptian, or the chairs being put up on tables. When one of us leaves, he turns around at the door and says, to no one in particular, 'Well, see you t'morrow.' The others nod, and the Egyptian woman says, 'Thanks.'

Yesterday Babacar dropped in unexpectedly. 'Babacar, what are you doing here?' I asked.

'I'm looking for a job,' he said. 'Maybe you need a dishwasher?'

The Egyptian woman shook her head.

'I thought you were a cab driver?'

'My brother drives a cab. My brother and I look like each other. When my brother is sick, I drive in his cab. But he's not been sick in two months. That's a problem,' Babacar said.

'That *is* a problem. If he doesn't get sick, maybe you should make him sick,' I suggested. But Babacar shook his head. He thought that wasn't what Jesus had had in mind.

When he'd left, the Egyptian woman came over to me. 'How was your day, Mr Bagel Lox?' Not only is she very beautiful, but she's also naturally friendly. A rare combination.

'Medium,' I answered, 'like your hamburgers.'

★

We had to write an essay about our first experiences in the United States. This is what Claudia wrote:

'We bought tickets for a truck. There were three of us:

me, my sister, and a young man we didn't know. We were hiding under the hood. It was so hot I was afraid we would suffocate. But I was even more afraid of being discovered. It was daylight when we were let out. "This is San Diego," the driver said, "Good luck in America." We were covered in soot from the engine. Our hands, our hair, our clothes. San Diego was just like Mexico. The streets were dusty, it was hot, and many people spoke Spanish. I could hardly believe this was America. We cleaned each other up. I had twenty dollars. The young man took us to a bar. There I bought a green card for three dollars. Now I was an American. We rented a room in a boarding house. The young man and my sister went out. But I was so scared that I locked the door and stayed in the whole day until they came back. My sister became a dancer in a club. After a week she said, "You have to work too, or we'll starve to death." The young man found me a job in the kitchen of a bar. Fortunately, everybody spoke Spanish there. I met my husband in that kitchen. He spoke Spanish too, but he was a real American. He took me to his room. I had never seen a bathroom before. He said the sink was for Number One and the toilet for Number Two. I didn't believe him. You didn't need such a big bucket for your Number Two. I asked his friends but they all said it was true. Then I believed him. Everyone spoke Spanish and nobody was blond. I lived with my husband in secret. My sister danced, and the young man got stabbed with his own knife. After three months they found me out. I told my husband, "You have to marry me, otherwise I must leave." Then we got married. Two years later we came to New York. We heard life was better there and that it looked less like Mexico. I'm very happy that I'm American now, and that I am doing this course. When I speak good English I will find a job that makes more money. Then my husband and I will see each other more often. My sister is still dancing in San Diego, but she doesn't have a phone.'

'That's good,' our new teacher says. Last week Mrs Hodgson had disappeared. Now we have a tiny woman from

Brooklyn for a teacher. She has a daughter who wants to be a ballerina and she would love to live in France. She speaks very softly, so that we have to sit close to her.

This is the first day of spring in New York. It feels like a summer day in Amsterdam. Claudia is wearing a new dress and is handing out M&Ms. 'Do you know why you don't have to give your phone number and address when you register here?' the teacher asks. Some people know, others don't. 'So that students are harder to trace,' she answers. 'Apparently they raided the place once, but that was before I worked here.'

I look at Claudia, her new dress, her white sneakers – the proof that she's American.

Next to Claudia is Anatoli. He's a balding Russian who used to make movies. The first time he came to class some of us said, 'Take us to Hollywood, Anatoli.' He has a camera. We'll be making a film about our class. The new teacher said it was all right. She apparently was an actress once. A long time ago. She doesn't want to talk about it.

We all have to say something about ourselves. In English. And Anatoli will make that into a movie. A movie about Edgar, who's from Ecuador and whose pants are always sagging and who always starts talking about himself in the middle of a lesson, when we're trying to grasp some complicated grammatical structure: how he needs an operation on his leg but doesn't have the money; how he clears dirty dishes off tables and takes them into the kitchen; how once he speaks English he'll be able to take dishes with food from the kitchen to the tables and he'll get tips; how he's in love with an American girl. Then he starts searching for words and lapses into Spanish. A movie about Mariejola from Poland, who has two children and looks like she lives in a labour camp and who leaves the classroom three times during every lesson to phone someone – we don't know who. About Mustafa from Casablanca, who, almost every week, wears a new pair of shoes that we all admire. About the Romanian,

Dorin, who always wants to play soccer with me. He's a giant, so I tell him I want to play with him, but only if some of the girls join in. He prefers to play soccer with men. About Claudia, who makes me copies from her grammar book because I don't have one yet, and who's always handing out M&Ms. About Babacar, who has no interest at all in coming with us to Hollywood. When asked what he wants most for the future, he answers, 'Sleep, sleep, sleep.'

There's a karaoke bar in the basement of the Pennsylvania Hotel. Our new teacher thought it would be a good idea for us to do some karaoke singing to improve our pronunciation. We have a new one again. We go through teachers like some people go through underwear. It's not our fault though. The American Language Communications Center is a haven for fallen artists.

The new one's named Edward. He's proud and Jewish. The first part is directly related to the second part. He wears cowboy boots and colourful shirts with a tie. He thinks he's the funniest New Yorker this city has seen in forty years. I've tried to explain to him that people who were not born in New York can be very funny as well. I would have been more successful at initiating him into the workings of the hydrogen bomb.

After he came back from his Easter vacation he exclaimed, 'My mother-in-law cooked for forty people – it was great, great.' Then he turned to me. 'Did your mother-in-law cook for you too?' He thinks I'm married and I refuse to tell him otherwise. When I didn't reply, he asked, 'Did you survive her?'

'Yes,' I said, 'And she survived me too.'

Ever since then, he's thought of me as a cynic. I once heard him mumble, 'Let the cynics stay in Europe – they've messed it up there really badly anyway.' America isn't a country for cynics, he thinks, but for healthy young Jews, and for healthy young blacks, and for healthy young Mexicans who are willing to work their fingers to the bone. Every time the topic of his grandfather comes up he says, 'He's worked his fingers to the bone to give his family a future.'

His grandfather comes up at almost every lesson. His whole family comes up. His wife writes songs nobody wants to sing. Sometimes she rents an ocean-view apartment on Long Island and writes songs. Ever since Edward called me a cynic, I've been tapping on his desk before I leave the classroom and saying, 'Have a great day, teacher.'

I was the first to arrive at the bar. An elderly lady brought us a menu listing the songs we could sing. I'd already announced, 'I will sing Randy Newman or nothing at all.' Of course there wasn't any Newman on the menu. Two black girls were singing, but they'd clearly been hired. Finally, after half an hour, someone from the audience went on stage. It was a balding man in a three-piece suit who looked like he'd come straight from work to the Pennsylvania Hotel. He sang a sad song. Meanwhile, the elderly lady was walking through the audience encouraging more people to sing. 'Even he can do it,' she called out.

I noticed that there were very few tourists for a hotel bar. I did, however, think I recognised the Italian consul I'd once met at a party. It's hard to tell consuls apart. Especially when you meet them all at the same time. I'm always introduced as the young writer at those kinds of parties. Nobody asks for more information. It's like being a consul: a totally vague occupation that apparently enables you to go to parties where young Latinos run around with lox and champagne. Once I even saw a consul who started singing a national anthem at the end of the party. Strangely enough, it wasn't the national anthem of the country he represented.

Edward had brought along his accountant to sing a duet with. He'd left his cowboy boots at home and was wearing big sneakers. Besides Jews, he likes women and basketball.

Claudia was wearing a dress that none of us had ever seen before. Her hair was hanging down over her forehead in thin strands and she had a big cross dangling from her neck.

'Are you Catholic?' I asked.

'I believe in the Virgin Mary,' she said, 'I was leading a boring life in Bogotá. Because life without money is boring. So now I'm here, and it's still boring. My husband says, "Do you love me or my money?" But he doesn't even have any money.'

'Do many South Americans wear this?'

'Only a couple,' she said. 'Do you know what *amigo* means?'

The elderly lady announced, 'Now Airnun will sing *The Answer is Blowing in the Wind*.'

As I released the necklace I accidentally touched the top of her breast, which Claudia had revealed especially for this evening.

'I'm on,' I said.

The act was a great success. Lots of girls were waving their arms, even though most of the time I came in with the words way too early. Edward just couldn't stand it. Halfway through, he came to stand next to me to sing along, so it looked like they were also waving at him.

'You're her ticket to heaven,' the Egyptian said when I told her about Claudia the next day. 'Blond, young, and you might even have money.'

I shook my head.

'There's a little dust on every ticket to heaven,' the Egyptian said. Then she waved at somebody outside. 'He comes by every day and asks what time I get off work,' she explained. 'I've got fourteen admirers. I had fifteen, but one of them moved to Texas.'

Friday was my last English class. John Cray, the Irishman, hugged me when we said good-bye. It wasn't the most voluntary goodbye: I'd been pressured into never coming back.

John Cray had been our teacher for the last two weeks.

He's kind of fat and his hair is sort of a dull orange. On the first day he announced that the Irish love talking about death. Since then, he taught us at least twenty different expressions for dying. Personally, I prefer 'kick the bucket.'

At the beginning of class one day, he looked out the window and said, 'What a nice, sunny day – the perfect weather for talking about death,' piercing us with his beady little pig eyes the whole time.

There were fewer people in his class every day, but that didn't seem to bother John Cray in the least. He always ended with a ghost story. During his story he would pace around the classroom, dragging his left leg a little.

Cray had forbidden us to take notes. He said, 'You learn a language with your ears, not by writing things down in little notebooks.' He never used the blackboard, either. He said, 'I'm not very good at spelling, especially on Mondays.' After every two sentences he'd take a swig of Coke. He had to keep pouring liquid down his throat. Sometimes he'd press the can of Coke against his forehead.

Once, on an exceptionally hot and humid afternoon, he said, 'My father tried to strangle me once; can anyone tell me about similar experiences?'

There were only four of us left by then. The cab driver from Pakistan was one of the most loyal: every afternoon he greeted me with the words, 'Tell me something about Paris.' I had already told him several times that I wasn't from Paris, but he seemed to forget that every time. Finally I gave in and started telling him about Paris, even though I'd only been there twice, on both occasions with a woman ten years older than I was – not the same woman, by the way.

Once I saw John Cray putting an issue of *Backstage* in his backpack. 'Are you an actor?' I asked.

'That's a secret,' he said. 'My parents think I'm a teacher. Thank God I'm not famous.' From that day on, he always had his guard up with me, as if I had something on him. Besides, he predicted that my hair would turn a dull orange too.

People started complaining about John Cray. He'd tell morbid jokes and fool around about death. The latter especially annoyed people. But John Cray's motto was that if, as a teacher, no one filed complaints about you, your life wasn't worth a plug nickel. So he encouraged us to file even more complaints. Only the Pakistani and I hadn't filed complaints yet. Neither had Sabrina from France, but she seemed a little lost to me. She said her parents had sent her to New York. She talked about herself like she was a post-office package. She was seventeen but looked twenty-five. She was from somewhere near Bordeaux. Whenever she panicked, she started speaking French. She panicked pretty often. Then John Cray made the rule that anyone who spoke French in his classroom had to pay him a buck. One afternoon she lost about six bucks to him. When I said good-bye to Sabrina, I asked her, out of politeness what she did all day while she was in New York.

'I walk in the park,' she said.

'Central Park?' I asked.

'No, Union Square.'

On my last day, John Cray taught us twenty different words for tits. And what fuck-me pumps are. At the end of that class he said, 'Today we've learned that a dictionary is no help when you want to pick somebody up.' He also taught us to say, 'You just want to get laid.' That made Sabrina laugh. She took pictures of John Cray with one of those disposable cameras. Also of me, by the way. John Cray said, however, 'Listen, I'm not a model, I'm a teacher. At least that's what they think around here.'

Two days earlier Cray had taken me aside after class and said, 'I'm throwing you out. This isn't for you. You've got your whole life ahead of you. Go to Columbia. Go to NYU. Go to hell, as far as I'm concerned. But *do* something.' He thinks that I'm copying articles from *The New York Times* in my own words for a small Dutch newspaper. He really seemed to be taking my future to heart.

That Friday I also said good-bye to the Egyptian. I wouldn't be coming around every day anymore. She told me she'd just made a date with a guy for a picnic the next Saturday. He'd written her a letter once a week for the last six months. She'd never answered the letters, but he'd kept insisting, and eventually she gave in. 'He has a mansion on Long Island. He's not ugly, he's well-off, and he wants to take care of me. And he's forty-five. Is that old, d'you think, is that old?'

'Well, it's not young,' I said, 'Do you have feelings for him?'

'None at all,' she whispered. 'He's just coming in now.' We watched him, a distinguished older gentleman. He seemed awfully polite. 'This is a dead-end job,' she whispered, 'What else am I to do?'

Ingoh Biegmann,
Discoverer of Talent

There was a time – not even all that long ago – when I couldn't even peddle a decent toothbrush to anyone, and now, people are lining up to buy poems and collections of letters I haven't even started writing – like I'm some part-time prophet.

It was during the time that I couldn't peddle a decent toothbrush to people when I met the poet Ingoh Biegmann. Rather, when my mother met him.

In those days my mother used to frequent – as she still does – a small temple in the centre of Amsterdam. I, too, used to frequent this temple when I was younger, but then I decided to give it up in favour of coffee houses. I had a suspicion bordering on certainty that I'd have a much better chance of finding salvation in a coffee house than in a temple. Praying is something you're supposed to practice in solitude, accompanied on the sofa by a dying mouse, at the most, and the sound of squeaking bunk beds.

Many a lost soul visited this synagogue in the centre of Amsterdam. One can find lost souls anywhere – parks, trains, public toilets – but you find the highest concentration in houses of prayer and brothels. That, at least, is my experience.

My mother, who likes to make herself useful – and usually succeeds at this – could spot a lost soul from miles away and when she did, she'd take the person home for lunch.

We've had several of them: Mr S., a fifty-five-year-old

medical student who proudly turned his room into a museum for mandarin orange peels.

Mr H., who decided to move back in with his mother after spending six years in an institution. He had something wrong with his hormone levels and was tormented by an insatiable desire for sex. But he was a lost soul, so my mother put up with a lot from him.

Mr K., an Austrian man whose father had single-handedly finished off some sixteen Jews. K. wanted to become a rabbi; he set off for Israel, where they kept him in prison for three years, having mistaken him for a spy. He was then kicked out of the country and ended up throwing himself down an elevator shaft back in Austria.

One day my mother said, 'We have this poet coming to temple now, Ingoh Biegmann. I think I might bring him over for lunch next week.'

And indeed, the following Saturday, Ingoh Biegmann, accompanied by his girlfriend, appeared at my parental home.

Biegmann was wearing tennis shoes; the crotch of his olive-green trousers hung down to his knees and the legs had been cut off unevenly, as if in an act of blind fury. He had a menacing tic: he kept fooling around with one of his eyes. At times, it was as if his whole face was one big, menacing tic.

While everyone else was seated, Ingoh Biegmann lingered at my father's bookcases.

'Why don't you come sit down, Mr Biegmann,' said my mother, who's been around the block. 'Dinner is served.'

'No, no,' Biegmann called back, 'I can hardly breathe.'

He was wearing a tiny yarmulke that kept sliding off. Each time this happened, his girlfriend would call, 'Why don't you fasten it with a pin, Ingoh?'

Ingoh's girlfriend had long black hair. Her chin was covered in down. I find this fantastic in older women, but in her case I thought it was rather premature. Whenever she opened her mouth wide – and for some reason she did this frequently – you could see countless tiny strings of slime moving down from her upper teeth to her lower teeth. She took quite liberal helpings of the smoked salmon; all the smoked salmon ended up in her little belly.

'Poets are a pitiable people,' my father said kindly. 'Do you happen to be poet too?'

'No,' Ingoh Biegmann's girlfriend answered. 'I work with children. But I can feel that I'm destined to become an actress.'

'Indeed,' my father said. 'Very good.'

At that moment Ingoh Biegmann started calling from over by the bookshelves, 'Water, water, soda water!'

'What's the matter, Mr Biegmann,' my mother asked. 'Is there anything you need?'

'Water,' Ingoh cried. 'Quick, water!'

My mother ran to the kitchen and came back with a bottle of soda water.

'Why don't you just sit down, Ingoh,' the girlfriend said. 'Don't be anti-social.'

Ingoh Biegmann spent the following ten minutes emptying the bottle of water, and then he finally sat down. He was gasping.

'My little elephant,' the poet said to his girlfriend, 'let's go home. I'm not feeling well.'

I wondered if the girlfriend liked being called 'my little elephant'. Wouldn't she rather be a little squirrel or a little goat? But then I figured that someone whose chin is covered in white hair and who opens her mouth unexpectedly, showing a web of spit between her upper and lower teeth, doesn't exactly have a lot of choice when it comes to pet names.

'Let's stay a little while, it's so pleasant,' the little elephant said.

A feeling of compassion for the little elephant started creeping up on me. In my spare time I do feel sympathy for other people. And she looked so sad.

123

The poet put his arm around the little elephant's shoulder, saying, 'Her eyes have witnessed all of Jewish suffering.' He looked around triumphantly, as if he had just delivered a tremendous performance.

My father let out a deep sigh; and for me, too, it was getting to be too much. When no one responded, Biegmann cried again, 'Water, water, quickly!' But the poet had already finished all the soda water we had.

I occasionally read *De Volkskrant* when I had nothing better to do, and in the paper's cultural section I had seen poetry reviews by Ingoh Biegmann. In those days, I still had great respect for people who wrote for the newspaper. I thought, that Ingoh Biegmann isn't just anybody − he must be a man of opinions, of sound judgment, somebody well-read, somebody who's seen the world. That Ingoh Biegmann, I thought, must be really somebody.

And that afternoon, the same Ingoh Biegmann, *De Volkskrant*'s poetry critic, was sitting right across from me yapping away about the wonderful riches of the Jewish religion, while the good man couldn't even read Hebrew. Oh God, I thought, here's another one of those people ready to go to Israel and become a rabbi and then end up at the bottom of some elevator shaft in Austria.

My father offered him some wine, but Biegmann gave him a look as if he'd been offered rat poison.

Then Biegmann began to talk: 'My parents are from Rostock. They fled the Communist regime in 1966. Rostock, the Baltic, my homeland, no home, melancholy, melancholy.'

None of it made any sense, there was nothing to hold onto, because Biegmann mumbled the whole time. The only decipherable word was 'melancholy' which he used in almost every sentence. That and, of course, Rostock and the Baltic, where, if we were to believe Biegmann, people still knew what happiness was.

'My parents didn't want to know, from being Jewish, but I am Jewish, Jewish, Jewish like hell,' Biegmann continued, and he grabbed the little elephant's arm with both hands, squeezing it firmly as he spoke: 'We're made of the same stuff.'

His girlfriend opened her mouth, showing not only the countless strings of slime between her upper and lower teeth but also a large serving of mashed carrot salad. My father let out another sigh. I don't know whether it was because of the carrot salad, the poet, or because of my mother who had apparently embraced the motto: the more lost souls, the merrier.

When all the others had finished their dinner, Biegmann decided to start his. He threw himself at the beet salad like a starving rat. He didn't eat *per se*, but crammed down half a bowl of beet salad in less than two minutes. When it was all gone, he looked up from his plate and said, 'A man must eat.' He slammed his fork on the table and cried, 'My grandmother survived the Nazis and the Communists; and my grandmother also used to say: "A man must eat."'

This made my father reply, 'We, too, survived the war, Mr Biegmann, but that's no reason to shout like that.' And he added in a whisper, 'Nor to eat like an animal.'

But Biegmann paid no attention to this and delivered a fifteen-minute monologue about his grandmother, who was apparently capable of all sorts of wonderful things, and who was the only person the poet really loved, until my mother finally interrupted him. 'Shall I serve some strawberries, Mr Biegmann?'

The poet ignored my mother, rummaged in a plastic bag he'd under his chair and pulled out a tiny book. He looked at me and said, 'There's something artistic about you. This is my latest collection of poems, *Faded Letters*. It's my best one so far. Here, for you.'

The poetry critic for *De Volkskrant* personally handing me his poetry – I didn't know what was happening to me.

'You should come over to my place sometime,' the poet said, extending his hand like a priest blessing the Jewish people. 'Right, my little elephant? He should come over for dinner, right?'

The little elephant mumbled something inaudible and my mother asked, 'Would you like some coffee?'

Biegmann shook his head. 'Water,' he cried, 'water, water!'

My mother had already started for the kitchen, but Biegmann beat her to it. He raced past her and, once in the kitchen, put his head to the tap and spent at least two minutes slurping water.

'What a boor he is,' my mother whispered, 'guzzling at my tap like that.'

'He's a poetry critic,' I whispered back. 'People like that often have something strange about them; they're bohemians.'

My mother didn't know what bohemians were, and she didn't want to know, either. 'Mr Biegmann, take this glass please.'

The poet's shirt and trousers were soaked by now – there was even water running down his ears.

'I feel dizzy,' Biegmann said. 'The world keeps spinning round and round. It's making me dizzy.'

As soon as the poet and his little elephant had left our house that afternoon, I ran up to my room to read Biegmann's faded letters.

'I started a poem / but my love got in between,' was the first line I read.

Peculiar lines.

Why not: 'I started a research project to cure cancer / but my love got in between.'

At least that would have meant something.

Or: 'I started building a sports centre / but my love got in between.'

After only five minutes of reading, I started feeling terribly sorry for the Dutch audience that love didn't get in between the poet and the poem a little more often.

Further along I read: 'Your hair curled up / and despite your presence / relationships of great sadness came up.'

Relationships of great sadness that came up. What kind of relationships? Relationships with the postman or the meter reader, or simply with relatives and friends?

Anyway, it became quite clear to me that the poet's life was one huge relationship of sadness. Coming up or not, that didn't really matter. I didn't really understand the lousy, vague language that followed; I guess the poet thought that lousy, vague language was poetic.

Poetry and love were his themes, and these two activities felt most like knitting a sweater in front of the telly, with a nightcap on your head and the indispensable cup of peppermint tea within reach. But then I guess that's what most Dutch poetry feels like.

'Pointless it is for me, who, so often / relates to a body, unreliable / to not give water,' was the last thing I read before I gave up entirely.

Two weeks later I visited the poet in his attic room on Agamemnonstraat. In my childlike innocence I thought: They don't make you the poetry critic for *De Volkskrant* for nothing.

I was carrying a briefcase containing four plays that I had written over the years. The poet wanted to read all of my work, or so he had told me. So I had made an appointment with him.

When I rang the doorbell, I could hear muffled shouting. The little elephant opened the door.

It seemed like the down on her chin had multiplied. She was trying to keep the hallway door closed; behind it I could hear trampling and shouting.

'This isn't a very convenient moment,' the little elephant said.

'I have an appointment,' I answered.

At that moment, the hallway door swung open. There was the poet in his underpants and shirt, shouting, 'Out! Both of you.'

'It's not a very convenient moment,' she said a second time.

And to Ingoh Biegmann she said, 'Put on some clothes.'

'Hello, Mr Biegmann,' I said. 'I'm only dropping by to hand you my plays, like you asked me to do.'

The phone rang.

I advanced a few steps into the home of the poet and the little elephant.

'No!' I heard Biegmann shout. 'You can reject anything from me, but not a poem. Not a poem, do you hear!'

Did all poets shout like that, I wondered. Biegmann tore the briefcase from my hand.

'Come back some other time,' he lisped. 'I'll make you a star. I'll write about you. I'll get famous and take you with me.'

I didn't think it would be a picnic, going along with the poet, but I thought it wise not to mention this.

After a last glance at the little elephant's down, I left the poet's house.

For the next four years, I didn't hear back from Ingoh Biegmann.

On a nice spring day I ran into him again on the Spiegelgracht in Amsterdam. He was accompanied by a blonde woman. As far as I could tell, she didn't have down on her chin.

'How's your father?' Biegmann asked, grabbing my hand.

'He's dead,' I said.

'It makes me wanna throw up,' he said, 'She wants to leave me.'

He pointed at the blonde woman.

I continued along my way, thinking that poets probably preferred to throw up by themselves.

After that, there was a silence surrounding Ingoh

Biegmann.

But then, years later, when I was reading *NRC Handelsblad* one afternoon in New York, I came across an extensive interview with Ingoh Biegmann in the paper's book section.   It put a big smile on my face to learn from the interview that Ingoh Biegmann and I were friends.

How nice, I thought. At last, I have a friend.

My Mother's Men

On Friday nights, my mother hosts single men. The oldest is ninety-four, the youngest is in his fifties. Some of them only come for the food; others hope for more.

My mother was offered several men after my father had died but she prefers to stick to her Friday-evening routine.

Occasionally, one of them has managed to get to sleep over. My mother, a cautious woman by nature, would carefully lock her bedroom door. This didn't always work, however. Once she had a bear of man staying over (this was her description of him) – even though I had told her that she shouldn't invite anyone who looks like a bear in the first place. In the middle of the night, she heard someone banging on her bedroom door. My mother, who thinks you should always consider the worst-case scenario first, thought there was a fire or a burglar. But it was only the bear in pyjamas standing at her bedroom door and muttering, 'I want to talk to you about your son.'

'Surely not in the middle of the night?' my mother answered.

That put an end to the sleepover parties.

'I'm not running a hotel!' she told me. 'Besides, he's always trying to press his dirty mouth onto my lips. And he eats like an animal.'

My mother thinks mouths are dirty in general, and she keeps an accurate account of her visitors' eating habits. She calls me sometimes and says, 'Mister X didn't touch his half chicken,' or, 'Mister Y spent an hour on the toilet again. His bowel movements are getting more and more difficult.'

Nothing gets past her, and I am kept fully up to date. 'Maybe you can use it in your writing,' she sometimes adds, prompted by her unvanquishable fear of her son ending up as a bagman under a bridge. She considers it her maternal duty to provide me with material. That way, we can join forces and push ourselves further away from the poverty line. 'People say you get that from me,' she says.

My mother refers to anyone who isn't a relative of hers as 'people.'

'Quick,' she used to say, 'People are coming. Clean everything up.'

Her own relatives are apparently somewhere on the periphery of the human race and my mother saw herself as a barely disguised subversive entity.

My mother wanted her children to become acquainted with her men, and to that end, she invited us to Amsterdam. My mother's men, each in his own way, are also somewhere on the periphery of the human race. That was not the reason, however, for my hesitation in accepting the invitation. I don't mind seeing the occasional relative, but all of them at once is asking too much.

I arrived in Amsterdam with trepidation. Perhaps it was better not to get acquainted with my mother's men. There is no need to know everything. It is better if you don't. Besides, my sister was going to be there.

My sister lives in a settlement on the West Bank, has six children, wears tent dresses and strange hats. Her husband knows a lot about God, his beard is old and his eyes are fierce. My oldest cousins see in me the sinner that I may very well be.

I greeted my relatives and went to great lengths to become a relative myself. I took a baby in my lap and tossed it into the air a couple of times.

'Be careful,' my mother cried, 'it will fall on the floor.'
But it didn't fall on the floor.

'Don't worry,' I said, 'she has six of them.'

My mother, too, feels a certain distance towards her grandchildren. 'I can't help it,' she remarked about one of them, 'but he makes me puke.' There is no doubt, however, that she loves her grandson. You can love even those who make you puke. Even I have made people puke, and yet I have never been at a loss for love.

'How is it possible,' I asked my mother, 'that you had two such crazy children? One takes God's word literally, the other takes his own words literally. One treats the world like a ritual bath house, the other like a bazaar filled with flea market junk. One thinks love comes from God, the other that love is a bargaining chip. It may very well be that your children have watered and fertilised the seeds of insanity, but couldn't it be true that you and Dad planted those seeds?'

My mother wouldn't hear of the seeds of insanity. 'There is no such thing in our family.'

And my sister says, 'There's nothing wrong with me – you're the one who's bananas.'

So we both think the other one's crazy, and that creates a bond as well.

On Thursday night, my mother began cooking for her men; reservations were made for the senior citizens' taxi service. Not all of the guests were particularly mobile anymore.

I tried very hard to come up with an excuse for getting out of the Friday night appointment, but my guilt got the better of me. And so I arrived at my parental home well on time. My mother was running back and forth between the kitchen and the living room, my sister was reciting prayers, and I was pacing around the garden. One by one, my mother's men arrived, some of them on foot, some of them by bicycle, and a few via the senior citizen's taxi service.

'Why don't you go and talk to the guests while I finish the potato salad?' my mother said.

It's not being that is unbearably light – it's despair. Like

133

a balloon, the despair rose and hovered against the ceiling.

I barely managed to keep one conversation going. It was about haemorrhoids. My contribution was: 'Haemorrhoids are just like tonsils: you take them out with scissors.' Apparently my mother liked men with haemorrhoids (everyone looks for his own periphery). I was playing the role of my mother's son, but I'd had better days.

Dinner was served, and my mother ran like an athlete, for fear her men might leave her home hungry.

'So,' one of her men said, 'now the family is complete?'

Even if we were a family, it was quite an experimental one.

My mother cut the meat. 'I bought a new shower head especially for him,' she called out, 'he likes a hard spray.' The men turned their attention to me. Well, well, I could hear them thinking, the writer likes a hard spray. I shrank further and further, but there was no emergency exit here. I had to play family member for a little while longer.

'I like a hard spray too,' said the youngest of my mother's men, 'but the water pressure in Amsterdam isn't good enough. There's no use getting a new shower head.'

'This one has three settings,' my mother answered, serving generous portions of meat. 'You should all come up and see for yourselves after dinner.'

After dinner, those assembled indeed climbed the stairs to admire my mother's shower head.

At the bottom of the stairs, my mother whispered to me, 'Be nice to Mister Z, will you, he's on death's doorstep.'

Even the dying expressed an interest in shower heads. Nothing surprised me anymore; all I longed for was to get off the stage and into the dressing room where I could remove my make-up.

And as my mother demonstrated the hard spray of her shower head, I wondered why we dare not choose happiness for ourselves, why, instead, we do everything to run away from it, in order not to risk losing it again.

Chastisement

I don't think of myself as someone who deals in female Jewish slaves. Old Mrs Nassweiler obviously does. Ever since I was able to convince her that we are related, she calls me regularly to tell me that her son Jack is thirty-five and still hasn't found himself a nice Jewish girl. 'If you meet one, let me know,' she said to me. A quick glance at the personal ads here tells you that the place is teeming with Jewish men looking for Jewish women. And vice versa. Especially Jewish men – with brown hair, of average height, between twenty-five and thirty-five, earning a good income – are in great demand.

Two weeks earlier she had started inviting me to her Seder. 'The whole family will be there,' she said, 'and surely you're part of that.'

'Thank you,' I said.

'And my son will be like a brother to you. He's a delightful boy.'

'The family I have at the moment is enough for me,' I answered. 'Please don't get me wrong, but I have no need to expand my family.'

'Do you have something against Jewish families?'

'To be completely frank, I have something against families no matter what their denomination, so please don't take it personally.'

'But you do want to have your own family later, don't you? Do you have any contact with Jewish girls?'

'All the time, Mrs Nassweiler.'

'Don't call me Mrs Nassweiler, sugar,' she exclaimed. 'It's Edith.'

'I don't mind calling you Edith, but then please don't call me sugar,' I proposed.

I remember Jan Wolkers telling me once, 'You sure know how to chastise your people.' Suddenly I felt God had chosen me to chastise my people. Why me, I thought, there must be better candidates. But I guess that's what they all think.

Some women fool with men's desires as if their lives depended on it. Others do the same with guilt. Edith Nassweiler clearly belonged to the latter category. In the end I gave in and promised to come to the Seder on Friday night.

That Friday I skipped my English class. I bought a six-pack of Miller Light and a *Playboy* to see if it had Nancy Sinatra in it yet. But I was one *Playboy* too early. At six o'clock I took a cab to Forest Hills.

Edith Nassweiler was a slender woman with grey hair. 'My daughter just came in from Los Angeles,' she said, full of pride. I shook hands with her daughter, a stout brunette with a baby in her arms. She had two other children and a husband who looked like he'd walked right off the set of *LA Law*.

'And this is Jackie,' she said. 'Jackie, shake hands with your cousin.' Jackie emerged from the kitchen. His head was rather puffy, just like his body. He was balding, and the way his eyes were set in his face, they looked as if they'd gotten lost, as if they really belonged in a completely different face.

'And that's Mrs Blum,' Edith said. She was pointing to a tiny, heavily-made-up woman who spoke with the accent of someone who'd gotten off the boat just two days before. I couldn't help being reminded of Amsterdam-South. We sat down on the couch.

'Have you been to Las Vegas yet?' Jack asked.

'I'll be going there soon.'

I noticed big red blotches showing through his black

hair. And they weren't birth marks. Every flake of skin he had ever had was gone from his head. What was left under his hair could best be described as 'crust'. It must have been incredibly itchy; he kept scratching his head. Whenever his mother caught him doing it she hissed, 'Jackie!'

'Are you Jewish?' asked Mrs Blum. She leaned closer to me and now I could even smell Amsterdam-South.

'No,' I said, 'I'm just very good at pretending, but then again I've been practicing for over twenty years.'

A brief silence fell. Then Jack started laughing. He was laughing for so long and so loudly that finally his mother called, 'Jackie, Jackie, wipe your mouth.'

That's when her husband came in. He was even smaller than she was. But that might have been because he stooped. I stood up and shook his hand. 'I'm a relative of your wife's,' I said.

'Mazel tov,' he said.

Jackie whispered in my ear, 'Never mind that. He says that to everybody.'

Suddenly I was certain that God had chosen me to chastise His people. I also knew I wouldn't resist any longer. I would do as I had been commanded.

'Jackie,' Mrs Nassweiler called. And then, 'We can sit down now.'

I was seated in between Mrs Blum and Jackie. I could hear his mother hiss, 'Jackie for God's sake, tuck your shirt into your pants,' stamping her right foot on the ground. Jackie's hands did move toward his shirt, but that was all.

Mr Nassweiler started the blessing.

'Do you have a girlfriend?' whispered Mrs Blum, who seemed to have her own ideas about blessings.

I nodded.

'Jewish?'

'Aryan as hell,' I whispered in her ear. 'Her father was called "The Butcher of Poznan". Now she's practising spiritual and physical *Wiedergutmachung*. I know, life can be so grim.'

The smile on Mrs Blum's face died away as I picked another radish off the Seder plate.

★

Halfway through the meal a sudden, horrendous scream came from the bathroom. Ten minutes earlier Jackie and his mother had disappeared into that same bathroom.

'They're killing each other,' Mrs Blum whispered triumphantly, as if she regretted it hadn't happened much sooner.

'It's not so bad,' I said, 'they're just playing around a little.'

From the exact moment we had sat down at the table, Jackie had been getting up every five minutes. He'd lie on the couch in another part of the room and practice some kind of gymnastics with his legs. As soon as his mother saw this she'd slam her hand on the table, making the glasses clink. Once or twice she had gotten up to pull her son off the couch, shouting at the grandchildren, 'Don't play with your Uncle Jackie – get off Uncle Jackie.' Her grandchildren ignored this completely. Mrs Blum was calling, 'Let him be, Edith, he's just excited.'

Mrs Nassweiler was chasing her son, who was now running around the small glass table and shrieking, 'Catch me, catch me!' This was not meant for his mother, but for his nephews and nieces who were also chasing him. Even though Mrs Nassweiler was running quite fast, she still had enough breath to shout, 'Jackie, stop, I tell you, we'll lock you in again, I'm warning you.' Her grandchildren were having a lot of fun too, shrieking like warriors, making it even harder for everyone at the table to understand Mr Nassweiler's prayers. Just as Mrs Nassweiler was about to catch up with her son, one of her grandchildren crashed into a vase. For a moment, an astonished Mrs Nassweiler looked at the pieces of broken china on the ground and at the water that was seeping through her carpet. Then she shrieked so loudly that even her husband – for one brief moment – looked up from his prayer book. She was just about to produce another such sound, but Mrs Blum cut her short. 'It brings good luck, Edith,' she said cheerfully, 'Come join us at the table again.'

Jackie had turned red with exertion. Sweat ran down his cheeks. 'What a good-natured giant he is,' Mrs Blum whispered. Jackie took a bottle of wine from the middle of the table, but his brother-in-law slapped his hand, hissing, 'I'm not taking you to the emergency room tonight, and your sister isn't taking you to the emergency room tonight either.'

I thought it was rather inappropriate to slap a young man of thirty-five on the hand. Apparently, Jackie was someone who needed to be taken to the emergency room after only one glass of wine.

Mrs Nassweiler brought in the food. Her son was playing with the children and she whispered, 'He loves his sister's children; he hardly needs anyone else.'

'Where do you live?' Mrs Blum asked.

'I live in Queens too,' I answered.

'If you're successful you live in Manhattan,' she concluded. On the other side of me, Jackie had started eating. He ate so fast and with such gusto that it seemed like food was the only thing that could keep his nerves under control.

'Marcia Clark,' Jackie's brother-in-law said, 'has a new hairdo. An LA radio show is taking a vote on whether the first hairstyle is better than the second.'

'The second is better,' his wife said.

'I have to use the bathroom,' Jackie said.

The children followed him.

'Ewald, do something,' Mrs Nassweiler cried, 'He's going to the bathroom with the children.' But her husband sat silently hunched over his meat.

'He's such a good-natured giant,' Mrs Blum said, no

longer to anyone in particular. Mrs Nassweiler ran to the bathroom. Her fluttering dress and her stocky figure reminded me suddenly of a bullfighter.

We continued eating. The discussion about Simpson's prosecutor was not resumed. Now and then we heard Mrs Nassweiler's hoarse voice, but we'd been hearing it all night long.

It could have been ten minutes later, it could have been fifteen. Jackie came running out of the bathroom. His mother was running after her little bull; his sister got up too and started running after them.

'Why don't you go home,' Mrs Nassweiler said to Mrs Blum and me after passing us three times. 'Come back some other time.' Her hair was all messed up. Two streaks of blood ran across her face. Somebody had dug his nails into her forehead.

We were handed our coats. Mr Nassweiler and his son-in-law had started saying grace. On my way out I passed the kitchen. Jackie no longer looked like a good-natured giant; more like a rat in agony.

'Go now, go,' said Mrs Nassweiler, pushing us to the exit.

'The food was delicious,' Mrs Blum said anyway.

From the living room came Mr Nassweiler's voice, singing that song about how it would have been enough if God had merely freed us from Egypt and given us the Ten Commandments. That would have been just fine with us. But not with God. For Him, it wasn't enough. That's how the song goes. For God, it just never is enough.

Tina II

I had kept myself locked inside the men's room of French restaurant 'J.' for twenty minutes already, thinking it might be better if I stayed there for the rest of the day. Despite the venison steak that was awaiting me there, I felt no urge to go back inside. Opposite the venison steak, a lady was seated. I'm not in a position to mention her name here, so I'll just use her initial, E.

In June of 1995, I had received a letter from E. in which she introduced herself as the editor of a literary encyclopaedia, specifically the letters F through H. I understood the letter G was also her responsibility and she had the intention of dedicating an extensive entry to Grunberg. It was for that reason that she was hoping to meet with me in New York in November. She was even offering me lunch, at the expense of the encyclopaedia of course. The letter had been postmarked 's-Hertogenbosch, in the southern part of the Netherlands.

I must have been flattered by the idea of having a large entry in a literary encyclopaedia, because I wrote back that she was welcome to share a simple yet nutritious meal with me.

During the months that followed, I received two more letters and a postcard from her – all three of them very formal. The only part that stood out a little was the remark that she often dreamt about me. I thought it might be common for editors of literary encyclopaedias to dream of the writers about which they're writing wonderful little essays. She had mentioned that several times, that it was going to be a 'wonderful little essay'.

She turned out to be much older than I had expected. She carried a large plastic bag and was dressed in black trousers and a V-neck sweater; the skin around her eyes, in particular, was completely weathered.

We sat down at a table near the window and talked about the price of ladieswear in New York. When she was about to light a cigarette, I kindly pointed out that in New York restaurants, smoking was virtually impossible. She extinguished her cigarette and started putting on lipstick. I suggested that now might be a good moment to talk about the literary encyclopedia, but she answered, 'You don't remember me, do you?' And she continued working on her lips.

Did I meet her at some literary event, I thought, or at a book-signing session? Maybe she interviewed me once. Was she insulted by my poor memory?

'I'm sorry, but I don't,' I said.

She was still working on her lips. 'Brederodestraat,' she said.

The strange thing was that Brederodestraat didn't mean anything to me at that moment – nothing whatsoever. I started to remember all the readings I had ever given in the Netherlands, especially those down south.

At that point, she pulled out a wig from the plastic bag and put it on. People in the restaurant were looking at us, especially at her; some were even nudging each other. But she seemed not to notice it, or not to mind it. She was looking in her make-up mirror and straightening the wig.

'You still don't recognise me?' she asked.

I shook my head.

'It's me, Tina.'

I only knew one Tina, and that was Tina from *Blue Mondays*. I thought it must be some kind of joke. Why wouldn't the editor of a literary encyclopaedia have the same sense of humour I have?

'But my real name is E,' she said, 'so you can call me E.'

I started to laugh. Who, in my place, wouldn't have laughed? I said, 'This is fantastic, E. You really got me there. I fully trust you with the essay. I do. Write whatever you want.'

We were served our fish soup.

E. took my book from her bag and opened it to the chapter called 'Tina'. I could see that certain parts were underlined in pencil. Meanwhile, I was trying to remember what the real Tina had looked like, but I couldn't. It had been too long ago; it had only been for an hour; and the room had been poorly lit. All I remembered was a certain garment, a smell, and everything I had written about her. But these don't count as real memories.

'You never thought this would happen, right?' she laughed. 'Us sitting across from each other eating fish soup. And how do you like that one about the literary encyclopaedia? You never expected that either, right, from an old hooker like me?' She tapped my book with her finger. 'I guess that's how I can best summarise your impression of me?'

The only thing that came out of my mouth was, 'That's great.' I was still hanging on to the idea of this being a joke, some kind of colossal joke. But I was starting to wonder who would ever think of a joke like that.

'Here, read,' E. said. She was pointing at a part that was underlined.

I shook my head.

'Read,' she said.

A lunatic, I thought, a fanatic, a radical feminist. Yes, that must be it. Every group has its own disturbed terrorists.

'I've always been very positive about the feminist movement,' I started. 'I think you completely misunderstood my book if you think…'

'Stop that nonsense,' she said.

'What on earth do you want from me?' I complained.

She took off her wig and started laughing again.

'You'll soon find out, my little writer.'

I took a gulp of wine and said, 'You don't work for a literary encyclopaedia at all, and your name isn't Tina, either. Please leave this restaurant.'

I was trying to sound tough.

'You still have the same coat you had back then,' she said, pointing at my black leather raincoat.

She's bluffing, I thought, she's just bluffing. She's mentally confused and she's picked me as a target for this confusion.

'Is it money you want?' I asked. 'Have you come here for financial reasons?'

She shook her head.

'Is there something you don't like about me, or about the things I write?'

'No,' she said. 'I'm not much of a reader. But I'm gonna make you an offer you can't refuse.'

'Which is?' I enquired.

'You shall write,' she hissed. 'You shall write everything I have to tell you, because you don't have anything to tell. And under my name. You've used me long enough until now; you've made enough money on my account.'

While she said this, she pinched my lower arm so hard that it started to bleed, and I said that she'd better start right away, but that I had to go to the bathroom now.

After spending half an hour in the bathroom, I called my friend S. in Chicago and told him what had happened.

He started to laugh. 'A great idea for a story,' he said, and hung up.

When I finally came back to the table, E. had finished her venison steak. She had put a stack of old notebooks beside my plate. 'You must help me,' she said. 'You owe it to me.'

That's how Tina came back into my life.

Fish Hunting

On Tuesday, October 29th, I went hunting. Fish and birds. I don't have any moral objection to hunting, especially not when you intend to eat the meat.

I had been invited by a French cook.

'I have a cottage in the Catskills,' he explained. 'I'm going up there tomorrow; if you feel like it, you're welcome to come along.'

'That's fine,' I said, 'but I don't have any hunting clothes.'

'Don't be ridiculous,' he said, 'I'm wearing my street clothes.'

Tuesday morning, quarter to ten, I was waiting outside his house. He owns a Jeep. A large Jeep. His name is Gérard. And the license plate reads GÉRARD 1. You can buy license plates here with your name on it, but then you have to pay extra. But it can be done.

In the back of his Jeep he had all kinds of guns and pistols. And six fishing rods.

It's fascinating: a two-hour drive from New York takes you into a totally different world. In the old days, in the Fifties, New Yorkers went on vacation to the Catskills; now, they go to Florida or Europe. That's why the Catskills are peppered with little towns that are dying out.

The cook had a house on a remote hill, facing a lake. It was in the middle of the wilderness. At least to my mind it was the wilderness. Some people travel all the way to China to see the wilderness, but I can find wilderness two hours outside of New York. Perhaps that's why I'm a happy man.

Once in the wilderness, we unloaded the rods and the guns. Gérard has two kinds of guns: one kind is for burglars, the other for wild animals.

First, we went fishing. We had to sit in a canoe. To go fishing. I had never been in a canoe before. I had been in a pedal boat, though, and that had been enough of an adventure for me. A canoe isn't quite the same as a pedal boat.

Each of us had our own canoe. I had asked him, 'Couldn't we share a canoe?' but he had answered, 'No, there won't be enough room in one canoe.'

At first I was afraid to handle the paddles; I thought I might tip the boat over. That wasn't very smart of me. I should have paddled because the lake had a current. I was fishing. The sun was shining. I thought, the fishing line is in the water and I'll leave it there until we go back. I wasn't counting on any currents. Nor on any wind. The wind blew me and my canoe into a jungle of reeds. And that's where I got stuck.

Among those reeds were geese, wild geese. Not one or four geese, no, at least fifty of them. And there I was in my canoe holding my fishing rod, surrounded by wild geese.

Don't let anybody tell you that geese are such cute animals; I hope that when parents take their kids to the petting zoo, they'll explain to them that geese are dangerous.

They came right at me. The geese. I was sitting in my canoe and started waving my paddle like a wild man. Because geese have large bills. It almost seemed like they were drunk. They were all looking at me as if they had never seen anything like it in their lives. Why didn't they just keep doing what they were doing? I really wasn't bothering them.

The cook was out in the middle of the lake, fishing, and I was stuck in the reeds, completely out of sight, except for the geese. I thought: If they eat me, I won't be found until years later.

So I kept waving my paddle. It unleashed some strange

force in me, as if my life were in danger. The geese were honking loudly. But somehow, they never touched me. I guess it was because of the paddle. I eventually managed to free myself – and my canoe and fishing rod – from the reeds as well. The fishing rod was slightly damaged, but the cook didn't mind very much. He hadn't caught any fish and neither had I.

We paddled our way back to shore.

He said, 'Now we'll hunt some birds.'

I said I didn't mind just sticking to the fishing part, but he said we had to get some meat to take home.

'Why don't we get it from the butcher?' I suggested.

That was out of the question.

He handed me a shotgun. It was loaded.

There was a tall tree that had a hut built into it. Actually, you couldn't really call it a hut; it wasn't much more than some planks nailed together. He said, 'That's the hunting stand.'

I said, 'There's not room for both of us up there. I'll take the canoe.'

'No,' he said, 'just follow me.'

'It had been a long time since I had climbed into a tree. But when I was halfway up, I thought: I have to go on now, otherwise I'll fall down.

After a while, we were lying next to each other on a few planks at the top of the tree. It was a fascinating experience. I kept my eyes firmly closed so as not to see the ground beneath me.

Every now and then I heard a gunshot. That made me hold on to my plank even tighter. Then he said, 'Shoot.'

So I just fired away.

There was a crashing sound. I thought I had hit a wild boar. But it was nothing but a branch.

We hadn't hit anything; we had only scared the birds away.

When darkness fell he said, 'It's time to go home.'

I have no recollection of how I managed to climb down from that tree.

Rabbit Warren

In November of 1995, I moved from Queens to Manhattan. The move was preceded by many weeks of searching and a thorough initiation into the world of real-estate.

There was a dead dog in the parking lot.

We were standing on the balcony and every now and then Joan Folson touched my shoulder. 'What colour is your hair?' she had asked me. 'I can't tell in this light.'

'Maybe it was fed up with the other dogs, or with people.'

'No,' she said, 'dogs don't jump. I have a dog myself.'

She called herself Joannie.

A superintendent came by: he tried to remove the dog by pulling it by its legs. It didn't work, but it did look funny, seen from above. Just like a movie.

'I won't do it,' I said. Now, two people were tugging at the dog's legs.

'And how about the jacuzzi?' Joannie said.

'It's a rabbit warren. What's the point of having a jacuzzi in a rabbit warren?'

We looked at the dog again.

Joannie was crying. I could tell from her mascara and the rest of her make-up.

It made me feel uneasy: my real-estate agent was crying. I was her first client, so she had told me, but I didn't think that was a reason to start crying.

'We'll find something, Joannie,' I said, 'we'll find

something.'

She was actually a singer. That very afternoon she had a meeting planned with a record producer. That might have had something to do with it.

'Let's go inside,' I said.

I was afraid she might follow the dog. After all, I didn't know anything about her other than her name and her profession. That, and the fact that I was her first client.

'I'm so sorry,' Joannie said. 'I'm really sorry.'

'It's okay. Someone has to be the first.'

We had another look at the jacuzzi. A couple of days before, she had offered me the opportunity of becoming neighbours with Al Pacino, even though it involved my moving into a rabbit warren with a view of a Chinese restaurant's kitchen.

'I'll give you my tapes.'

'I'd like that,' I said.

'Singing means the world to me.'

'I can tell.'

'You can?' Again, she touched my shoulder.

They had now managed to drag the dog away. 'Maybe it did jump after all,' I said. 'They say dogs are very intelligent creatures.'

She then put in her ear plugs. The New York City noise drove her crazy, so she had told me. It made me think of someone who had written that the only things sacred to people are those they have to make a sacrifice for, either through work or desire. And that he now knew who the real saints in this world were.

We walked back to her office. 'I'm so glad you're not leaving me by myself right now,' she said. She had told me she was nearly thirty, but her hands looked like they had spent their time submerged in dishwater for the better part of her life. Maybe she had used all of her savings to get her face redone.

The office was a small room containing ten tables where

fifteen real-estate agents were doing their job. Joannie shared a table with a young Russian man who sat reading Russian newspapers all day long, waiting for the phone to ring. Like most of his colleagues. Occasionally, his pager went off, but that was usually his wife. Every couple of hours he'd look up from his newspaper and say, 'Capitalism sucks.' Then he'd turn back to his paper.

Joannie, too, had one of those pagers. Whenever I paged her I had to press 333. 'That's your number,' she had told me.

The other real-estate agents were sitting at their desks, reading real-estate ads in the *Times*. That was a hopeless task, because many agents listed non-existent apartments. 'Ads have become a basic need for me,' I had told Joannie. 'They can offer you anything you long for that doesn't exist. And that's precisely what life is about.'

I was considering becoming a real-estate agent myself. I was getting more and more interested in finally finding the real saints in this world.

When she wasn't singing or working as a real-estate agent, Joannie made pens in the shape of roses. She had given one of them to me.

'They invested three grand in me,' she said.

We were waiting for the light to change.

'And then what?'

She took my hand. I could tell she was about to say something very important.

'I also speak French,' she said.

After that, we moved on. When we got to her building she had to sit down on a bench. We were right across from Central Park. That was one of my preferred neighbourhoods, so I had mentioned to them.

Her throwing up came unexpectedly; it rather looked like diarrhoea.

At first, I stepped back, but then I started slapping her on the back, gently.

A man in a suit brought over some napkins.

'Expecting a baby?' he asked.

I got her a bottle of water at a hotdog stand. She used it to clean off her shoes.

'It must be stress,' I offered.

There was nothing left of her make-up.

Two tourists got out of a horse-drawn carriage. 'Or the lunch.' I was talking like a madman. The last thing I wanted was to sit next to her silently.

Fortunately, she spoke after a few minutes. 'I still have to walk the dog.'

Before parting, she said, 'Singing means the world to me.'

For the first time, I now also touched her shoulder and whispered in her ear, 'I know, Joannie. I know.'

A Fine Trade

Mr Vogel had red hair, two grandchildren, and a cane, which he used for slapping on his desk when something wasn't to his liking. A lot of things weren't to his liking. Besides that, he'd told me more about his life in the half hour since we'd met than my own father had told me in twenty years.

I was actually in a meeting with Mr Vogel, but that meeting had to be interrupted for a minute, because he had to call the police. Just before, he'd said, 'You should've seen me fifteen years ago, I was such a depressed old dog.'

There was not much left of that depressed old dog. On the contrary, Mr Vogel was the picture of liveliness. He was working five phones at once; he was also working two secretaries, and he paced his office incessantly, even when he was in a meeting with you. He even had time to orchestrate when his employees were allowed to go to the bathroom. He was the only one who had the key to the bathroom, and he kept careful track of how much time everyone spent there.

'Just hold it in,' I'd already heard him call out twice. 'Just hold it in. You have to learn that in this business.'

Mr Vogel was a late bloomer in his career. And it was too late, perhaps, because in addition to his career and his business, he was gripped by a paranoia that now controlled his life. Of course he was also controlled by his two grandsons from his second and third marriages, but that was only on the weekends.

Even then he had a hard time trying not to think about how everything he'd built up would be taken away from him.

An understandable concern, but just as with death, it might be better not to think about it all the time.

Right at that moment, Mr Vogel was shouting, 'Get out, get out or I'll kill somebody.'

The person who was supposed to get out didn't pay much attention to this. I had never seen two real-estate agents go at each other, but in Mr Vogel's office this apparently was not unusual. I later heard that Mr Vogel was in the habit of poking you in the stomach with his cane, driving you out of the office that way.

He didn't want it to come to that in my presence, I think, so he called the police.

'There's an intruder here,' he said.

The intruder was sitting next to me, also calling the police on the other line to report physical abuse. He was a tiny little man, balding, with a few tufts of black hair left, who slapped his forehead every now and then, pointing at Mr Vogel. When they had both persuaded the police to come, the little man whispered to me, 'Don't do business with him, he belongs in a nut house.'

The police must've gotten pretty confused by the two calls, because when they arrived, there were six of them. And once they were there, they didn't want to leave. Neither did the little bald man. Mr Vogel was getting more and more excited, but that didn't impress the police. I – and the whole staff along with me – was afraid it would lead to a heart attack. They were running around with glasses of water, which Mr Vogel would knock out of their hands as if it were a perfectly natural thing to do.

The police announced that they were ready to start listening to both parties, and that this could take a while. They wanted me as a witness, but I kept repeating that I didn't know anything about it. How the police ultimately got out of there I'll never know, because Mr Vogel's youngest assistant, Noah, took me away.

In a bar across from the office we had a couple of beers

at Mr Vogel's expense and Noah said, 'It's a great business, but you have to know when to quit.'

'That goes for any business,' I said.

When, two hours later, we went upstairs again, Mr Vogel had undergone a complete transformation. Sometimes you sleep with someone and the next day she acts like nothing happened. That's what Mr Vogel did. He was in an excellent mood when he greeted us and even hugged me like a prodigal son. He was about to make a few thousand dollars on me, which might explain his strange behaviour. But maybe he'd developed a sincere affection for me.

'I do hope we haven't given you a bad impression of our business,' Mr Vogel said.

'Not at all.'

I signed the lease. There wasn't much time to read the contracts, but I could trust Mr Vogel. There was nothing but a few pieces of broken glass in the corner to remind me of the event of an hour ago.

As I got up Mr Vogel said, 'Would you like to come and work here?'

I didn't say anything, but Vogel laughed and grabbed my hand.

'Yes,' he said, 'it's an eight-day course to get your license. And if you promise to come and work here I'll be your sponsor.'

I still didn't say anything.

'I can see you've got it in you,' Vogel said triumphantly. 'And a few extra bucks wouldn't be bad either, right?'

'I'll think it over,' I promised. Maybe this was why I'd come to New York. To become a real-estate agent.

'You've got talent,' Vogel called after me. 'I recognise talent.'

I remember hearing those words before. When I stepped out of the elevator I saw the little bald man. Apparently, he'd been waiting for me.

'I have something to tell you,' he said. 'I'm sure it will interest you.'

Refrigerator

'People don't buy my books because of my good looks,' I said softly. I'd already said it three times.

'No, no,' the photographer said, 'just leave everything to me. I've done portraits of Genet, Beckett, Sharon Tate. Could you open that button?'

He'd been sent by my Italian publisher. It was a sweltering Saturday afternoon and he'd been working on me for an hour and a half. Every time I wanted to bring this fact to his attention he called out, 'Freeze. *Freeze.* This is beautiful.' Then he slowly approached me, grabbed my head, and twisted it a few degrees. He had also wanted to have a look at my wardrobe. I thought it was a little odd for a photographer, but he kept repeating the bit about Beckett, Genet, Sharon Tate. I wondered whether he'd rummaged about in Beckett's and Sharon Tate's wardrobes; maybe he couldn't take pictures without doing that.

'If I open another button, people will see my nipples. Italians might get a totally wrong impression of me.' The photographer put his index finger in his mouth, then brushed some curls off my forehead.

'It is a sensuous book, right?' he said.

'No,' I said. 'It isn't. It's quite the opposite of a sensuous book. You've been misinformed. Or maybe you misheard over the telephone. Italian phone connections are terrible, that's for sure. I'm not even a sensual writer. I'm not even sensuous in my private life. More like a refrigerator. Yeah, that's how you should picture me, a walking refrigerator. A living freezer. Who would be interested in seeing the nipples of a living freezer?'

He didn't answer and went into the bedroom.

'Now let's have a few shots lying down,' he said.

'I don't work in bed, I'm a writer. At least I'd like to think so.'

'I always take a few lying down – I did Beckett and Genet and Sharon Tate.' He'd tried to cover the bald spots on his head, without much success. He was wearing purple glasses, which he constantly took off and put back on.

'Now hold your hands behind your head and pull up your knees a little,' he said in a friendly voice.

I could visualise myself lying there, and suddenly it occurred to me that the photos were getting more and more erotic. It had started out quite innocently. He'd asked me to put on another shirt. At least I thought it was rather innocent. When I was in the middle of changing, he'd suddenly said, 'Freeze. This is beautiful. This is *so* beautiful.'

He loaded his camera with new film, came over to the bed, fell down on his knees, and pressed his nose into my sheets, somewhere near the end of the bed. I was astonished – didn't know what to say for a few seconds. I'd never met a photographer who got on his knees in my bedroom to stick his nose in my sheets.

'You shouldn't be doing that,' I finally muttered, 'I have a kitchen drawer full of tissues.'

He straightened up. 'I'm sorry,' he said, 'I got dizzy, I don't deal with heat so well.'

'Neither do I,' I said.

Only then did I realise that Beckett, Genet, and Sharon Tate all were dead, and that Sharon Tate in particular had died a gruesome death.

'My girlfriend will be home soon,' I said. 'She only went to walk the dogs. We have two German Shepherds. Abraham and Isaac – we named them after the patriarchs because they're so, well, aggressive. They can tear up a baby in less then two minutes. A small adult takes only a little longer. They have to wear muzzles in the street. But we love those dogs. If I had to live my life over again, I'd want to be a dog.'

I tried to climb out of my bed, but the photographer gently pushed me back. 'Let's just do the lying down part,' he said.

'Can't we do that some other time?' I whispered. He shook his head.

'So you knew Sharon Tate?' I asked while he was arranging my legs. I was thinking that it wasn't so bad as long as I could keep my pants on, and that I was just being childish. Maybe taking erotic pictures of writers was some kind of trend.

'Very well indeed,' he said, 'and I also knew Polanski. I once walked into the room when he was screwing this black woman. So I quietly left again.'

'That's my idea. When it comes to screwing I always leave the room quietly. You shouldn't interfere with people's concentration.'

After taking the last picture, he washed his hands in the kitchen and put on his hat.

Two men in the street were spraying each other with a hose.

'You'll have to come over to my house to choose the best one,' the photographer said. He took little swigs from his glass of water. After each swallow, he wiped his mouth with a chequered handkerchief.

'Sharon Tate also came over to pick out the best one. They've all come over, the greats. You can't miss the party.'

'I'd be delighted to come to the party,' I whispered.

There was a scuffling sound in the hallway. 'The dogs are coming home,' he said, and for the first time, I saw him smile.

Money Plague

In June of 1994, I met a man in Amsterdam who had read my first novel and had recognised a lot of himself in it; enough, at least, to address me in a café. He claimed to be a professional gambler. I invited him to my house a few times and he, in turn, invited me to come see him in Las Vegas where he spent six months every year and where, so he said, he was treated like a king.

In December of 1995, I completed my move from Queens to Manhattan. It had taken me four weeks because I used the subway to move. This was still in my frugal days. Not long after the move, there was a fire in my building and I had to evacuate the apartment in which I had just settled. I thought this was a good time to accept the invitation of the professional gambler and to travel out to Las Vegas.

When I went out one Sunday morning there was a man sleeping on the stairs. His head was on the upper step. It was a miracle that anyone could sleep in this position. He had on boots and a black scarf. He wasn't a tramp, more likely a leftover from my Norwegian upstairs neighbour's party. She throws parties every Saturday night. I've been invited too, but I never go. Once, when I ran into the Norwegian, she said, 'You're new here, right? Then you should throw a party.'

The man in boots was blocking the way, but it was still early in the morning, so I stepped over him carefully. When I came back he was still there.

I hardly know anyone in this building. I know there's an

Italian below me, but he's never home. I used to hear meowing coming from his apartment every time I walked past. But recently the meowing has stopped. I'm almost positive that a cat has starved to death right below me. But I'm new here and I don't want to make myself impossible.

At eleven, when I took another look, the man was still there. He had changed position a little, though. Now he was no longer on the steps, but in front of my door. Specifically, he was on the doormat I had bought a few days before. It had been the first time in my life that I had bought a doormat.

He was still there at twelve. I whispered in his ear, 'Please get up, it's noon. Why don't you get into your own bed, it'll be more comfortable than my doormat.'

At one o'clock he was still there so I decided to call the Norwegian. I wanted to tell her, 'One of the guests at your party last night has fallen asleep in front of my door on his way home and he doesn't want to wake up.' But the Norwegian didn't answer.

The only other person left to call was an elderly lady who lived all the way downstairs. I was in her apartment once. She lives in a kind of museum.

'This is the tenant in 4A. I'm sorry to bother you, but there's a man sleeping in front of my door.'

'He'll go away,' the lady said.

Maybe I was being a little childish. How was it hurting me to have a man sleeping on my doormat?

I tried to read, but it was addictive – every ten minutes I went to the door to see if he was still there. At about two-thirty I noticed it was wet in front of my door. I stepped outside and saw that the man had peed in his pants in his sleep. I could smell it, too.

I called the Norwegian and got her answering machine again, but this time I left a message: 'Good afternoon, this is the tenant in 4A. One of the guests at your party has peed on my doormat, and he's sleeping on it, too. I know this isn't your problem, but maybe you can call me as soon as you wake up.'

I took a bottle of after-shave from my bathroom and sprinkled it over the sleeping man. I was having guests at four and was embarrassed about the urine smell. The after-shave didn't wake him either. It was as if he was in a coma.

At four I was outside waiting for my guests. It was a man and a woman who were getting on in years. I didn't know them very well.

'Please come in,' I said. 'But I must tell you that there's a man sleeping in front of my door. But it shouldn't bother us. If we close the door we won't notice him.' I noticed the man raise his eyebrows.

'Let's just go to a café,' he said. So that's what we did. I couldn't keep my mind on the conversation.

When I came back an hour later, the man was still there.

Despite my after-shave, there was a strong urine smell.

By four-thirty the Norwegian still hadn't woken up and I decided to call the police. 'There's a man sleeping in front of my door,' I said. 'I have a feeling that maybe a doctor should have a look at him.'

'Are you a relative of this man?'

'No,' I said.

'Do you know him personally?'

'Well, he has been sleeping in front of my door for ten hours, but not more personally than that.'

'Give him some water to drink, and if he's still there tomorrow you can call us back.'

I filled a glass with water and sprinkled some on the man's face. I wasn't daring enough to pour a bucket of water on his head.

I couldn't stand to be in the house so I went to the movies. When I came back, the man was gone. The glass of water I had set down next to him was gone as well. The smell of urine was still there, though.

The next day I rang the Norwegian's doorbell. 'One of your guests, a man wearing black boots, peed on my doormat yesterday and slept on it, too.'

She looked at me. 'Oh, that's strange. There were no men at my party. I only invited some of my girlfriends. And you say this man peed on your doormat?'

'Yes,' I said, 'you can still smell it.'

She came downstairs. I waved the doormat under her nose.

'I don't smell a thing,' she said.

'Well of course I scrubbed it,' I said. But it did sound kind of lame.

★

It was Christmas and it smelled like gas in my apartment. Not only in my apartment – the whole building smelled like gas. But I had an appointment in a hotel bar and thought, 'When I get back it'll be gone. Maybe they're painting with some strange stuff somewhere.'

I came home at three-thirty the next morning. I'd downed four bottles of champagne. Or five. It might've been seven: I don't remember. I'd lost count. All I know is that I'd tried to treat all sorts of ladies to champagne as well, and that occasionally I succeeded.

Two girls were standing in front of the door. 'Do you live here?' they asked.

I nodded.

'So do we,' one of them said. 'Don't go in. It isn't safe. It smells like gas and the walls in our apartment are burning hot. We've already called the fire department.'

'And nobody's home,' the other said.

'Maybe somebody committed suicide. That seems to happen a lot at Christmas,' I said.

The fire department was very busy that night. We had to wait forty-five minutes. But finally they did arrive, with four fire engines.

Twenty guys went into the building and after five

minutes, all twenty were outside again.

'We turned off the main valve,' a fireman with a moustache said. 'Just go to sleep, but do open the windows for a while.' I thought I'd open the windows in the morning. I was so tired. Half an hour or an hour later, the bell woke me up. Somebody was ringing the doorbell like a maniac. I went to the intercom. 'This is the fire department,' I heard, 'There's a fire. Come down as quickly as possible.'

'Listen,' I said, 'the fire department was just here. If you want to rob me, you'll have to think of a better story.' Then I turned around and saw a fireman on a ladder in front of my window. He was shining a flashlight inside. From his gestures I could tell that he would lift me down if I wouldn't leave my apartment voluntarily – immediately. Not that I'm afraid of heights, but I didn't feel much like hanging out in a fireman's arms. So I ran down the stairs.

I know that most people in a situation like that remember to grab something valuable: money, a picture of their nearest and dearest, the manuscript of a new book. But I'd had too much champagne to worry about it. The only thing I took with me was a shawl. Besides that shawl and my underpants, I was naked. And it was five below that night.

In the movies, there are always nice firemen standing by with blankets. In reality, they're much too busy with the fire. I said to a fireman, 'Would you happen to have something for me to wear?'

'We'll have the fire under control in a few minutes,' he said.

'I understand, but I'll be dead in a few minutes.'

A woman in the building next to mine opened her window and threw down a pair of tennis socks.

'Thank you,' I called, 'I'll get them back to you – washed. But could you possibly spare a sweater too, because I'm not gonna make it with just the socks.' Her generosity had apparently run out with the socks, because she slammed the window shut.

I went up to the doorman.

'Listen,' I said, 'I live in this building. As you can see, it's on fire. May I please come in for a while to warm up?' He looked at my socks, my underpants, and then my shawl.

'You're drunk,' he hissed, 'Get out of here.'

'That's just an unfortunate coincidence,' I said. 'My being naked has nothing to do with my being drunk, and everything with that fire. Believe me. I do get drunk sometimes, but I never undress in public. And the reason I sound strange is my lips are freezing.' Just then a man with a video camera came out of the building. He started filming the fire. Not just the fire – me, too.

'I'm sorry to bother you,' I said. But he didn't stop filming. 'Would you have some clothes for me to use? I'll get them back to you washed, but if that grosses you out, I'll give you money for them instead.'

The man with the video camera didn't answer. I guess he didn't speak English. I walked over to Park Avenue. Maybe I'd be arrested by the police for public drunkenness.

I looked up at the cloudless sky. I don't normally give a damn, but now I said, 'Listen, God, I understand you don't like Jews who celebrate Christmas, but all I'm asking you for is some pants and a sweater.'

I still hadn't been picked up by the police.

'Listen God,' I repeated, 'did my parents survive the camps so their son could collapse from pneumonia in the streets of New York? If that's your intention, just let me know. Then I'll take off my socks and my shawl. But don't keep me guessing anymore.'

From their apartment windows, people were watching me talk to God on Park Avenue.

'Am I the only Jew celebrating Christmas? Is it because of the whores? Do you still hold that against me? All right, so maybe I had ten bottles of champagne today. Should I have given the money to the JNF?'

Then I put up my two fists, like I'd seen Arafat do on

TV, and I said: 'But I swear to you, if I get out of this alive, I'll drink one whole bottle of champagne every day of my life.'

When the fire had been put out, I went back into the building. I knocked on the door where the two ladies lived. A policeman opened the door.

'Is it safe?' I asked.

The policeman looked at me, at my underpants, at my socks, and at my shawl. I still wasn't wearing more than that. He took a few steps in my direction.

'Is it safe?' I quickly asked again, to make it clear that I was living in the building and didn't deserve to be beaten by his baton, despite my clothes.

'Yes, it's safe,' the cop said. 'And this young man,' he was pointing at me, 'is going to his own bed in his own apartment, really fast.'

The elevator wasn't working. They think I'm a rapist, I thought, dragging myself up the stairs. I survive a fire and then I'm accused of being a rapist. I started to laugh. It echoed through the stairwell. Then I noticed one sock was all bloody. I'd stepped in something, but the funny thing was I didn't feel anything. I just felt cold.

Back in my apartment I discovered that the heating was broken. Instead of warm water, a brown dribble came out of the tap. A little later, I found the same brown dribble when I tried to turn the cold water on. Then I fell asleep.

The next morning I woke up to the sound of shouting down the hall. 'Magic, get down those stairs,' somebody was calling. Magic was my upstairs neighbour's dog. He was more like a young calf than a dog. His head came up to my nipples. Another fire, I thought. I ran out into the hallway. My upstairs neighbour was trying with all his might to push his dog Magic down the stairs.

When he saw me, he stopped. Without even realising it, I was exposing myself to the world in nothing but underpants, socks, and a shawl – again.

'The elevator isn't working anymore,' my upstairs neighbour said, 'And poor Magic is afraid of the stairs. But he's gonna have to do his thing somewhere sooner or later.'

I went up a couple of steps. Then, in front of my upstairs neighbour's door, on a newspaper, I saw a pile of dog shit. At twelve we were informed that it would take a few days before we'd have heat and hot water. At two I started calling hotels. I eventually found a room in the Hotel S., diagonally across from my building. I threw my clothes and shaving stuff into a plastic bag. The smell of dog shit filled the corridor. The only one left in the building was my upstairs neighbour. 'I won't leave my Magic alone,' he called after me.

The desk clerk was Russian. When he heard my address he looked at me mischievously and asked, 'Rendezvous?'

'No,' I said, 'No rendezvous. Fire.'

He smiled. 'Yup, fire,' he said.

I had a wonderful view of my own apartment from my hotel room. It really is a beautiful apartment, I thought. I went down to the hotel bar, where I ordered a bottle of champagne. There weren't many people. That didn't surprise me, because of all the hotel bars I knew, this one was the most depressing. I offered everybody champagne, including the bartender.

'On vacation?' he asked.

'No,' I said, 'Driven out of my place.'

'By your wife?' he whispered.

'No,' I said, 'by fire.'

For the second bottle of champagne, a girl named Lisa joined me. She was in the fashion business and wanted to design clothing herself.

'Why do you drink so much champagne?' she asked. What was I supposed to tell her? That I'd promised myself I'd drink a whole bottle of champagne every day of my life – but this was already my second?

'I can't stand the garbage they call wine and the nice thing about champagne is that you can drink as much as you want and still feel human the next morning. That's very useful in my profession.'

'What *is* your profession?' she asked.

'I'm a private detective, Private Detective Greenberg.' I put out my hand.

'What's your specialty, private detective?' Lisa asked.

'Divorce,' I said, 'People who want to get divorced but don't yet know why come to me.' I ordered another bottle.

'Do you have the money plague, private detective?' Lisa asked.

I looked at her. 'The money plague? I've never heard of that disease.'

'It has to do with trying to get rid of your money as fast as possible.'

I suddenly noticed how feverish I felt. My shirt was soaked with sweat and my cheeks were burning. So this was the money plague.

'You're right, Lisa,' I said, 'The money plague.'

When the bar closed, she wanted to come up to my hotel room, but I said 'No, a bar, let's find another bar.' We walked down the street. I could hardly keep up with her. In the morning, you don't notice the champagne, but at night you do; it's such a remarkable drink.

We went into a building on 31st Street between Park and Madison Avenues.

The hallway was leaking. 'You need an umbrella to survive in here,' I tried, but she didn't answer. We passed a woman in a purple track suit – or a man, I don't remember. We stopped in front of a door that had '4F' chalked on it.

'Now I have to check you for weapons, private detective,' Lisa said.

'What?' I asked.

'I'm sorry,' she said, 'That's the rules.' She apologised: 'This is a funny country.'

'Sure,' I said, 'Firemen let you freeze, the cops think you're a rapist, and you have to check me for weapons.'

'Open your coat,' she said.

I opened my coat.

'Pull up your shirt,' she said.

I pulled up my shirt.

'Roll up your pants.'

I bent over to roll up my pants. I remember thinking, what's this all about. Someone's gonna knock me over the head.

And that's all I thought.

My first thought was, they've taken away my furniture. And they've bashed in a window so now it's raining in. Only then did it occur to me that I wasn't lying in bed, but on the floor in some hallway. The ceiling was leaking. There was a steady drip right beside my head.

When I lifted my head a few inches, I noticed I wasn't wearing shoes anymore. The coat and vest I'd bought at B's department store the other day had also disappeared. Fortunately, I still had my glasses. You can't always afford the luxury of pessimism.

I got up. Just in time: I'd hardly gotten to my feet when I started throwing up. I didn't remember having eaten corn in the last 24 hours, but a small cornfield spewed from my mouth. Maybe the stomach takes large quantities of champagne and turns it into corn. But if that was the case, I'd discovered the solution to World Hunger. Soon everyone could produce their own corn.

I had to lie down again. The floor was really filthy, but I had to. Besides, I was pretty filthy myself.

The money and bank cards had disappeared from my breast pocket, but what worried me more was that the key to my room in Hotel S., where I'd been staying since the fire, was gone too.

I'd have to ask for a new key at the desk. And desk clerks in fancy hotels like the S. are known for not wanting to give out spare keys to filthy-looking guests who can't identify themselves.

I tried to get up again. I saw the wooden door with '4F' on it and suddenly remembered that her name was Lisa and that she was a fashion designer, or wanted to be, and that she'd brought me here. I had met her in the Hotel S. bar.

I walked down the stairs. Slowly, so I wouldn't fall. The building seemed deserted to me. There were leaks all over. The walls were scrawled with graffiti I couldn't read. When I got out to the street, I saw it was early in the morning and that I was on 20th Street, fifteen minutes from my hotel. It was the second time in 48 hours that I had to walk the streets half-naked. This would be a memorable winter.

I was walking step by step. Not because I was afraid to step in glass; I just couldn't go any faster. Nobody watched me, nobody noticed me.

Back at the Hotel S. I had to use the night bell. The night clerk opened up for me. Before he could open his mouth I said, 'It's my own fault, I take full responsibility. I drank so much champagne that it turned into a cornfield in my stomach. But the truth is, I've been robbed. They even took some of my clothes – see for yourself. I don't mind that. I was about to give my old clothes to the Salvation Army, but now I can wear them myself. But they also took the key to my room. Number 508. Could I have a spare key?' He let me in without a word, and handed me the key silently.

I ran into the elevator as best I could, afraid he might change his mind.

I kept hearing the sound of water in my sleep, until the noise turned into the phone ringing. By that time I'd been asleep for more than sixteen hours. I answered. It was the desk clerk: Could they clean my room?

The headache was less intense now, but still there. It was like a ferocious storm that had raged for 24 hours and then turned into a strong wind.

I got dressed and put on some old sneakers. Then I went

to the hotel bar, hoping to find Lisa there again. But I didn't think she'd be that stupid – and she wasn't.

'How are you, private detective,' the bartender greeted me. I remembered saying I was a private eye. It's remarkable how other people have to tell you what you've said. Like you've become somebody else.

'What was your name again, private detective?'

'They call me The Cockroach,' I said.

'Then you're a cockroach with the money plague.' It was true. Lisa had told me I had the money plague.

'There's only one place for people with the money plague,' the bartender whispered, 'Las Vegas.'

Sometimes, a tennis player who's about to win the match suddenly starts missing every ball. I knew I was missing every ball, but I enjoyed it. It was like a victory, even though I had no idea over what or whom.

I bought a plane ticket to Las Vegas for that same night. I was on a high, but it wasn't from champagne or any other booze. It was the kind of high you feel when you conquer your fear with all your strength. Like you're floating in the clouds after breaking the sound barrier, singing loudly: the fear's been destroyed, then comes the rest.

'Where you going?' the cabbie asked.

'Vegas,' I said, 'Former private detective becomes a fortune seeker in Vegas. Does that satisfy you?'

'Private detective?' He couldn't believe it.

'I'd better introduce myself,' I said, 'They call me The Cockroach and I have the money plague.'

'I've had lots of animals in my car, but never a cockroach with the money plague.'

'Just drive,' I said, 'or I'll miss my plane.'

★

'Mister,' said the lady with two dried flowers glued to her hat. 'Mister, I can see you've got a good heart. I'm a little psychic. See. Not all the time, but it's not always easy knowing when people are gonna die.' She grabbed my hand.

'Mister, I came from Los Angeles by car and now I don't even have enough money left for gas. You're not gonna let me walk back, are you? I come up here every weekend. Five hours by car, and five hours back, but this never happened to me before.' She opened her handbag.

'You see,' she said, 'nothing left. Some lipstick. From France. When my husband was still alive we went to France. But what's in France for me now? The only place I come is here. Every Friday. If you could use it, I'd give you the lipstick, but what good is a lipstick to you?'

A waitress in the shortest skirt I'd ever seen asked us what we wanted to drink. We ordered two cocktails and a pack of cigarettes for the lady. The drinks and cigarettes were free. I moved up two machines. She followed me. Her skin reminded me of an apricot forgotten in a fruit bowl.

'Mister, I'm from a good family. If my husband could see me now he'd turn over in his grave. But I don't think we'll ever see each other again. I don't believe in life after death. That's why I've been living it up since he died. If you're not gonna see each other again anyway, why hold yourself back, don't you think? He had his own plane, and cows. If you only knew how many cows he had... There's nothing left of it, because I've been living like mad. My husband took good care of me, Mister, but he never touched me. In all the thirty-four years we were married. He touched me a few times before our wedding, but never since we got married. He touched cows and bulls and dogs and strippers, but never me. I never complained, Mister. I went through life with my head held high.'

Our drinks came. She lit a cigarette with trembling hands that had brown spots on them.

'Not until he was dying, Mister, did I have the courage

to ask him. He was drugged – morphine – but he was still screaming from the pain. Why didn't you ever touch me, I asked. I never had the time, he said. That gave me peace of mind. It wasn't because he hated me or thought I was disgusting or because he secretly didn't like women. That would've been the worst, if he'd told me he didn't like women.'

I wasn't watching her anymore, just the machine I was playing.

'Mister,' she said, 'you could have been my son. I never had children. Three of our maids had a kid with him. I was like a mother to them, which was hard, since they had their father's meanness and their mothers' ignorance. Illegal Indians who couldn't tell A from B. I'm no racist, Mister, but those people are three thousand years behind in evolution. I knew my husband would die soon – I'm psychic. That's why I stuck it out with him. Now there's nothing left. The ranch, the plane, the cows, nothing. All I want is thirty bucks for gas. So I can get back home. You're not gonna let me walk back, are you Mister? I can see you're an artist, a very sensitive one.'

I put another hundred-dollar bill in the machine.

'I'm a cockroach with the money plague,' I said. I think those were my first words.

'No, no, Mister,' she said, 'I've seen a lot of cockroaches. You're not a cockroach. Maybe you want to be one. You're not gonna let me walk back, are you, Mister, I can see that in your eyes.' I took a fifty-dollar bill out of my shirt pocket. She put it away in her purse without saying anything. Then she took off her hat. She was as bald as a guy. Only a few grey strands stuck out of her head.

'Do you want to touch me?' she whispered.

'Where?' I asked.

She bent her head. Her scalp felt like a frying pan where hundreds of eggs had been fried.

I got up.

'Your name?' she whispered.

'My nickname is The Cockroach – that should do it.'

I went over to the roulette table. A chubby man with a sweaty head put up five thousand dollars, lost it, and walked over to the next table. An hour later the lady with the hat walked by. 'Go home, Cockroach,' she said, but I shook my head.

By six the next morning, I'd blown all the royalties from *Blue Mondays* – except for 160 KPN shares. I got up and went to the restaurant in the corner of the casino and ordered a hamburger.

'Is this your breakfast, lunch, or dinner?' the waitress asked.

'Make it brunch,' I said.

I felt neither unhappy nor happy. Slightly amazed, at most. Reality had definitely turned surreal.

I finally took the elevator to my room on the thirty-sixth floor. Las Vegas stretched below me. And beyond that, the desert. As far as the eye could see, the desert. Nothing but the desert.

★

'If you don't love weapons, you don't love people,' the young man said. He had a cheerful face. 'I guess you don't usually hear these kinds of things in New York?'

'No,' I said.

'Look, the liberals say if you have a gun, innocent people will get shot. That doesn't show much faith in people. That's badmouthing your fellow man. That's cynicism. What are your hobbies?'

It was an unexpected question.

'I go to the movies now and then,' I said.

'What if someone all of a sudden said you couldn't go to the movies anymore. Wouldn't that make you mad?'

I nodded.

'I grew up with weapons,' the young man said. He was

my age. 'I was in the navy. I love weapons.'

He looked at me in his rear-view mirror.

'Weapons aren't just weapons. They're also beautiful, like women can be beautiful. When you know more about weapons, you learn that they all have a history. Just like people. They don't tell you that in the newspaper, right?'

'No.'

The sky over Las Vegas was blue. It was the day after the night I gambled away most of my money. I'd gotten up at eleven and gone to the hotel hairdresser for a haircut. 'You have dry hair,' the hairdresser had said, and tried to sell me some lotion. He'd succeeded.

'I won't shoot just like that, you know, if someone wants to rob me I'll shoot, but that's another story.'

He produced a small box from beneath his seat. The kind of box I recognised from music school. They had flutes in them.

'Have a good look at it,' he said.

I looked at the weapon. It was shiny, lying on a bed of green velvet.

'Beautiful?'

'Beautiful,' I said.

'Do you know why there's so much crime in New York? Because people aren't allowed to carry guns there.'

We stopped for a light.

'You wanna buy one?'

'Do you think that's wise?' I don't know how I managed to utter this phrase. It was meant as a prelude to saying no. But for the young man, it was a done deal. He turned left. We were now on a sandy road. I felt dizzy, but maybe this was because the road was quite bumpy and we were going rather fast. We finally got to a sandy field surrounded by some scraggly bushes. There was a rusty car, which apparently got shot at pretty frequently.

The young man opened the trunk and took out a whole collection of weapons. Most of them were wrapped in cloth.

Only the odd weapon was lying on a bed of green velvet.

'Are you a cab driver or an arms dealer?' I asked.

'I'm Tim,' he answered, 'and you?'

'My friends call me The Cockroach.'

He laughed. 'All right, Cockroach,' he said, 'have you ever fired a gun before?'

I didn't think it was wise to lie. 'Never.'

'Then we'll start with the smallest,' Tim said.

He loaded a silver gun and fired a couple of shots at the car. Then he passed it on to me.

For at least a full minute I just stood there motionless, with the weapon in my hand. I held it as if it were a poisonous snake.

I realised that I wasn't in danger of being shot by Tim; I was in danger of shooting myself. In my feet, for instance. There was something tempting about the idea of shooting myself. It seemed so easy to do.

'Shoot.' He had pulled the trigger with one finger. I couldn't do it with one finger. I had to use both of my forefingers. The bullet hit the sand a few yards away from me. I'd never realised how much noise firing a gun can make.

'Do you have something for my ears?' I asked. He took two wads of cotton out of his pocket. They looked like they'd been used before, but I popped them in my ears anyway. He now handed me something that looked more like a rifle. I had to hold it against my shoulder. The recoil was incredible. It felt like my shoulder was being ripped off my body.

'I'll take the little one,' I said, 'I'm a little guy.'

He held the silver weapon in his hand. 'It's a beauty. Five hundred dollars.'

What's five hundred dollars if you've just lost tens of thousands the night before? Besides, I wanted to get rid of him. I pulled the cotton out of my ears and took the money from my breast pocket.

He kept the green velvet box. He did give me ten bullets as a promotional gift, though. They were just over an inch long and weighed next to nothing. My forefinger was bleeding. I'd hurt myself pulling the trigger.

Tim drove me back to my hotel.

'Man is as free as the weapon he carries,' he said, 'that's my philosophy.'

'Mine too,' I said.

I walked across the lobby to the elevator. The weapon in my pocket was rubbing uncomfortably against my crotch. Back in my room I threw it on the bed, next to the lotion for dry hair.

The sky was still blue.

I took a bath. When I was drying myself off I noticed my teeth were chattering. They didn't stop for at least an hour. I have to get rid of it, I thought. I don't have a licence. If they find out, I'll be thrown out of the country. I wrapped the weapon in an old newspaper and put the newspaper in a plastic bag. It looked just like I'd bought some carrots at the market. I was determined to throw it in a garbage can out on the street. I left my room. It looked innocent, I thought. Only I'd forgotten to take the bullets out of my pocket.

The sign said: Hungry. The man holding it was pacing up and down if front of the casino. He had a yellow bucket dangling from his arm. The kind of bucket kids take to the beach. I dropped some change into it and held on tight to my plastic bag.

'God bless you,' he said. And then he looked down into his bucket. I continued along my way, but he caught up with me.

'Excuse me,' he said, 'but I believe this belongs to you.' He opened his hand. There was a bullet in it. It's odd how innocent bullets look. Just like something the plumber would carry with him to fix your drain.

'I'm sorry,' I said and put the bullet back in my pocket.

'God bless you,' he said for the second time.

There were others pacing around with signs saying

'Hungry'. Maybe the signs were provided by the local council. I ignored them. I was looking for a bin.

At last I spotted one next to a nice little bench that was occupied by three ladies sunbathing. I walked back and forth a couple of times, but then I realised that this was not a suitable bin. The ladies looked as if they wouldn't hesitate to rifle through a bin. I tried some other bins, even went inside a MacDonald's, but none of the bins I saw met the requirements. The only thing I had to do was to deposit the plastic bag into a bin, but somehow, it didn't work. I was worried that people would search through the bin and come after me just like the beggar and say, 'I believe this belongs to you.'

After two hours I went back to the hotel. I ordered a cocktail at the bar. This time, I had to pay because I wasn't gambling. I also had to show my passport to prove that I was of age. I had put the plastic bag on the bar so as not to lose track of it.

'Is this you?' the bartender asked, pointing at the picture in my passport.

That's when I saw Mariette. She was wearing a tiny green hat and was completely focussed on the one-armed bandit she was playing. It's too time-consuming to explain who Mariette is, but I can say this much: if I had seen God riding a donkey through the streets of Las Vegas crying, 'We're off to free Jerusalem!' I would have been less surprised than I was at seeing Mariette in her green hat playing the one-armed bandit.

I felt a terrible headache coming up. I was grabbing around my left pocket for some aspirin, but when I fished out another bullet, I just left it. Slowly I moved over to the one-armed bandit, holding my glass in one hand, the plastic bag in the other.

Either she didn't notice me or she didn't want to notice me. From her mouth dangled a filtered cigarette, which she hardly ever took out. Despite the little green hat there was no doubt: this was the very same Mariette who used to serve me night after night at the Italian restaurant, P.

'Hello,' I said.

She looked up from her machine. For an instant, she raised her eyebrows. Then she started to laugh. I just stood beside her holding my glass in one hand and the plastic bag in the other. People stopped to see what I had done to make somebody laugh like that, but I gave them little nods, trying to tell them they should move on.

Eventually, I sat down next to her. I put a dollar in the machine to make it look a little more casual.

'What are you doing here?' I asked. I knew it was a rather silly question, but I couldn't think of anything else.

'Vacationing,' she said, without taking her eyes off the machine. 'How about you?'

'I'm looking for a friend,' I said, which was, in fact, the truth.

The machine started making a noise. It was a sign that she had won something. 'What do you have in that bag? You're holding it like it has poop in it.'

'I accidentally bought a gun,' I whispered. 'And now I have to get rid of it.'

She started laughing again. The one-armed bandit was still spewing coins. She put them all in a plastic cup and moved over to the next machine.

'This is quite a coincidence,' I called a few times. 'What a coincidence.' She didn't respond.

I didn't have the guts to ask her where she'd gotten the little green hat, in case it was a present from her lover.

'Listen,' she said, putting on some sunglasses. 'When I'm playing I want to be left alone. But if you come down to the bar at ten tonight, I'll be there too.'

'All right,' I said. 'I'm known here as The Cockroach.'

Again she laughed, but this time I didn't wait for her to finish. I went outside. Most of the people carrying the 'Hungry' signs had disappeared. Only the most hungry among them were still there. I dropped my plastic bag in the first bin I came across. I took the bullets out of my pocket as well; one of them, I kept as a souvenir.

Back at the hotel, there was no sign of Mariette. I did hear someone call, 'Friend, friend.' It was the bartender. He was waving my passport at me.

Two hours before my meeting with Mariette at the bar of the Treasure Island hotel, I bought a pair of snakeskin shoes. I felt like dressing in snakeskin top to bottom. I felt remarkably cheerful. The fact that I had gambled away most of my money didn't seem to bother me at all; on the contrary.

'I'll keep them on,' I said to the sales assistant.

That's how I ended up walking through the casino in snakeskin shoes for two hours. They were loafers, so I had to walk carefully so as not to lose them. I wasn't wearing any socks. I felt like Don Johnson. I was at the agreed-upon place way in advance. It may have been merely imagination but I thought my toes had gotten all smelly inside my snakeskin shoes. The fear of being smelly is universal, but, just like happiness, hunger, beauty and wealth, unevenly distributed.

A Hawaiian woman sat down next to me; after a while she said, 'Would you like to see me pee, Jew boy?'

I looked at her.

'Sure,' I said, 'but not today.'

I remembered all those other days and I realised how wonderful and valuable they were – simply feeling like Don Johnson. They should be turned into small parties, those days.

She greeted a man who was walking by. He was wearing a large necklace. She whispered to me, 'Could you go and sit somewhere else?'

I said I was waiting for someone, but that I didn't mind moving up to the next bar stool.

A little later she and the man went upstairs; ten minutes later they came back down again.

'That was quick,' I said.

She put on lipstick and whispered, 'Las Vegas Jews like black women. Do you like black women?'

'Listen,' I said, 'I'm not a Las Vegas Jew and you're not a black woman. And as far as Jewish rituals are concerned, they vary from place to place. And I'm not a rabbi, either.'

'Let's sit down somewhere else,' Mariette said. I hadn't noticed her approaching. She looked exactly as she had earlier that afternoon, only the little green hat was missing.

I followed her. With each step I took my shoes produced the sound of the glue coming loose; I hoped she couldn't hear it.

We went over to a cafeteria in a remote corner of the casino. She ordered two glasses of orange juice, which she drank all by herself. I was thinking of God, the greatest storyteller in the universe, and I realised how He, like many people, must hate competition.

'This has to stop,' she said after she'd finished her juice.

I was looking down at my snakeskin Don Johnson shoes. 'How did you end up in this town?' I asked.

'I'm on my way to Hollywood,' she said.

That cheered me up. Wasn't I on my way to Hollywood as well?

'That's a coincidence,' I said.

She took my chin in her hand. 'No.' she said. 'Your life can be described in three words: one great escape. And I no longer want to have any part of it. In no way whatsoever. Writing all this stuff about me has to stop.' She released my chin. She had given it quite a thorough squeeze.

'It's quite innocent,' I whispered.

'You wrote,' she hissed, 'that I was the most beautiful woman in Amsterdam, but with the heart of a coffee maker.'

'No', I cried. 'The heart of an espresso maker. The heart of a coffee maker is not at all the same as the heart of an espresso maker. People who can't see that have no sense of nuance. Besides, I love espresso makers, so I also love their hearts.'

I looked at my bare ankles.

'I'm gonna be nasty now,' she said.

I didn't ask how. I said, 'You're right. It's so strange how people can act so pathetically when it comes to hormones. If there's anything we shouldn't be pathetic about it's death and hormones. So, no more hearts of espresso makers. Not if you find that objectionable. It's about time we start thinking about ourselves in an open and honest way. You're a living hormone. Your admirers are living hormones.'

She grabbed my chin again, making it hard for me to speak, but now that I had started, there was no stopping me. 'There's nothing wrong about that. I, too, am a living hormone. And Hollywood is *the* place for living hormones to flourish. Trust me, there's nothing bad about being a living hormone. I've experienced it myself. At most, realising this creates a mild sense of melancholy.'

It was a miracle she hadn't broken my jaw yet.

'Listen,' I said, 'maybe we can make it in Hollywood: the two Dutch hormones!'

She slapped me across the face, knocking off my glasses. At the same moment, she grabbed my right ear, squeezing it between her fingers, and dragged me out of the cafeteria.

'My glasses,' I cried, following her with my head bent forward.

'They'll be there when you get back,' she said. 'My boyfriend wants to meet you.'

'Is he a living hormone as well?' I added. That wasn't a wise thing to say.

Someone was squeezing my hand. It was the gentleman lying on the sunbed next to me. He was wearing a red bathing suit. Only now could I hear what he was whispering: 'Little Lolita, my little Lolita'. I looked around. We were the only ones at this beauty parlour.

I felt the ear that Mariette had dragged me out of the casino by and remembered her saying, 'Just lie down here; I'll go and find your glasses and I'll be back with my boyfriend soon.'

The man in the red bathing suit was stroking my hand. As I was still without glasses, I raised myself to have a better look. He had grey hair. On his chest, too – a substantial amount of it.

'Little Lolita,' he said softly.

'I'm not Lolita,' I said in a friendly voice. 'I'm The Cockroach, but today I feel like Don Johnson.'

I put my shoes on the floor. They were smelly.

The man got up. He put on a pair of slippers and a white bathrobe. Then he knelt down beside my sunbed. He stroked my cheek with the back of his hand.

'How old are you?' He was whispering so softly that I could barely hear him.

'Twenty-five,' I said.

'You hardly have any growth on your chin, and you have tiny pimples and your skin is soft. Feel my skin.' He pressed my hand against his cheek. 'Sandpaper,' he said, a little louder this time. 'Sandpaper.'

'It's not so bad.'

'What are you doing here in this dead city?' the man in the red bathing suit whispered.

'I want to conquer the world,' I said. I realised that I had spoken the truth and I found my self-exposure somehow very moving. It was as if all my desires had been reduced to just this single emotion. As if my longing had bankrupted itself.

The man wore a necklace, but I couldn't see what was hanging from it.

'May I comb your hair?' he asked. I said that was all right. He sat down beside me on the sunbed and started combing my hair. As he slowly combed the knots out of my hair, he said, 'I'm the wealthiest man in Las Vegas. That's why nobody knows my name. I'm only known as Mr Z.'

'Mr Z.,' I repeated. Pronounced like Mr Zee it didn't

sound all that bad.

He then put his mouth right next to my ear. The same ear Mariette had pulled so hard that I thought it was going to rip.

'I started off as a porn star,' Mr Z. whispered. He tugged at my curls gently. 'I worked myself up to the richest man in Las Vegas and I can't trust anyone.'

A phone started ringing in the pocket of his bathrobe.

'The first time you notice that people are afraid of you,' Mr Z. said, 'it's wonderful. But by the tenth time it's merely exhausting. As you get older, you lose your edge; you got to have an edge when you're in the currency business. That's why I no longer deal with currency. Only with desire.' Because he had combed the curls out of my hair it was now five times its normal length – and it was in my eyes.

I could smell peppermint every time Mr Z. moved closer to me.

'Lolita,' I could hear in my ear. 'Little Lolita.'

'I started off as a porn star,' Mr Z. repeated. He laughed. Only after a couple of minutes I noticed he wasn't laughing, he was crying. Again the phone in his bathrobe rang. Nobody answered.

I heard a loud voice. It was Mariette. She didn't seem surprised to see Mr Z. handling my hair. She gave me my glasses. One of the lenses had some dried-up ketchup stuck to it. I didn't notice her boyfriend until I had put on my glasses. Immediately, I could see why she would have picked him: he looked like a young god, and even that is a euphemism. How can I blame others for basing their choices on looks when I do exactly the same? Then he opened his mouth. The young god turned out to have a thick Dutch accent: he was from the Southeast. 'We want to be left alone,' he said.

'Allow me to introduce you,' I said, 'this is Mr Z.'

Mr Z. got up. His robe fell open. His belly protruded over his red bathing suit. I looked at the young god's shoes.

They were boots. No snakeskin.

Mr Z. sat down again. His hands had returned to my hair and he whispered, 'Would you like to be my personal secretary, Lolita?'

I watched Mariette looking at us with a mixture of surprise and disgust. She was everything people would want to be: young, beautiful, desired, and maybe even talented – I prefer to leave judging other people's talents to someone more qualified.

The young god walked towards the exit. 'We have to catch our plane, Mariette,' he said. 'We have an appointment with the agent in LA.'

I grabbed my shoes and ran after them. I could hear the voice of Mr Z. calling after me, 'Lolita, stay with me, you could be my personal secretary. You'd never have to work again.' I finally caught up with them in the lobby. It's not easy to run in snakeskin loafers.

'Who do you think you are, anyway?' she asked.

'A porn star.'

Only then did I realise that, finally, I'd nailed it.

And from the far end of the lobby Mr Z. appeared in his white bathrobe; he was waving.

Carrots

The dealer was a lady in her late fifties. Her hair was permed and she was wearing jogging pants. She'd brought along her husband, who was dressed in shorts. He kept dipping his hand into the bowl of peanuts beside my bed.

The dealer's name was Elizabeth. In real life she was a porter, which meant she worked in a fancy hotel lugging around other people's bags. To make some extra cash, she and her husband had this small business dealing marijuana – and maybe a few other things I didn't know about.

The dealer threw a little plastic bag on my bed. It smelled of baby food. Baby food made of carrots.

I noticed the smell was nauseating me, so I moved as far away from the bag as possible.

'Those curls look great on you,' I said, stalling for time. I had no idea what else to say. I'd had all kinds of things in my hotel room, but never a drug dealer.

'How about I open a bottle of wine?' I said.

'That'd be nice,' her husband said. He was an elderly man, but very well preserved.

I went into the bathroom to open the bottle. They never show you this in the movies: a dealer married to a senior citizen with a peanut addiction having a glass of wine with you. The man had already eaten half the bowl I'd ordered from room service.

'Here we are,' I said, 'Cheers.'

'Don't you want to check it?' Elizabeth asked. I walked over to the packet. It really did look like pieces of carrot that had turned brown after soaking too long. The same thing happens to tree leaves: if they soak for a long time, they turn brown on you.

'It's excellent quality,' I said, 'I can smell it.'

I was starting to wonder if they'd ever leave. Her husband had finished his first glass of wine and was pouring himself another.

'At first we just imported it for ourselves,' the man said, 'but then we noticed we could make other people happy with it too, so we thought, why not? Make other people happy and make some cash on the side.'

'Exactly,' I said, 'that's my philosophy: make other people happy and make some cash on the side.' Now I turned to the dealer herself, but she was busy putting on red lipstick. 'It's funny,' I said, 'us having two totally different professions and exactly the same philosophy.'

Her husband put his hand up. At first I thought there was something wrong with the ceiling, but then I got it – I was supposed to slam my hand against his, like they do in sports. I slammed my hand against his.

When you're dead, I figure you can quit adjusting to other people, but until then life is all about adjusting. I even think it's the cornerstone of our society, adjustment. Not that I'm seriously worried about society; I'm no pessimist. But I don't want to end up with people saying about me, 'He was one of those maladjusted types who fucked up our society.'

'If you feel like lighting one,' Elizabeth said.

'No, no,' I said, 'Not yet. I have to take a shower first.'

A friend of mine had suggested that I buy some marijuana, since I'd gotten sick a couple of times on wine. Australian wine, to be precise. But the smell of fermented carrots was turning my stomach before I'd even touched the stuff.

'Is there anything else we can do for you?' Elizabeth said.

'No, thanks,' I said, 'I'm taken care of for now.'

'We really like doing it for you,' she said. 'You remind us so much of our grandson.'

'Hell yeah,' her husband said, 'He looks just like Dave.' He'd managed to eat the whole bowl of nuts all by himself. Maybe he was hungry. Maybe dealing drugs makes you extremely hungry. Most of his clients wouldn't have given him nice nuts like that, of course. Again he put his hand in the air and I slammed mine against it.

'To meeting you,' the man said.

'Yes,' I said, 'To meeting you.'

'And to Dave,' Elizabeth said.

I sat down, since nobody made any move to get up. I'd already gone over to the door a few times, and even opened it, but neither one of them had gotten the hint. I was afraid that if I walked to the door again they'd say, 'It was nice meeting you,' and close the door behind me.

By this time my bottle of wine was also empty.

'We mostly use it before we have sex,' the man said. I wondered if the smell of fermented carrots didn't detract from the pleasure. Then again, sex itself could also smell like fermented carrots.

I tried to open the window, but it was stuck.

'Those tiny sloping shoulders,' I heard my dealer say, 'they're just like our grandson's.'

I turned around. It was a good thing my mother wasn't there – she thinks I'm broad-shouldered. If she had any idea who Arnold Schwarzenegger was, she'd have called me the Arnold Schwarzenegger of Amsterdam. But she doesn't even know Arnold Schwarzenegger.

I felt the dealer's hands on my shoulders.

'Give in to it,' she whispered.

'That's exactly what I've been trying to do all my life,' was the last thing I could think of.

Watermelon

My contribution to the barbecue was a watermelon, which I thought was an appropriate gift in this heat. I had picked out the biggest and most beautiful one. Only when I was back out on the street did I realise that it was impossible to lift it. I waited for a cab for twenty minutes, but it was a Friday afternoon and there were no free cabs. Some people mistook me for a lost vendor, waiting to unload his last melon. 'I'll take it for two dollars,' they'd say. Others simply started squeezing the melon. When I asked them, 'Could you please stop doing that?' they'd look up at me, surprised. Sometimes they walked away shaking their heads, like I was some cranky fruit salesman.

Finally I realised there was only one way that I could reach the barbecue in time: I'd have to roll the melon there. Fortunately, sidewalks in New York are quite suitable for this – they're made for people in wheelchairs. Another advantage is that dog shit here has to be cleaned up right away. The only thing I wasn't able to avoid was a dead mouse. I could have steered the melon a little to the right, but then it would have rolled over an old lady's shoe. In a flash, I envisioned how the old lady would bash me and my melon with her umbrella, and how other exhausted and thirsty passers-by would whip out their umbrellas and bash me with them. The newspaper had said the heat was causing a lot of aggression among New Yorkers. So I went for the mouse.

We headed down a small hill, and every now and then the melon went faster than I did. Most commuters, with battle-weary expressions, avoided the melon. They'd accepted the heat, this city, and all the hopeless cases that live here. A small minority refused to avoid the melon and kicked it instead. Some people just looked at it maniacally.

Then there were the beggars who offered to help me push for a couple of bucks. But I was afraid that would only make things worse.

Important people would be at that barbecue. I wanted to show them that I knew how to act with important people – maybe even give the impression I was one of them.

When I finally reached the neighbourhood where the party was, it seemed the street number I had didn't exist. I was soaked and had a feeling that the melon – and even I – smelled like dead mouse.

I went into a bar to find a phone book. The neighbourhood was fancy and quiet; it seemed fine to leave the melon right outside the bar for a few seconds. The bartender was an elderly woman with reading glasses who looked like she belonged in a nursing home. I was the only customer. When I asked to use the bathroom and the phone book for a second, she said, 'Would ya believe it?' I decided to take this as encouragement. When I came out of the bathroom, I noticed an old Chinese guy sleeping on a napkin in a dark corner of the bar.

'It's nice and cool here,' I said, by way of saying good-bye, but the bartender didn't answer me.

Back outside, a couple of middle-aged gentlemen had taken charge of my melon. They were in the process of beating the melon with a small rock. A lot of juice had already leaked out. They hadn't even bothered to run away with the thing.

I said, 'There must be some mistake – this is my melon. I rolled it all the way down from 14th Street.' They didn't even bother to look at me, but kept hammering at the melon, and finally, it burst open. They fell upon the melon as if they were completely dehydrated. The remarkable thing was that one of the men was wearing a tie. Neither guy looked like someone who'd give in to this kind of behaviour.

'This must be a mistake,' I tried again. The man with the tie broke off a piece and held it up. At that moment the door of the bar opened and the Chinese man emerged. From the way he'd exited the place, it didn't look voluntary – it seemed to me that somebody had pushed him. The Chinese man looked at the two gentlemen on the ground eating my melon, then he looked at me. He turned around and went back inside the bar.

Three seconds later, he was back outside. He was wearing a straw hat someone had taken a bite out of.

Their thirst quenched, the gentlemen left me alone with what was left of my melon. I sat down on the sidewalk. About fifteen minutes later, the door of the bar opened.

She saw the remains of my melon and froze. She went back inside and returned with a bucket of water. I jumped aside just in time. She started scrubbing my melon off the sidewalk with incredible energy. I felt sorry for her, having to scrub in this heat, but then I decided she liked cleaning compulsively.

'It was an accident,' I said.

'Would ya believe it?' she answered.

In the distance, I could just make out the straw hat of the Chinese man.

Tuesday

Everyone called him Tuesday: the regulars, the cook, his brothers, and even the suppliers. He was the waiter at Luna, the Italian restaurant on Mulberry Street, but he had tried everything to become a monk instead.

Tuesday's parents had started the restaurant in the twenties and they had named it Luna because they had found a sign for a dollar that said Luna on it. Someone had ordered the sign but never picked it up.

It was Wednesday night and Tuesday was leaning over table eleven where a couple were taking their time with their lasagne. 'I don't mean to bother you,' Tuesday said, 'but we'll be closing any minute now; I have to get home; my cat is hungry.'

Tuesday lived with his cat. He used to live with seven cats, but when the neighbours threatened to sue him, he got rid of six of them. Mostly because his brothers talked him into it.

Tuesday had five brothers and one sister, all of whom had become successful in life. His brothers had all made it in business and his sister had her own beauty parlour. Tuesday's brothers said, 'If you get along with Tuesday, you've got a screw loose.'

When he was eighteen, Tuesday had gone to the monastery. His mother was from Manchester and his father from Naples; Tuesday said he had the best of both cities in him. According to some, his choice for the monastery had something to do with an unrequited love, but most people thought something had gone wrong long before that. His birth had taken an unusually long time.

After spending four years in the cloister, he got a phone call from his mother: 'We need you here,' she said. 'Your brothers are in Vietnam and Europe, your sister is about to get married, and your father's in hospital. You need to help out in the restaurant; Luna needs you.'

Tuesday left the monastery that very day. 'It'll be for several months,' he told the brothers at the monastery. 'My mother needs me.'

It actually took a couple of years before his brothers returned from Vietnam and Europe – all but one of them. The official line was that his elder brother had gone missing during combat. Missing in action, it said. But everyone had given up all hope of him ever showing up again. Except for his mother, who put up pictures of her missing son in the kitchen. When she started addressing the customers as her son, the whole family got together and decided it would be better not to let the mother serve anymore.

For the third time, Tuesday leaned over the young couple's table. They seemed to be having a fight. 'My cat is hungry,' Tuesday said calmly, 'I really need to close now; I can have this wrapped up for you.' He pointed at the leftover lasagne on their plates while a malicious grin spread over his face.

When his brothers had established that in fact their mother was more or less legally incompetent, they asked Tuesday if he would stay and work at the restaurant a little longer. 'That monastery isn't going anywhere,' they said. So Tuesday called his brothers at the cloister to tell him his return had to be postponed a while longer. It was at that time that he started to collect cats.

His brothers treated Tuesday as if he had some disease. But when the neighbours threatened to sue Tuesday, his brothers paid for the best lawyer they could get.

'The family must stick together,' the now-eldest brother said.

'Aren't you an actor?' the young man asked Tuesday. 'You look so familiar.'

'No,' Tuesday answered. 'I'm a monk.' He handed them a plastic bag with what was left of their lasagne.

In 1986, Tuesday's younger brother had been accused of assaulting an under-age girl. The whole family got together and rounded up the money to hire the best lawyers available. They had all taken time off to be present at the trial. In their Sunday best, they sat in the front of the public gallery, waving at their brother and giving him the thumbs-up. One hour before the verdict was to be read, Tuesday had gotten up and said, 'Excuse me, I have to feed my cat.' The next day, a picture of this scene had appeared in the newspaper. The caption read, 'The tension of the trial becomes unbearable for one of the brothers.'

Tuesday had written a letter to the newspaper saying it was not the tension of the trial that had forced him to leave, but his cat almost starving to death. Nobody had ever answered his letter.

Tuesday turned off the lights. Only the sign saying LUNA was still lit up.

His mother lived in a retirement home, but in her mind, there was no difference between the retirement home and the restaurant. So she kept preparing large quantities of pasta in her tiny kitchen, much to the dismay of the nursing staff.

When Tuesday got home that night, there was a message from one of his brothers on the answering machine. Halfway through the message, he turned the machine off. He took his cat onto his lap, and began to sing a hymn.

Left Shoe

During the summer of 1995 I took an eight-week intensive course at the New York Film Academy. You were supposed to learn all about making films there: from writing a film script to operating a camera, and from directing actors to creating special effects with lighting and make-up.

I

On the night of Friday, June 16th, I lost my left shoe somewhere near Mulberry and Grand Streets. Or else it happened in a taxi. I made the discovery the following afternoon when I tried to put on my shoes. It was the Italian pair I'd just had re-soled – the ones I'd bought in Venice. A Moroccan shoemaker had charged me a special price because his wife had just had a baby.

I went back to Mulberry Street that same day. First to the Café Roma, where I went for iced cappuccinos; it was the place I'd been the night before. I thought it was polite to order a coffee first, and not to blurt out that I'd lost a shoe. When I settled the check, I said to the waitress: 'Can I ask you something? I think I lost my left shoe here last night... maybe you found it?' She was silent, so I said, 'While cleaning up?' She looked at my feet. They were both covered.

'No,' I said, 'these are different shoes.' Fortunately, I had thought to bring along my right shoe. 'It was a shoe like this – but the left one.'

She turned around and went into the kitchen. Apparently

she didn't communicate my message correctly, because her mother, the boss, came over and asked, 'Is something wrong? Have you got a complaint?'

'Not at all.' I explained again why I'd come, at which point she showed me a box of everything that anyone had ever left behind. I sifted through a few bracelets, a watch, some wallets; somebody had even left his electric toothbrush at Café Roma. But there wasn't a left shoe in the box.

I thanked them for the help. But as soon as I left the place, I noticed the boss eyeing my feet suspiciously.

The café next-door had just opened. I sat down at the bar and ordered a beer. The night before, I'd met an Italian priest there. We'd started talking and didn't part company until six hours later. His name was Brother Louis and he told me the Pope was coming to New York soon – he'd be holding an open-air service in Central Park. The Mass was actually only meant for Catholics, but Brother Louis didn't mind making an exception for me. He asked for my address so he could mail me the tickets. I could hardly imagine Brother Louis taking off with my left shoe.

'I was here last night,' I told the bartender. I leaned in close and whispered, 'I lost my left shoe here.'

He took a step back after hearing this information; it might have been my breath.

'Are you sure it happened here?' he asked. 'And just your left shoe?'

I nodded. He bent over the bar to have a look at my feet, and for the second time that day I explained, 'These are different shoes.' I took the mate out of a plastic bag and placed it on the bar.

He examined it. 'That's a nice specimen.'

'Italian,' I whispered.

He took off his glasses and said softly, 'I was at a wedding once where we drank champagne out of the bride's shoes. Are you sure somethin' like that didn't happen to you last night?'

I couldn't say for sure that Brother Louis and I hadn't drunk beer from my left shoe, but it seemed unlikely to me. 'I don't think so.' Just to make sure, I did ask whether it was customary among Italian priests to drink from each other's shoes to, y'know, celebrate brotherhood or something.

The bartender whispered in my ear, 'I'm Italian, but whatever Italian priests do, I don't wanna know about.'

He put a drink in front of me. 'On the house.'

'Did you take off anything at all?' he asked. The case had apparently captured his interest.

'I don't remember. I did dance. When the cross-eyed harmonica player came in.'

'Frederico. You better watch out for Frederico – he'll steal your wife right out from underneath you.'

I hadn't brought any women. 'How about shoes?' I said.

He shook his head.

'I'd give up if I were you,' he said, 'you're never gonna find it.'

'I bought them in Venice,' I explained, 'That shoe has sentimental value for me.'

'You don't need shoes for that,' he told me.

'I do,' I insisted. Then I took a look around anyway – under the table we'd been sitting at, in the bathroom. But everything had been cleaned up.

'He's looking for his shoe,' I heard the bartender say.

'Does the name Brother Louis mean anything to you?' I said weakly.

'Nothing. I only remember faces, no names.'

A guy who'd been watching a baseball game on TV the whole time said, 'Every time I find a single shoe in the street, I figure there's been a murder. Now I know how they really get there.'

'Right,' I said, 'Now you know – another mystery solved.'

'Remember,' the bartender called after me, 'to drink

champagne from the bride's shoe. It's good luck.'

I walked up and down Mulberry Street a couple of times. Finally, I pulled out the other shoe and put it next to a lamp post, hoping that whoever had my left shoe would somehow find the right one.

II

There are sixteen of us: fourteen men and two women. Khaled claims he's related to the King of Jordan; John is from upstate New York and said he wanted to get rich making porn flicks. He gets paged all the time. He also falls asleep during almost every lesson. He burps, loudly and frequently, but he says he can't help it. And then there's Bruce, a model from Miami. Bruce looks like Superman. When he comes over to talk to me he doesn't sit down on the chair next to me, but squats down on the ground to lower himself to eye level. Some people say his shoulders are as wide as my legs are long. The only thing that doesn't quite match is Bruce's voice: it's the voice of a mouse. I guess that's the main reason he never tried to become an actor. He's been a model for twelve years and has worked for every major magazine in the world. He's lived in Florida, Paris, and Italy, but now he's had enough. He wants to make movies and that's the reason he's here. Bruce claims he has a girlfriend, but rumour has it that he's more interested in tiny, scrawny guys like me. When Bruce and I walk down the street, people stare at us. We also attract attention when we go to restaurants. Last Thursday, Bruce said, 'We're not a comedy team; we can't help the way we look.' His mousy voice really did it: even the waiter doubled over laughing. He later apologised profusely.

I shouldn't forget to mention Steve Friedman. He's eighteen and from Manhattan. He's bald all over, except for a tiny moustache. He wears a red rain jacket and carries a rucksack – he never takes off either of these. Steve always sits towards the side of the room. Sometimes the teacher says,

'You can't see from there.' Then Steve tilts his head a little and waves his hand in a friendly gesture as if to say, 'Take it easy.' No one has ever heard him say more than fifteen words at a time. And that was on the first day, when everyone had to get up and introduce themselves and when Steve had said, 'My name is Steve Friedman and I want to make movies.' But last Thursday he managed to astonish everyone by answering a question that no one else knew the answer to. Steve remained himself and simply stared ahead.

'How can that be?' we asked.

'Just watch,' he said. In a short movie, Steve played the role of a man who puts out steaks on his balcony because he likes sun-dried meat. I was surprised to see how convincing Steve was in his role. For ninety seconds, Steve was transformed into a mildly dangerous fool who's obsessed with sun-dried meat.

I don't have much to say about Karin from Berlin. Maybe just that I wish her an imminent demise. And that's not because she's German.

Pablo Berger, one of our teachers at this film academy, won a prize at the Oberhausen film festival.

Heng-Tatt Lim, another teacher, speaks so softly that you almost have to crawl into his lap to hear him. He always looks as if he's about to attack the whole world, as if it's costing all his energy not to. He's our best teacher. He said, 'I once asked Scorsese, "What is it that you know, that I don't know?" Meaning, Why do all of my films fail? Scorsese thought that was a good question, because most people approached him to find out how to become famous.'

It was on the day the papers had called the hottest day of the summer that we had to shoot our first movie. My crew had three Mexicans in it, plus myself. The oldest of them is half-Lebanese and used to import French clothing.

Even though my idea was quite brilliant, it didn't turn out the way it was supposed to. Perhaps because I hadn't yet mastered the effect of the 10mm lens. When we were done shooting, everyone had sunburn. We went to get some dinner at a French restaurant right near Houston Street. It's one of the best places I know in New York City. I wouldn't mind at all having to live there.

Nearly everyone had left the city. We were the only ones there, except for the owner, who was spritzing her child with water in the street for some refreshment and offered to spritz us as well. We were quick to accept the offer. Completely soaked, we then finished our gazpacho. The waitress, too, took a turn getting spritzed. She was reading a book that opened with the sentence, *I'm young, unhappy, and neurotic.*

I told her, 'Come and move in with me for a week; then you'll find out more about that kind of person than you will from reading a hundred of these books.'

Because the Mexicans had trouble remembering my name, they called me by the task I had when we were shooting the movie. Edgardo put his arm around me and said, 'Cameraman, you completely fucked up my movie, but still, I'm happy.'

Later, on our way home, we noticed that the colour from the seats in the restaurant had stained our wet clothes. At first I tried to scrub it out, but when that proved futile I decided to just leave it like that. There are certain things in life you should commemorate. With tombstones, Italian shoes, or white jeans that have changed colour in a French restaurant.

III

The only person waiting for us in the parking lot at Coney Island was a Black lady who had bared her highly-pregnant belly. She was dancing to music playing on a car radio. It was six in the morning, and it wasn't until we got out of our rental car – which was really too small for seven people – that we noticed two men either sleeping at the Black woman's feet, or dying there. At the hottest time of day, Coney Island smells of hot dogs, urine, and sweet perfume, but early in the morning you can still smell the sea.

We saw the scorched rollercoaster that no one had bothered either to burn down to the ground for good or to rebuild – the result was a botanical garden for wild flowers.

'Watch car?' the highly-pregnant lady asked. I couldn't keep my eyes from wandering down to her belly. It was as big as a bomb. I gave her fifteen dollars: there were more car thieves on Coney Island than hotdog vendors. One of the men at her feet was lying in his own urine. It would dry up as soon as the sun was a little stronger. Everything here dried up.

There will no doubt be many more hot days and hot months and maybe even hot years, but I wonder if any of them will ever feel as hot as the two days we spent at Coney Island, trying to shoot a movie about a man who'd lost his left shoe. We dragged through the dirty sand, schlepping the camera, the tripod, the reels of film and all the other crap with us. Saadi, Mejia, and Garcia, our cameraman, assistant cameraman, and light man respectively, walked in front, followed by me and the actors carrying cups of coffee that spilled over.

Under the boardwalk where we were shooting, an entire family had taken up residence – grandparents, grandchildren, uncles and aunts. They were rather annoyed by a whole camera crew marching into what they considered their bedroom at six in the morning.

It was our second day of filming on Coney Island, and the Mexicans that I had to put up with for the eight weeks of film academy classes hated each other. They hated each other in Spanish, so I had no idea why they hated each other. Each one in turn did occasionally go to the trouble of explaining to me in English that the other two were corrupt Mexican rats. 'It's not all that bad,' is all I could think of to say. Garcia was the younger one of the threesome and he seemed to generate a lot of interest from men. As soon as the beach filled up, all kinds of men came up to him and offered him hotdogs; some of them even wanted to bring him home with them in return for some money. He was sixteen, and because he didn't have a toothbrush he used a washcloth to brush his teeth. All three of them had come to this city because they wanted to make movies. They were hoping to become great filmmakers who would end up in Hollywood – and if not in Hollywood, then at least at the Academy Awards. This is what they had in common with a dozen or so others who had come to this city. Or who happened to be living here already but who now had given up their jobs and had taken all of their money to the film school where the director always sported a five-day-old beard.

I, too, had adopted the idea that I wanted to make movies. To be more precise: I wanted to make a movie about a shampoo salesman who is taking a nap on a bench in Coney Island. When he wakes up he discovers that he's missing his left shoe. He needs to go to a meeting with his boss, but he'd rather die than walk into that meeting with only one shoe. So he starts searching for his left shoe, but there's no trace of it. Eventually, he tries to buy a new left shoe, but people think the man is crazy because he's walking around in only one shoe, and when he insists on buying only a left shoe, they knock him down. A lady even has a go at him with her parasol. By the end of the day he no longer looks like a shampoo salesman, but more like one of the bums who inhabit Coney Island during the summer. He finally decides to give up his right shoe as well, and hurls it into the sea.

'What is it with you and your left shoe?' one of the teachers who read the script asked me.

'It's just something that happened to me,' I said. 'So I know what I'm talking about.'

'Did you lose that left shoe in a brothel or something?' another teacher asked, trying to be clever.

'No,' I said. 'I never lost anything in a brothel.'

My original idea was to play the part of the shampoo salesman myself, but that turned out to be somewhat difficult. Eventually I found a friend who was willing to do it. He's a philosopher, and he sacrificed the only good suit he owned to the film. I'll be grateful to him for the rest of my life.

We were all standing in the water. Because the shampoo salesman thinks he saw his shoe floating in the sea. We were standing there, getting scorched by the sun while some children who were trying to catch crabs with chicken wings stared at us as if we were wild animals at the zoo. Everyone was waiting for my instructions, but I was thinking that I'd never seen anyone fishing with chicken wings and an old paper basket. I was trying to remember what had possessed me to think that I had to make a movie about a shampoo salesman who'd lost his left shoe. It's like waking up in the morning with all your clothes on and trying to remember where you spent the night before. And whose perfume you're smelling, and when you feel your inside pocket, you try to remember who stole your passport.

During the third take of the shampoo salesman running into the ocean to find his shoe, we heard a strange rattle coming from inside the camera; it was followed by a plopping sound, and then silence.

'Stop,' I called to the actor. 'You can get out of the water. The camera's given out.' He was too far out in the ocean to hear me.

Saadia and Mejia drove back into the city to have the camera fixed. I stayed behind with Garcia and the actor. We took off our wet clothes and put them out to dry on the tripod and lay down in the sand under the pier. Right next to the family from Puerto Rico – as we had by then discovered.

I looked at Garcia, who was lying next to me with his eyes closed. He told us that his father was a homeless good-for-nothing, but that his mother was the most beautiful woman that he knew, and that she was about my age. I told him that implied she must have been about eight when he was born, but he told me strange things happened in Mexico.

I saw his brown teeth and tried to imagine what he would look like when, someday, those teeth were gone. Would he have his mouth filled with silver or gold, or nothing at all? I saw his brown skin and his pimples and the hairs on his cheek. I thought he'd be great playing a homeless person. I still needed a homeless person. And the homeless people of Coney Island were too homeless to do anything at all.

When the film was eventually shown, everyone congratulated me on the casting of the homeless person. They congratulated me on many other things as well, but this was the kind of party where everyone congratulated everyone – regardless of what you'd made or done. They were still busy congratulating all over the place when they no longer knew where they were, and some people started clapping their hands and demanding that they speak to Robert de Niro, that it was urgent, and that someone had to put them through to Robert de Niro immediately.

People often ask me: 'What's your best experience in New York?' I think the best thing was those five hours we spent lying under the pier waiting, drinking lukewarm Coke and eating half-decayed hotdogs. The moment I secretly thought I was doing something that hadn't been done since Chaplin or the Marx Brothers. The shots we did in the ocean were great – they took about eight hours or so. I had to throw all of those out in the end because they didn't really contribute anything to the movie. One of the best moments was me lying there trying to imagine Garcia brushing his teeth with a washcloth. But it remained unimaginable, and eventually I decided that it must be one of his principles to not brush his teeth at all.

The absolute best moment was when Garcia asked me

to take him out to a strip club – he promised to wash his clothes for the occasion. I found out later what he meant by 'washing': he put the clothes out on his balcony, in the sun, to dry.

'The sun washes too,' he said.

I did take him out to the strip club, on the opening night of our movies. I lost track of him after about two hours. We had been standing at the bar, talking pinball, and when I came back from the bathroom there was no sign of him. I did make a brief attempt to find him, but in vain. Perhaps he'd gone off with some girl, or maybe someone had taken him along.

I was thinking of the movie about the shampoo salesman in search of his left shoe. It hadn't really turned out like something that hadn't been done since the Marx Brothers. But then, you can't survive without some blind spots. The good thing is that, every now and then, a shot of reality makes it past those blind spots. Only those who steal your passport from your inside pocket can't afford this kind of luxury. They embrace you gently and simply lift your passport from your inside pocket. It's still a complete mystery to me how they manage this trick with a left shoe, though. As far as I'm concerned, it should be called an art.

A man who had read my stories once wrote to me, 'I'm always interested in knowing the motive for the crime.' I wrote back, 'There is no crime, and there is no motive.' No, there's no time for self-pity here. You just avoid certain neighbourhoods; stay out of certain bars; ignore certain people. Everyone knows that. So there's no point shouting, 'Stop thief' when your passport or your left shoe is stolen. God gives and God takes away.

Only when you wake up in the morning with your clothes still on do you ask yourself, 'What was I doing there? What in God's name was I doing there?'

And then later, in the bathroom, you suddenly remember you were singing into Brother Louis' ear, 'If that's all there is my friend, then let's keep dancing'.

Slapped

'My father's a private detective,' a girl at the optician's office said. I was holding my broken glasses and said that I thought this was an interesting profession. I realised that even without my glasses I could see she had large breasts. The optician wore a white coat; when it was finally my turn I showed him my broken glasses. He slowly shook his head.

'These can't be fixed anymore,' he said.

'The person who recommended you said you were excellent at repairs,' I tried.

The optician smacked his lips. 'You're lucky the lenses weren't damaged. Did you fall?'

'Something like that.'

I hadn't fallen. I had been slapped across the face. A good friend of mine had slapped me across the face. That's nothing to be ashamed of. It is my opinion that, among good friends, an occasional slap across the face is acceptable. But this was the first time I had been slapped with such disastrous consequences. My glasses had ended up hitting the wall with great velocity. To be fair, I should mention that my glasses were still alive even then. Only one of the arms was completely bent. And when I tried to bend it back, my glasses snapped. That was at four in the morning. I panicked, more so than necessary when breaking your glasses. Usually, there's no particular cause for panic: it's always been a mystery to me why so many people spend such a large part of their lives in a panic.

'What am I gonna do without my glasses?' I cried over

and over again. This was strictly rhetorical, because there was no sensible answer to this question. Initially, we tried to fix the glasses with tape and plasters. When that didn't work, I started running around the house from the front door to the window, not forgetting the bathroom of course. Eventually, I ended up banging on the walls, causing some ruckus at the neighbour's. All along, I kept crying, 'What am I gonna do without my glasses?'

Before going to bed, I also smashed a bottle of rum in the kitchen.

'Now I'll have to find you a frame exactly like this one, otherwise the lenses will be of no further use to you,' the optician said.

He disappeared in the back with my glasses. The girl whose father was a private detective said she had switched to contact lenses because her glasses kept breaking as well.

That morning, on the subway, I had held the left part of my glasses in front of my eye so I could tell what stop we were at. Nobody paid any attention to me, although the seat next to me remained empty.

On my way to the optician, while I was holding up my half pair of glasses and walking along a crowded Park Avenue, someone at the traffic light asked me if I had had a rough night.

'I've seen rougher nights than this,' I answered.

At that moment, I considered myself lucky for living in New York, and not in Amsterdam, where I might have run into people I know who would have asked me why I was walking around town with a half-pair of glasses. Jacques Prévert, the French poet, wrote a film script in which a man says, 'I don't wear a hat. Not because I want to be fashionable, but because I don't have a hat.' But no one believes him.

'You'll need a new frame,' the optician said. 'So we can't use these lenses anymore either.'

'How long will it take?' I asked.

'Three days, maximum,' the optician said.

'That's impossible, I can't see a thing.'

'We need to order the lenses,' he said. He asked for my prescription and went into the back to make a phone call.

'Offer him money,' the girl said.

I looked at her. She was a little shorter than I.

'Offer him money,' she said once more, 'then he'll do it in a day.'

I hesitated. Then I whispered in her ear, 'How much?'

'Twenty dollars,' she said, 'at least.'

I continued looking at the frames, but my left hand was already grasping a twenty-dollar bill in my pocket.

'Three working days,' the optician said, 'if you choose the frame today.'

I took the twenty dollars and put it on the counter. I whispered, 'Could you do it in one day?'

I had a feeling everyone in the store was watching me. But nothing happened. I couldn't tell whether the optician was looking at me or at the money. All I know is that he didn't say a word.

So I put down another twenty-dollar bill, pushed it across the counter, and said, 'You think they could be ready by tonight?'

Another silence fell. I wondered if it still wasn't enough. Then the optician pushed the bills back in my direction. 'I think you've misunderstood,' he said. 'It takes three working days before I can have your lenses.' I put the twenty-dollar bills back into my pocket.

'I didn't say a word,' I said in a rather husky voice.

'It's not so bad,' the optician said. He yanked open a drawer from a chest and said, 'Let's see if we can find you a frame then.'

Mopping Up

After hesitating for weeks I finally decided to place the ad: 'Young man seeks cleaner – one day a week.'

Nearly everyone in this neighbourhood has a cleaner, usually three times a week. In the apartment below me, the cleaner even comes every day except Sundays. So why shouldn't I allow myself some help once a week?

I had asked around the neighbourhood if people knew of a reliable cleaner, but most people are very stingy when it comes to sharing their cleaner. They want to keep their cleaners all to themselves. 'Mine isn't available,' they'd say. Or, 'Mine is so old, she's not taking on any new clients.' One woman even said, 'Mine's afraid of men.'

So at last I decided I couldn't go on like this and placed the ad. It appeared in *The New York Times* on Sunday, January 19th.

On Monday, January 20th, forty-three people called – two calls were from Connecticut, three from New Jersey. On Tuesday I only received eighteen calls. But on Wednesday the number increased again to twenty-seven. One call was from South Carolina. It was a woman who didn't mind moving to New York. She thought the offer included full board. I followed a neighbour's advice and met people at a nearby café. Out of the eighty or so responses, I selected twenty people for an interview. My criteria for selecting them were actually rather vague. In fact, the only criterion was whether or not I could understand them at all. There had been quite a few callers I couldn't understand – and who apparently couldn't understand me either.

I had set aside a whole Monday afternoon for the interview sessions. I had drawn up a very strict schedule, allocating ten minutes to each potential cleaner. That way, it could all be done in three hours.

I had arranged for the first one to arrive at two o'clock. By two-fifteen, there was no one yet, but at two twenty-five, six of them showed up all at once. One potential household helper had brought along her whole family, including five children. I treated everybody to lemonade, and coffee or tea for the adults. Tables and chairs were pulled up. It was cosy. Everybody was talking; some potential helpers apparently knew each other from previous interviews and embraced each other like lovers.

'All right,' I called out after ten minutes. 'Could those of you who are planning to work for me sit at the left side of the table, and those who just came along for the reunion sit at the right side of the table?'

I had to repeat this three more times, but then a small migration started.

At last they had split into two groups.

I started off with a lady who had dyed black hair and a pockmarked face.

'So,' I said. 'We're talking about light domestic work: mopping the floor, cleaning the bathtub, sponging off the window sill. Have you worked as a domestic before?'

'Cashier,' she said.

'That's all right,' I said. 'Anyone can mop a floor. On what days are you available?'

'I'm not a thief,' she said.

'No, no,' I said, 'of course not. But on what days are you available?'

'Pedro,' she called. A tiny man at the right side of the table got up from the crowd and moved over to the pock-faced woman.

They spoke to each other, and then the man said, 'The

afternoon is good for us.'

'What afternoon?'

'Any afternoon,' the man said.

I took down their number and said I could pay ten dollars an hour.

'Should I bring cleaning supplies?'

'No,' I said. 'I have everything.'

After three conversations like that I gave up. All I did now was take down their phone numbers.

At four o'clock, I paid the bill and sent everyone home.

The next day, I picked a random number from my list and made an appointment. And so a lady appeared at my apartment at eleven o'clock on Monday.

She was in her late sixties and extremely rotund. She puffed with every move she made.

I made her some tea and when she had finished drinking it, I suggested she start by mopping the floor.

She looked around.

I handed her a mop and cleaner.

'Don't you work?' she asked.

'I work from home,' I explained.

'I see.' She seemed a little suspicious of this.

After she had mopped a square metre her face turned totally red. She sank into a chair and said, 'Time for a cigarette.'

Sweat was dripping down her forehead. It wasn't all that hot, but given her proportions, I could understand.

When she had mopped half of the room in an hour and a half, I couldn't take it any more. Besides, she was huffing like an old horse. Maybe she had a heart condition. She might have a heart attack in the middle of mopping my floor; I'd have to go through life branded a slave-driver.

'That'll be enough for today,' I said.

It was obviously torturous for both of us, and I thought it was enough torture for one day.

'Am I not good enough?'

'Very good,' I said, 'but it's enough for today.' I handed her the money and wished her a healthy and happy life.

Pliers

I was invited to tea by a Dutch couple who'd been living in New York for some time. For various reasons, I couldn't refuse the invitation.

They lived in a luxurious apartment on the Upper East Side; an elevator man took me all the way up to their front door.

In addition to the couple, there was the daughter; a retired diplomat; a gallery owner; and a gentleman who claimed to have been a colonel in the army. I did my very best not to offend anybody, although it was clear to me that these were the kind of people who were easily offended.

Soon after we'd been served tuna sandwiches, I felt an urgent need to use the bathroom. The hostess accompanied me there; she even switched on the light for me before whispering, 'You do realise how much we can do for you?'

When, after ten minutes, I started feeling a little better, it was clear that merely flushing wasn't gonna do it. I'd have to clean the toilet, at least if I didn't want to offend anyone. And that's exactly how I wanted it.

The bathroom was very well-equipped: I saw a blow-dryer, a few lipsticks, an old-fashioned razor – but I didn't see a toilet brush. I only found it after another five minutes. It was a toilet brush shaped like a palm tree. I started scrubbing the toilet with the toilet brush disguised as a palm tree like I'd never scrubbed a toilet before. I must have been scrubbing pretty enthusiastically, because the toilet brush broke halfway through. All I had left in my hand was the trunk of the palm tree. The brush itself was stuck deep inside the toilet, where the toilet connects to the drain. I used the palm tree to push against the brush, but that only made the brush disappear even further down the drain.

I realised I couldn't leave the bathroom like that; I had to fix the palm tree. I paced up and down a couple of times, saying to myself, 'Don't panic, don't panic.' Then it occurred to me to try flushing again. Maybe the force of the water would make the brush pop out.

I flushed the toilet, but the brush didn't pop out. In fact, the brush was now blocking the drain, so rather than going down, the water bubbled up instead. It filled the whole toilet, then gradually started to spill over the sides, onto the marble. It wasn't clean water; I could see the remains of my excrement floating in it.

I cursed myself and thought, You don't deserve to live. But then I thought, How can people buy toilet brushes that look like palm trees? I spotted the host's razor and it made me wonder why you always read about people committing suicide on account of love or because they're in debt, and why nobody in literature has ever killed himself over a toilet brush.

Suddenly, someone knocked at the door. 'Are you all right?' the hostess asked.

'Yes,' I answered. 'It's just starting to loosen up.' I realised I had no choice. I put my hand down the toilet; more water and filth trickled over the rim, and I yanked on the brush with every ounce of strength I had in me. But no matter how hard I pulled, the brush was as stuck as a rock. Besides, the brush was pretty slippery, so it kept sliding out of my hand.

My clothes were messed up, but I hardly noticed. I needed pliers, only pliers could save me. I searched the entire bathroom, but of course there were no pliers to be found there. Finally I opened the door. The bathroom was right next to the living room. I stuck out my head only. Everybody was watching me. 'I need pliers,' I said softly. 'Does anyone happen to have a pair of pliers?' For a few seconds it was quiet, so I added, 'It's urgent.'

They all started whispering to each other, but nobody produced a pair of pliers. I could hear the colonel whispering, 'I'm not at all surprised, having read his book.' Then I got it: they thought I was planning to masturbate with a pair of pliers.

'I have to fix something,' I shouted. At last the whispering died down and the hostess handed me a pair of pliers. She kept her distance and had a wild look in her eyes.

As soon as I had the pliers, I locked myself up again. Even with the pliers, I couldn't get a grip on the brush. All I managed to do was to push the brush deeper down the drain. When it was finally all the way in, the water level started to sink. It must have taken ten minutes for all the water to drain. I cleaned everything as well as I could with toilet paper. Since I didn't feel it was safe to flush the toilet again, I hid the dirty toilet paper in the back of a closet.

I sweetly thanked the hostess for the pliers and went back to my seat. All of a sudden, the gallery owner next to me gave a little shriek. I was right in the middle of putting a piece of sandwich in my mouth. She pointed to my sleeve. When I looked, I saw a little piece of shit sticking to my sleeve. 'It was an accident,' I explained, but nobody was listening. They opened the windows, and didn't offer me anything else to drink. I heard the colonel whisper again, 'I'm not at all surprised, having read his book.'

Five minutes later, I left the house. No one shook my hand. The elevator man was standing by in the hallway, but I left him standing there and went down the emergency stairs instead.

Meeting with the Consul, Pierre P. van der Velden

I

My first meeting with the consul, Pierre P. van der Velden, took place on Valentine's Day in 1995. I had arrived in New York six weeks before. Van der Velden wanted to have lunch with me, on the Queen's tab.

Some assistant of Van der Velden's had left a message on my answering machine one morning: 'I'm calling from the Dutch consulate in New York. We heard your book will be published shortly. Congratulations! My boss, Mr Pierre P. van der Velden, would like to invite you for lunch. Could you call us back?'

I called back the very same day. I asked for van der Velden. He had to think for a moment, but then he remembered. 'Oh yes, of course,' he said. 'Good to talk to you at last. Very nice. I've heard a lot about you.'

I met with van der Velden on the agreed-upon day at the Dutch consulate. There was a reception area with six windows, all in a row. A girl was sitting behind one of those windows. 'I'm here to see Pierre P. van der Velden,' I said.

'What's your name?'

I told her my name as loudly and clearly as I could.

'Why don't you sit down for a moment,' the girl said. 'Mr van der Velden will be with you in a moment.'

I sat down on a wooden bench and spent the next few

minutes examining the Dutch flag and a poster advertising Madurodam. Then the consul appeared. At least I assumed the man who appeared was van der Velden, the consul. He had put on his coat, as if he had just gotten up from his desk and run off.

'Those phone calls,' he cried. 'Those rotten phone calls.'

He then shook my hand. 'Pierre P. van der Velden,' he said. 'But please call me Pierre.'

We went outside to a nearby restaurant.

Van der Velden confessed that he hadn't read my book yet. In fact, so he said, he hadn't even heard of the book until four days earlier. But he would definitely read it.

'Do you think they'll have it at Book-of-the-Month club?' he asked.

'Yes, I'm sure,' I said.

'Great, because I'm a member. You can really save some money on those books.'

'I don't mind giving you a copy.'

'No, no,' van der Velden said. 'I really want you to get your royalties.' By then we had arrived at the restaurant.

'Van der Velden,' the consul said to the lady. 'I have a reservation for two.'

She showed us to the wardrobe where we could hand in our coats. When I put my coat on top of Pierre's coat, he seemed startled, as if my coat would create some permanent stain.

We were taken to a table by the window. The restaurant was rather fancy and was full of couples because of Valentine's Day.

'Oh, just look at all these lovebirds,' the consul said. 'We sure picked the right day.'

We sat down.

The consul took a pair of glasses from his pocket, glanced at me first, and then at the menu.

'I've been told,' he said after a short pause, 'that your

book is quite juicy.'

'That all depends,' I answered. 'There are juicier books.'

'Right,' the consul said. 'Right.' I wondered if he had even been listening. He said, 'I suggest we order a bottle of mineral water; that always goes well with lunch. I'm not having wine. Neither are you, right?' And as he said this, he closed the wine list.

'With or without bubbles, the water?' the consul inquired.

'Well,' I said, 'personally I like bubbles.'

'Now that is convenient. I also like bubbles very much. Non-carbonated has such a bad aftertaste, don't you think?'

'Really?' I didn't know; I'd never paid any attention.

'Yes, this awkward, solid taste, as if there's lead in it.'

Pierre P. van der Velden now started waving his right arm agitatedly and called, 'Waitress, waitress, a bottle of mineral water with bubbles.'

Then there was a silence; the consul was studying the menu. When he had made his choice, he took off his glasses, stared ahead for a few moments and asked, 'Do you know when your book will be published here?'

'No,' I said. 'It still has to be translated.'

'Right,' the consul said. 'Well, I hope they find somebody good, because some translations really make you wanna cry.' He nodded a few times, looking very serious.

Next, he pulled a business card from his inside pocket and put it on the table in front of me. 'This is me,' he said. I studied the card. It read: PIERRE P. VAN DER VELDEN. CONSUL FOR CULTURAL AFFAIRS.

'Put it in your pocket,' the consul said. 'It has my private number as well. But please, never call me consul. I find that very embarrassing. After all, I'm only human.'

'Of course,' I said. 'Of course.'

Once more, the consul stared straight ahead, a pensive look on his face.

He sat like that for several seconds before his first course was served: a green salad.

The consul sprinkled pepper, salt, and vinegar over his salad and said, 'I've been told that one should really be Jewish to fully appreciate your book; so I guess you're in the right city, then.'

'Yes,' I said, 'Fortunately.'

In silence, we hurried through our salads. He glanced at his watch several times, which gave me the impression that he had another appointment after this one.

When his plate was completely empty – except for a few shreds of lettuce – he pushed it away and resumed the conversation by saying, 'Salad is not really my kind of food.'

'I'm sorry to hear that.'

The consul wouldn't hear of any apologies. 'The Queen is paying, so enjoy.'

Our main course was pasta with tiny pieces of broccoli. For the sake of convenience, I had ordered the same as the consul. This dish didn't seem to appeal to him, either. After a few bites, he put down his fork and leaned towards me. 'Of course we'll organise a presentation for you at the Y on 92nd. That's quite essential, quite essential. Nooteboom did that. And Claus.' He took a big swig, washed the water through his teeth a couple of times, as if it were mouthwash, and then swallowed it. 'Wonderful. His work offers a magnificent world view.'

'Who?' I asked.

'Nooteboom,' the consul said. 'And Aunt Harry is coming over as well, so that'll be quite something.'

I fell silent for a moment, prompting the consul to explain himself further.

'I mean Harry Mulisch. I call him Aunt Harry; it's just a little joke of mine. I love jokes.'

'So do I.'

'Humour makes life bearable,' the consul said, after using the mineral water as mouthwash a second time. 'Mulisch's work is very baroque, but I still find it moving.'

I nodded.

'But,' the consul said, 'it's always nice to have something juicy for a change.'

I couldn't answer because my mouth was full.

'I mean your book,' the consul said, upon which he took out a toothpick. He held the toothpick in his hand for a few seconds, hesitating.

'Don't start playing the fool around here,' he said. 'This city has enough of them already.'

He started working on his front teeth with his toothpick now. I tried to be polite by looking the other way.

II

My contact with the Dutch consul for Cultural Affairs, Mr Pierre P. van der Velden, didn't end with that lunch. I started running into him mainly at consulate receptions that I attended out of mix of curiosity, vanity, and a sense of obligation. After a couple of receptions I found out that vanity could not really be considered a good motive for attending these gatherings. Neither could curiosity – they were all pretty much the same – and my sense of obligation didn't last very long, either.

The last reception I went to was organised for the Dutch Foreign Minister, Mr van Mierlo. They had rented a room somewhere in the United Nations building. Apparently, Consul Pierre P. van der Velden was attending the reception as well, but we must have missed each other. Van der Velden was somewhere in the back, but I never got that far. The minister was standing by the door shaking hands with the arriving and departing guests. I was introduced as 'the young writer'. The minister was a stouter man than the pictures in the newspaper had suggested, and he was sweating heavily. I actually felt sorry for him. Because he couldn't sit down anywhere and was expected to stay by the door, like a doorman. So I was not at all offended by his lack of interest in young writers. I was also introduced to Mr van Mierlo's wife or girlfriend. When she heard I was a young writer, she said, 'God, and you already sound like on old man.'

A journalist once quoted me as saying that I was embittered. I always adjust to my environment. Partly for reasons of safety, partly out of politeness, regardless of whether it's felt sincerely. I don't think it is important to even make that distinction. After all, politeness is politeness.

In the company of journalists I am embittered; in the company of Mr van Mierlo I am an old man. Of course I didn't mention this to his girlfriend. I simply gave her a polite nod. She then started complaining of a headache and insisted on some aspirin. Even though I knew for certain that I had none on me, I started searching all my pockets. I noticed that there were only Dutch guests at the reception. Mr van Mierlo didn't seem to have very many foreign friends in New York.

The minister was still standing by the door, shaking hands with people he didn't know and who he would probably never see again. He was getting visibly warmer. Again, I felt sorry for Mr van Mierlo. Even more so because he, too, seemed to be aware of the idiocy of standing there by the door. Tiny meatballs and toast rounds with caviar were served. I passed on both the meatballs and the caviar. Instead, I opted for a glass of white wine.

'Yes,' the Dutch ambassador said, 'for real food, you have to go to the Arabs around the corner.'

'So I noticed,' I said. I had accidentally walked into the Pakistani party earlier on. I only discovered that I was at the wrong party when it turned out they weren't serving any wine.

Nobody at the Pakistani party asked me what I was doing there. And they didn't have a minister standing by the door to shake hands with the guests. They did have three cooks cutting large chunks of chicken and beef into bite-size pieces.

About eight minutes later – the time it took me to get

hold of, and empty, a glass of white wine – I decided I'd had enough.

I couldn't escape without having to shake hands with the minister again.

'Is the young writer leaving already?' he inquired.

'Yes,' I said. 'Unfortunately.'

'You're not having a good time?'

'It's not that.'

'Oh, I understand,' Mr van Mierlo sighed. 'I find these receptions a horror, too.'

Only at that moment did the full extent of the drama sink in, but I was in no position to help him. 'This reception, too, will come to an end,' was the only thing I managed to utter.

'You can say that,' Mr van Mierlo said. 'I think I'd like to read that book of yours. What's it called?'

I gave him the title of the book.

'I'll buy a copy,' the minister said.

'You could also get it from the library,' I said before our final farewell.

When I was about to turn the corner, I glanced back over my shoulder at the minister: he was still at his post by the door. He waved at me.

In the elevator, on my way to the lobby, I overheard a Dutch woman wearing a hat say, 'This summer is never gonna end, God oh God.'

'Let's be honest,' her friend said, 'those receptions for van den Broek were much more elaborate, weren't they?'

A man, her husband perhaps, added, 'Right, but then he was a Christian-Democrat.'

Fortunately, I don't look very Dutch, so none of them could possibly have any idea that I understood what they were saying.

That was the last reception I ever attended.

As the publication date of *Blue Mondays* drew closer, Mr

Pierre P. van der Velden began visiting me at my home. He usually came around six-thirty and downed four beers, one right after the other. If I had forgotten to buy beer in time for it to chill for the consul, we'd go to a nearby café. He didn't like anything but beer. He was actually even allergic to everything else.

The consul's literary intake went hand in hand with his beer intake. Before emptying his first beer, he'd rave about all kinds of books. After about three beers, his appreciation would decline markedly. After six beers, it turned out that many of the books he'd been raving about a few minutes earlier were books he'd never finished because they were too boring. And once he'd downed nine beers, he no longer had anything good to say about any book, nor about any writer. Hugo Claus was a grumpy old man who insisted on drinking champagne at the expense of the Dutch consulate every time he was in New York. The consul wondered – not entirely unjustifiably – whether Mr Claus shouldn't in fact enjoy his champagne at the expense of the Belgian consulate, given the fact that he was Flemish. Nooteboom was on the phone every day with yet another request, and Mulisch, well, we'd better not even discuss Mulisch. And so we didn't. In short: the Dutch Consul for Cultural Affairs did not wish to be treated like a butler by any Dutch author. And if they did, then he really let them have it, after nine beers. But this treatment was not only reserved for writers.

After nine beers, the consul became more intimate. One night he told me that oral sex was his favourite form of sex. 'You're the only one I could tell this to,' he added. I never asked him why. Another night he told me, 'We had Princess Margriet visiting one day and her driver gave me such an amazing blowjob. I haven't had a blowjob like that since.'

That made me look at Princess Margriet in a very different way; in fact, it made me look at the whole royal family in a very different way.

When my book was published in the US, Mr van der

Velden wanted to make a video. There's not much to say about this video: it never materialised. And neither did the reception that Mr van der Velden had described to me more than once in such vivid terms. I have no regrets about that. I can understand that I'm probably not considered the best ambassador of Dutch culture.

This reminds me of the literary critic of the German paper *Die Zeit*, who wrote that my writing was so American and that I 'really belonged in New York'. Coming from anyone else, I would have considered this a great compliment; a German claiming that I belong in New York and that my writing is so American, however, makes me suspicious.

After the night when the consul told me about Princess Margriet's driver, I saw him one more time. I was doing a reading in the East Village. The consul was there too. He had on a baseball cap. At the end of the reading, he had vanished without a trace.

Kisselgoff

Even before he was twenty-four years old, Kisselgoff had a little story factory going that was doing so well he could easily have provided for eight large families. But apart from an unemployed girlfriend and himself, he had nobody to provide for. So that's why he lived a life that only retired company directors can live – and real-estate barons who withdraw from business at forty-five with their twenty-two-year-old girlfriends. The types that move to San Francisco and buy themselves scooters.

Kisselgoff got up late, bought a newspaper at the supermarket, and when the time came to have lunch, he took a cab to Manhattan. He was a regular at the kind of restaurant where only people who don't have to cover their own expenses eat. Except for Kisselgoff.

Kisselgoff was by no means a remarkable figure. He was skinny, and pale, almost to the extent of being unhealthy. And his eyes, not very large to begin with, looked even smaller through his glasses. In the summer, his nose was turned red by the sun, and in winter, by a series of consecutive colds.

We were eighteen years of age when Kisselgoff moved in next door, in one of those apartments that had gone unoccupied for three years. People with children tend to move out of our neighbourhood; their apartments remain empty. They're too unattractive to the rich, and too expensive for the poor. We fall right in between the two categories. We, that's Tito and Paul Andino. We've done all kinds of things in our lives. Last summer, for instance, we totalled a car. It was

233

not just any car. It was our mother's Toyota. It was her birthday and we had tried to explain to her that normal people don't drive around in a Toyota. She slowly came up to us, dragging the left passenger door along. 'Leave that door,' we called in an attempt to stop her, 'it's evidence.'

But there was no stopping her. Later on, she threw all the presents we had bought her onto the highway and shouted, 'If you ever dare to buy me another thing I'll fling it right back at your head.' We've known her for a long time, but it was clear that the police didn't have to deal with her on a daily basis.

We've wanted to do all kinds of things in our lives. Like totalling more Toyotas. And Tito's been considering marrying his biology teacher for the past five years. This nearly happened and would have, if it hadn't been for the interference of a computer programmer from Miami Beach. Paul put a personal ad in the paper, which only one woman responded to, and, at first, said she wasn't particularly slim and later she turned out to weigh 250 pounds.

A couple of years ago we found out we were writers. We don't exactly know how we found this out. All we know is that we were at a Pizza Hut with an uncle of ours. He wasn't really our uncle; he had been our mother's boyfriend for two months. We called this period 'the black months'. It was our intention not to eat any meat for two months each year, and to give a lot of money to the poor, and to refrain from drinking alcohol. This was only one of many intentions that we never stuck to, and that we never will stick to. Just because we like meat too much, and because we have too little money, and because it doesn't look like any of that will ever change. Besides, has anyone ever heard of people with important thoughts drinking nothing but Coca Cola?

We have very few memories of this uncle. Perhaps nothing more than him warning us about the dangers of toothpicks. He told us that he, too, had a habit of using toothpicks and that this had caused him some six infections.

We often chewed toothpicks in those days. We even went to bed with toothpicks in our mouths. What exactly made us so nervous, we don't know: life, our mother, her boyfriend, or the biology teacher. All we know is that we were nervous. We were always on edge. On one occasion, this uncle opened his mouth to show us his infections. It may very well have taken place at that Pizza Hut. Whether these infections had anything to do with us turning out to be writers, we don't know. All we know is that, in that Pizza Hut, we were able to feel that we were writers. We imagine this is the same feeling the prophets must have experienced when they discovered their power to see into the future.

It started in our mouths. We're quite sure about that. We had just put ten toothpicks into our mouths (five in each mouth) and some mushroom pizza. And then the laughter set in. Our uncle was just staring at us and we couldn't stop anymore. We had never laughed like that before, and everything came out. When we say 'everything', we mean everything. Toothpicks, pizza, even some Coke; and out of Paul's mouth a piece of orange emerged that must have been there for three days or so. Our uncle got up. And we said, 'We are writers.' We felt there could be no doubt whatsoever about us being writers. We got up as well and cried out at the top of our lungs, 'We may look like toothpicks, but we sure are writers.' A Pizza Hut staff member – probably the manager – approached us. But we shouted at him too: 'We are writers.'

'Just go to hell, you bunch of pimple-faces,' the manager cried. Through a remarkable combination of many, many cheeseburgers, lots of French fries, and even more Pizza Hut pizza, tiny infections had developed on our faces which, in our view, were no more than a metaphor of the world, our mother, and God.

How we eventually made our escape from the Pizza Hut, we don't recall. We do recall that, from that moment on, we saw the world through entirely new eyes, the eyes of a

Saul Bellow, the eyes of a Hemingway, the eyes of a Dostoyevski. Those were our eyes.

From that day on, we've gone to bookshops at least three times a week and there we imagine our book being too. What we want to say is this: having our book published means as much to us as meeting Jesus Christ must mean to a true believer. Or something like that. Just for the record, we are Christians, but not true believers.

Once our book is published, there will be many things we won't be doing anymore. That is what we want to say. It will no longer matter that our jackets are all frayed around the cuffs. It will no longer matter that our mother, despite our warning her a hundred times over, washes our pants at too high a temperature, so we will always show a patch of skin when we're walking. Once our book is out, people will no longer notice these things; they will only think, There are the writers Paul and Tito Andino. Imagine us walking on the very same pavement. That could be their final thought before they go into a swoon.

Even our odd-looking noses will no longer matter once our books have made it into the bookshops. We will no longer need to spell out our names; we will no longer have to show our passports in the bar. People in the street will spontaneously offer us cigars and the constant marriage proposals will drive us insane – we'll have to change our phone number every three days. And when we meet with our publisher and leave the premises after five hours, the entire staff will be waving out the windows. Nobody will ever say, 'What is to become of you?' or, 'Isn't it about time you bought yourselves some new trousers?' We shall be dancing with the most interesting ladies at important parties and converse with the mightiest men. Our lives will be called 'tragic' and will be turned into movies, three times. First in America, later in Europe, and finally, in China. We will no longer be insignificant ants.

We don't believe those judges who claim that they had

always wanted to become judges, and we don't believe the salesladies in the womenswear department who claim they had always wanted to be salesladies in the womenswear department. We think that they, too, had really wanted to be writers, because there is but one honourable calling in this world.

For the past two years, we've been trying to write down stories from our lives, but somehow we always ended up in a tangle. So now we've decided to write down everything we know about Kisselgoff. And that isn't very much. We think that we knew too much about our own lives, and that we could simply not decide on what to write down, and what to leave out, and that's why we filled up thousands of sheets of paper without producing even one single page that we would like to have anyone else read.

Perhaps it's a good idea to describe in a few words the things we have been trying to write down in the past couple of years. First, in hefty notebooks, and later on a typewriter we were given by an uncle who had gone insane and was locked up in an institution – this was a real uncle. He thought his drawings were of greater importance than Picasso's. Or at least of equal importance. Since nobody could convince him otherwise, he went to the Museum of Modern Art on a Tuesday morning and put up three of his drawings there. Then security came. 'Who could possibly say that a Picasso is worth more than an Andino?' he apparently said. Then they started kicking him. Our uncle installed boilers. He was very proud of the fact that he had installed over a thousand boilers. Whenever he came over for dinner he'd ask my mother, 'Do you think Picasso ever carried a boiler on his back?' 'Just finish your food,' our mother would say.

They had to kick him for a very long time, but when he finally stopped moving they dragged him outside. Five psychiatrists declared him insane. He now has to spend the rest of his life in an institution. He draws during the day, and at night he writes essays about art, God, and identity. Three

ARNON GRUNBERG

words, so he claims, that all refer to the same thing: nothing. At first, we thought him to be quite harmless, but ever since he bit a nurse's hand, he's spent his time in isolation. Occasionally we receive a letter from him, but our mother tears these up immediately. She's afraid insanity may be contagious.

We'd often skip school to finish the stories we had started the night before. During the summers, we sat in the park, and in winter, we rode the subway for hours on end, and when we now read what we were writing back then, we cannot but conclude that something went wrong somewhere along the way – we still don't know where. Our father died three days after our seventh birthday. Our version of his death has always been that he was a private detective who got killed in a gunfight with some of the most wanted criminals of the time. In reality, our father was an accountant's assistant; he died of a heart attack while reading a comic book during his lunch break. To be honest, all he ever read – apart from his clients' tax returns – were comic books. His heart attack struck him right when the cleaners were on strike, so they didn't find him until three days later. He apparently had tried to get up and unlatch the door, but didn't make it. They eventually found him with his face down in his comic book. We imagine that our father must have thought, 'Just leave that latch on the door,' and that he spent the last few minutes of his life lying on the floor, finishing his comic book. It's very likely he would have lived if the cleaners hadn't been on strike. But then, we always prefer to think of circumstances under which someone shouldn't have died – or maybe should have. Ever since, my mother hasn't gotten along with cleaners. We've tried to explain to her that, even though this is quite understandable, it is also not exactly reasonable. We never succeeded in convincing her. Our mother is a waitress and she still has a habit of spitting on the floor whenever she comes across a cleaner. This has gotten her into serious trouble on various occasions, but that's not the point here.

Three days after Kisselgoff moved in, our mother said, 'Tito, Paul, go over to the new neighbour and invite him over to dinner tonight.'

We live in an apartment building with corridors that feel like a poorly maintained hospital. It was three paces from our door to Kisselgoff's. So she could easily have gone herself, she could even have phoned him, but this was one of those errands our mother always sends us on. Even though we are adults now, and have needed our daily shave for the past three years.

Kisselgoff invited us in for a beer. Most of the residents in our building are old, and when they invite you in, it's to take out the garbage or to go to the drugstore or read out a letter from a cousin in Australia.

Aside from a few couches and chairs, Kisselgoff's living room was empty. There were some newspapers scattered about, and on the table stood a bottle of rum and a few cans of beer.

'Cheers,' Kisselgoff said. 'If you think it smells in here, you gotta tell me. I haven't brushed my teeth, you see.' He got up and closed the living-room door. 'I'm not alone here, you know. Someone's taking a bath in there.'

'Where are you from?' we asked. We already knew where Kisselgoff was from, but we're not really at our best when it comes to finding brilliant opening lines. Sure, we can always come up with things we could have said. But when we're on the spot, we always stammer and stutter; and things get even worse when people claim they can't understand what we're saying.

'I'm from Holland,' Kisselgoff said. 'From Amsterdam.'

Some strands of hair hung over his glasses, and he brushed them aside in a quick gesture.

'Why did you move here?' we asked.

'These things start off as a joke,' Kisselgoff said. 'And then you start to think about them, and in the end, you actually do them.'

'Do you work here, are you American?'

'No,' said Kisselgoff, 'I'm not American, but I am an honest, hardworking man.'

Then we both got up. We had heard our mother calling, 'Paul, Tito, have you two drowned?' Even though both of us have already gone through three girlfriends – one of whom was forty-two – our mother is still in the habit of calling us inside in a way that makes our blood turn to buttermilk. A few months ago, we came to the conclusion that we will never be able to function as young, healthy Americans as long as our mother opens the window upon spotting us returning from the bus stop and shouts, 'Tito, Paul! Am I making dinner here for the dear God?'

Before leaving Kisselgoff's apartment, we looked around once more, hoping to see who'd emerge from the bathroom. But no one came out.

Back in our own kitchen – we had to help make the soup – we couldn't stop talking about Kisselgoff. That funny little man who talked so fast that he was sometimes difficult to understand. And we said to each other, 'Perhaps Kisselgoff is the sign we've been waiting so long for. Maybe now we'll start writing books that will change the world, and change our lives.'

In terms of our popularity with women, we have nothing to complain about; but we'd be lying if we said there's no room for improvement. And then we're not only thinking of the biology teacher who married some sucker from Miami Beach because she was afraid she'd be left behind. We're also thinking of some twenty other women who clearly were in no position to make an independent choice when it came to men.

Once our book is out, no woman will be beyond our reach. Nothing will be beyond our reach.

One thing we have to hand it to our mother for: she really tried her best that evening. She had cooked skate, and made clam chowder. If there's anything she can do it's make clam chowder.

Kisselgoff came by himself. He apologised and said his girlfriend had an appointment she couldn't cancel. He handed my mother a box of chocolates.

'Godiva,' she exclaimed. 'That's the best chocolate there is.'

Kisselgoff was wearing a jacket which reminded us of the postmen in the fifties. From a distance, he smelled of aftershave, but from close by, of beer, and it looked like he had forgotten to shave some parts of his face.

While we were spooning up our clam chowder, our mother asked, 'Mr Kisselgoff, I hear you came over here for your work. You're a journalist?'

'Sort of, Mrs Andino…'

'Please don't call me Mrs Andino,' our mother interrupted, 'call me Marietta.'

Kisselgoff put down his spoon, wiped his mouth quickly, nearly knocking over his glass of water, and said, 'Marietta, now that's a coincidence. I once was in love with a girl called Mariette. She actually reminds me of you.'

Our mother started to laugh, and there's no reason to hide it: at that moment we thought Kisselgoff was a total creep, and we already regretted our decision to even attend this dinner.

We leaned closer into our plates so as not to see our mother laugh, and we were still bent over our plates when we heard her say, 'You're such a charmer, Mr Kisselgoff, a real charmer. You wouldn't have expected this…'

'From a little, insignificant man like me.'

And again, our mother and Mr Kisselgoff exploded into laughter.

Kisselgoff was laughing so hard that a tiny chunk of fish flew out of his mouth and landed on Tito's plate.

We were actually hoping that this man Kisselgoff would leave our apartment as soon as possible. We liked him a lot less than we'd hoped we would, and the sign we had been waiting so long, well, we'd given up on that, as well, by then.

'You were saying something, Mr Kisselgoff, please go on.'

Again, Kisselgoff wiped his mouth with an abrupt gesture, and this time he indeed managed to knock over his glass of water and spill the contents onto our mother's dress.

We could feel that what we most wanted to do at that moment was to punch Kisselgoff in the jaw to put an end to his visit. But our mother, who usually detests men who mess up her clothes, said with a smile, 'It's all right, Kisselgoff, it's water, it's only water. My husband was clumsy too.'

'The nicest men are clumsy,' Kisselgoff said.

This guy really had no shame whatsoever.

He finished his soup and said, 'This is the best clam chowder I've ever had, Marietta.'

'Before I serve the skate, you must finish your story, Kisselgoff. I know that my boys are dying…'

Now we were drumming our spoons on the table. We drummed our spoons on the table like that a lot. From a historical perspective, it is probably a mother's job to drive her children crazy, but our mother took this a little bit too far.

'Tito and Paul, I mean,' she said.

We stared at our empty plates and thought about the nights we had waited outside the restaurant where my mother was working, and we thought about the dishes we had washed during our summer vacations. We also thought about how we'd never told anyone she was a waitress. There were at least twenty professions that we had attributed to her, but waitress wasn't one of them.

'I don't write about politics or the economy,' Kisselgoff said. 'What I write is more like stories. They ask me to write something for the newspaper every now and then, because I wrote a book.'

Kisselgoff took a swig of water, and said, 'Let's drink to tonight.'

And Marietta Andino lifted her glass, and said, 'To a wonderful evening, Kisselgoff.'

'What kind of book did you write?' we asked.

'A novel,' Kisselgoff said. '*To the Oil Rig*, that's the title. It's about to be published in America as well.'

Kisselgoff rubbed his Adam's apple with his right hand; we didn't need to speak in order for us to know that we were thinking the same thoughts. How could a character like Kisselgoff possibly write a book? How could somebody who claims that all nice men are clumsy even be capable of producing two well-written sentences? We could only hope that Marietta Andino would keep her mouth shut about our notebooks, keep her mouth shut about all our notebooks in the name of everything that was sacred to us – and there wasn't all that much left that was sacred to us.

But our mother merely said, '*To the Oil Rig*, that's an interesting title.'

'What is your book about, Kisselgoff?' we asked, and we tried to stare him down with all the contempt we could squeeze through our eyes, until they started to tear, and we were forced to stare at our plates again instead.

'It's about life,' Kisselgoff said. 'It's always hard to explain what a book is about. But yes, I think I could say that my book is about life.'

He laughed, and we wondered if this was the shallowest summary of a book we had ever heard.

'And how many copies has it sold?' our mother asked as she was stacking the dishes.

'Seventy thousand,' Kisselgoff answered. 'It was a bestseller.'

'Do you hear that, boys?'

Again, we drummed our spoons on the table, louder than we had ever drummed before.

'I'm sorry, Tito and Paul, did you hear that? A bestseller. We must drink to that.'

She disappeared into the kitchen and returned with a

bottle of wine. We knew that bottle of wine had cost as much as she could earn in an hour, and we cursed life in general, and several people in particular, computer programmers from Miami Beach and a best-selling writer from the Netherlands among them.

'Enough talk about work,' our mother said, and she opened the bottle of wine. 'Tell us about Holland, Kisselgoff, tell us a good story.'

'There is a lot to tell about Holland,' Kisselgoff said, 'but you know what's funny? You remind me so much of Mariette. That girl, remember. She was a waitress…'

Our mother nearly dropped the bottle of wine. She threw her arms up in the air and cried out, 'Now that's what I call a coincidence. That's what I call a coincidence. I'm a waitress too.'

We thought we were about to have a heart attack. Frankly we would have much preferred having a heart attack at that moment over everything else that was awaiting us that evening. But there were no heart attacks. There was nothing. Just Kisselgoff's giggles, and our mother's laughter.

'Boys, do your hear that?' Marietta Andino cried. 'My boys…'

We drummed our spoons on the table, and we knew we'd be drumming for the rest of the evening if Kisselgoff didn't leave. Tito's spoon broke and flew in an arc onto the carpet, but we kept on drumming.

'Tito and Paul, that's enough,' Marietta Andino shouted. Her red hair had partly come loose from her ribbon and now draped her face. We – and only we – knew that hair was dyed. We were also the only ones who knew that she had put on a summer dress today, even though it was mid-January and she was probably half-frozen by now. But she said that you could already notice the sun getting stronger and that spring was in the air.

'Tito and Paul. You are not toddlers, so please. What is Kisselgoff to think of this?'

We stopped our drumming. Tito picked up the broken spoon. We took out our cigarettes and lit up.

'They're at a difficult age,' our mother said, but we could no longer hear her. We were smoking. And we casually tried to blow the smoke towards Kisselgoff.

'I'm at a difficult age myself,' Kisselgoff said as he winked at us.

We could hear it, but we didn't want to hear it. We could see it, but we didn't want to see it. We didn't want to submit to a man who goes after waitresses. We know writers shouldn't generalise like that, but we also know that there are no rules when it comes to writing. And we know the kind of men who come in to have lunch all by themselves and then linger at the bar to strike up a conversation with our mother. We know the way these men smile, and we know their entire repertoire of pick-up lines; we know the way they move their heads and the way they slide off bar stools. There are practically no words to describe how we despise these men. How cheap we find their colognes, their gifts, their ignominious retreat, and their cheap response to this retreat. Marietta Andino always smiles at these men; she knows them by name, and every now and then she winks at them, listens to their stories even when she's heard them a hundred times, because we can't get by without tips.

'I won't talk about Mariette again,' Kisselgoff said. 'In fact it's nonsense to compare you to her.'

We had finished our cigarettes. We cut the fish on our plates into little pieces.

'Why do you write for the newspaper, Mr Kisselgoff?' we asked. 'Why don't you write another book?'

'A few weeks after *To the Oil Rig* came out,' Kisselgoff said, 'I received offers to write from about ten different magazines and three newspapers, plus four anthologies. I was having lunch with the arts editor of this newspaper, and dinner with the arts editor of that newspaper. And I thought, God, I'm in demand. Journalists asked for my opinion on

Salman Rushdie, drugs, and capital punishment; a middle-aged woman from Amsterdam-West wrote me fourteen letters insisting that she was going to make me a happy man, for no charge whatsoever.

Some of these offers were very tempting because they looked like they could bring in some money, others because they gave me the opportunity to publish in prestigious magazines, and some because they involved trips abroad. I sometimes feel like a little story factory, literally. But I guess literature is only one pillar of the small-business economy.'

We savoured the words 'small-business economy', 'story factory', and 'pillar'. We ate our fish and we knew that it was only to spare our mother that we didn't let the food that our stomachs had already digested flow back into our mouth in order to spew it out. In our view, that would have been the only decent response to Kisselgoff. We looked at our mother; she was looking at Kisselgoff.

And Kisselgoff said, 'It's remarkable how we want to be respected by people who we ourselves don't respect.'

Intuitively, we understood that Kisselgoff didn't respect anyone in this world. We thought of the great French thinkers of our century whose books we'd read, we thought of the novels by the great Russian writers, and we thought of all those American authors we considered to be our heroes and there was no way we could imagine that Kisselgoff had anything of value to say.

'Do you ever see Mariette?' our mother asked.

'No,' Kisselgoff said, 'never. It's always tempting to imagine how one's life could have turned out, but that's hopeless.'

'Yes,' she said, 'that's hopeless.'

Kisselgoff had his third refill. His lips had turned red from the wine, and his nose was shiny with sweat.

'What was it that attracted you in her?' Marietta Andino asked.

We spotted two stains on her summer dress. This was the

dress that made it hard for people to tell her age, that's why she liked the dress. But we didn't like people who couldn't tell her age. Or ours.

'She worked in a restaurant where I used to have dinner,' Kisselgoff said. 'I actually don't understand why people prepare their own food when the city is teeming with people who prepare food professionally and who are willing to do it for you for a small fee. At this particular restaurant there was a girl who always winked at me when she served me. After having winked at me fourteen times I decided that there was some meaning in her winking. From then on, I went to the restaurant every day for two months. Except for Easter, because they were closed that day. At the end of those two months I knew the menu by heart and her colleagues started giggling as soon as they saw me. One night, I invited her out to lunch; she accepted the invitation with the words: 'Why don't you pop in sometime?' That was exactly the problem: I was already popping into her restaurant every single day. When I still hadn't heard from her after two weeks I called a courier service one Saturday. I only knew her first name and the address of the restaurant and I asked the courier to deliver a short note to her there. She called me that same Saturday and we made a lunch date. I reserved a table at a renowned restaurant near the concert hall, and was waiting for her there on Friday, the second of May in 1992, just as we had agreed. I'll skip the details. Neither I nor the restaurant managed to make even the slightest impression on her. When, at half past three, she said, 'I'd better be going now,' I felt that she had just ended a mutual torture session that had lasted for three hours. Later, I wrote her some eighty letters I can only think about with some embarrassment.'

Marietta Andino clapped her hands and said, 'Surely someone like you suffers no lack of attention from women?'

There was silence, and then Kisselgoff said, 'I have the same thing with women as my father had with his meat: I always feel I'm getting the smallest piece.'

Fortunately it looked like Marietta Andino hadn't understood this, or perhaps she hadn't heard it at all. She merely giggled and whispered, 'You are such a sweet man.'

We suddenly remembered how our history teacher had once said that, from a historical point of view, President Reagan was not inevitable, and we decided that Kisselgoff fell into the same category.

During the time that we spent in parks and in subway stations, and outside the restaurant where our mother works, we often spoke about our intellectual heroes. And we reached the conclusion that the question of whether or not man is free is pointless. We need to investigate what, in a person's life, is inevitable; whatever remains is freedom, or at least appears to be freedom.

When we sat down around the coffee table and ate our raspberry pie, we brought this up with Kisselgoff.

'I'm sorry,' Kisselgoff said, 'I've had a little too much to drink.'

'Do you ever discuss this with your friends?' we pressed.

'Friends,' Kisselgoff said. 'You know, to me meetings with other people are what the drum roll is to the trapeze artist. I put on a show. And sometimes it turns out better than other times. But even the most dedicated audience can't watch the same show over and over again.'

Then he fell asleep on our couch. He woke up after twenty minutes, and our mother said, 'You're a sweet person, Mr Kisselgoff.'

'Opinions vary on that,' Kisselgoff said.

He got up, checked out our book shelves and said, 'I must apologise, I haven't behaved very well; but then, my soul is inhabited by a salesman.'

'Do stay,' Marietta Andino said.

'God, how much you look like Mariette. You'd think the gods are sadists. Or maybe I'm just a masochist. I once had my palm read by a man who claimed I was super-intelligent,

248

and a neurotic masochist. In short, the perfect son-in-law.'

'Your words are like golden leaves,' Marietta Andino said.

'Golden leaves? I always thought that was something else. Anyway, people who've known me for some time always tell me that my nonsense no longer has any impact on them.'

'Can I offer you some brandy?'

When we heard the word brandy, all our muscles contracted. We did try to get through to our mother via all kinds of signals like winks, prolonged sneezes, and even fainting, but she didn't seem to notice.

Kisselgoff drank half our bottle of brandy. At three in the morning, he swaggered out of our apartment, indeed a sales representative – in soap and shampoos.

We now believe that in Kisselgoff's life, nothing is inevitable. As long as no one went as far as to threaten his life, it was all a game to him. And there was no one threatening his life. We think he'll never understand Marietta Andino, no matter how long he stares at her, no matter how much he writes about her. He has taken the position of the gods, and that's what makes him a stranger among the people. He doesn't understand that Marietta Andino needs to smile at the men who sit around the bar, and has to listen to their stories, and give them an occasional wink. Sure, she doesn't like doing these things, but she cannot simply decide to stop laughing, listening, and winking. Because we can't get by without the tips. He can stop laughing any moment, he can stop talking to Marietta Andino any moment. Kisselgoff thinks he's a fallen angel, but his downfall has yet to come. If we're around, we'll be there to watch. We'll sit where Kisselgoff always sits. It's the spectator's seat.

There's just one thing we haven't agreed on yet: whether or not it was inevitable for Kisselgoff to sit in the spectator's seat. We discussed this after he'd left, and the next day as well, but we couldn't agree on it. We think there's something inevitable in everybody's life, but we don't know what. And as long as we don't know this, we won't know which opportunities we've had to miss, and which opportunities we decided to miss.

Kisselgoff had kissed Marietta Andino on the mouth. When he left, when he thanked her for dinner. We still have to write this down, for the record. She denies it, but we've seen it. And we also heard how our mother was singing – for the first time in eight years. At two in the morning, for Kisselgoff who was just starting his sixth brandy. There are two things she excels at: singing and making clam chowder.

'Take Kisselgoff to his apartment,' she had told us. Because Kisselgoff was just about to break down the door of our other neighbour, Mrs Yuet Fong. We held Kisselgoff's arms, looked through his pockets to find his keys, and finally managed to open the door to his apartment. We then released him, gently, into a black leather chair. 'Stay a while,' he said. 'There's more beer and early in the morning is when I start to get really witty.' At that moment, a woman in a green nightgown walked into the room. 'Kisselgoff,' she said, 'are you putting on your sales-rep show again? Did you find a new audience?' They continued in a language we couldn't understand, and because nobody was paying any attention to us, we left, without turning back and without saying goodbye.

Naturally, we warned our mother about Kisselgoff. But she brushed aside our warnings, laughing and saying that we understood even less about men than we did about women, but that the day when we'd understand all about them would come sooner than we could hope for. To this she added that Kisselgoff was a sensitive person. All we could do was shake our heads. After all, what could we expect from someone who had voted for George Bush and who was in favour of capital punishment?

A few weeks later, a Dutch guy in our class read us a clipping from a Dutch newspaper. It was written by Kisselgoff.

It was about a family called Pempino. It wasn't so hard to recognise the Andinos in this. We never showed it to our mother. Despite the fact that we still feel compelled to drum our spoons on the table night after night, we don't want her to find out that a character like Kisselgoff is trying to disgrace her.

So now we've said everything about Kisselgoff that we wanted to say. Now we can return to our own stories that are awaiting us in hefty notebooks in plastic bags in our bedroom, like faithful dogs.

Of course there are other stories to tell about Kisselgoff, but we are the writers and we decide what is true.

We ran into Kisselgoff a few more times – in the street, and in the corridors of our apartment building.

He's invited us to drink a beer with him, and promised us he'd take our mother out to dinner soon. We feel he wants to hear us out about our father. It wasn't enough for him to drag our mother through the mud; he now wants to disgrace our father's memory. But we can disgrace that ourselves.

Marietta Andino said that if our father had read anything in his life other than comic books, he would have been able to get his law degree. Then he wouldn't have had to end up as an assistant accountant. And then he could have worked at a better office where the cleaners didn't go on strike at the drop of a hat, and then he would have still been alive.

We've tried to show her how absurd this line of reasoning is, but we haven't succeeded.

And last week, we swore that we'd rather jump off the roof than start a story factory.

There is no other way. We'll astonish the world. We'll be translated into twenty-three languages and we'll win at least that many awards. Pizza Hut will become a Mecca for every self-respecting writer.

We've read it in our father's comic books; we hear it in the rattling of the subway; we feel it in our bushy eyebrows, which we must trim even more frequently than our nails.

Who are we to ignore the omens?

Afterword

Amuse-Bouche brings together Arnon Grunberg's early stories which, according to the author himself, have either withstood the ravages of time or are curious enough to be considered when studying Grunberg's development as a writer. Most of these early writings cover the period 1991–1996, the time of Grunberg's transition from drama to fiction, and his move from Amsterdam to New York.

Grunberg's first novel, *Blue Mondays*, apparently came out of the blue when it was published in the Netherlands in May 1994. It was hailed by the critics as 'a grotesque comedy, a rarity in Dutch literature.' At last, there was once again an author who could be considered 'the voice of his generation.' *Blue Mondays* was also published abroad. The critic for *The New York Times Book Review* used the term 'gold mine', probably without realising that he had nailed it: this collection will clearly demonstrate that *Blue Mondays* was not merely a fluke.

Back in 1990, Grunberg self-published his poetry collection, *The Machiavellian*, under the imprint Stichting Casimir (The Casimir Foundation). This was followed the next year by *Johanna, The Book*, this time under the imprint Kasimir, in an edition of only 27 numbered copies; the publication's protagonist quickly tried to acquire as many of these as possible. This episode is described in Grunberg's novel *Silent Extras* (1997). With the inclusion of *Johanna, The Book* in this volume, Grunberg's debut in prose is now available for all to read. Kasimir also published *Letter to M*, in a rather optimistic print–run of 200 copies. It was later reprinted as number 13 in the Rothschild & Bach library, published by Jan Ritsema. This made Ritsema – who had earlier been instrumental in launching Grunberg's career as an actor – his first official publisher.

In addition to these early curiosities, *Amuse-Bouche* also contains a series of stories which originated during the writing of *Blue Mondays*, such as *The Accordion* (not published before, but read in part by the author in 1993 for the VPRO radio programme *Music Hall*), and *Ushi and Septembrius*, a fine sketch that was first rejected by the literary magazine *De Tweede Ronde*, and later published by Carbolineum Pers, owned by the Flemish bibliophilic printer Boris Rousseeuw. *De Tweede Ronde* did, however, publish the chapter *Tina* from *Blue Mondays*. For this story Grunberg received the Rabo-Bank Spring Award for Literature, an event that signalled the rise of Arnon Grunberg as a writer. The lesser-known sequel, *Tina II*, is another surprise to be found in this volume.

Grunberg also included a selection from his columns written for the newspaper *NRC Handelsblad*. Most of these had appeared as *Letter from America*. In *Amuse-Bouche*, he combines several of these shorter stories under new titles. Together with several humorous stories that were previously published in magazines like *Man*, and *Hollands Maandblad*, these stories form a wonderful introduction to Grunberg's novels *Blue Mondays*, *Silent Extras*, and *Phantom Pain*.

Frederik van der Kamp

ALSO AVAILABLE FROM COMMA...

The Silence Room

SEAN O'BRIEN

ISBN: 978 1905583171
RRP: £7.95

'Sean O'Brien does for libraries what Ursula Andress did for bikinis. Read and rejoice!' - Val McDermid

Chain-smoking alcoholics, warring academics, gothic stalkers and aspiring writers are just some of the visitors that browse the mysterious library at the heart of Sean O'Brien's fiction debut. Idlers and idolisers alike can be referenced, in body or in text, among the crepuscular alcoves and dim staircases of this seemingly unassuming building. The secret to a family curse, a dog-eared first edition of Stevens' Harmonium, the gruesome fate of a feminist literary theorist - all are available to simply take down from the shelf, as are the catalogue of genres and subject areas that O'Brien himself effortlessly deploys: from gothic horror to English pastoral, Critical Theory to Cold War noir.

'Sean O'Brien, like Graham Greene, creates his own instantly recognisable fictional landscape, where crime, mystery and disillusion lurk by the waters of the Tyne or Humber. His stories glint with black comedy and touches of the macabre and surreal. In O'Brien country you may hear the hoot of a train pulling out of the city, but you'll never be on it, because your place is here in the kingdom of backstreet pubs, tired, desirable girls and drowned men. Nothing is ever as it seems: it is much more frightening than that... First-class stories from one of our finest writers.' - Helen Dunmore

Under the Dam
and other stories

DAVID CONSTANTINE

ISBN 0954828011
RRP: £7.95

'Flawless and unsettling'
Boyd Tonkin, Books of the Year, *The Independent*

'I started reading these stories quietly, and then became obsessed, read them all fast, and started re-reading them again and again. They are gripping tales, but what is startling is the quality of the writing. Every sentence is both unpredictable and exactly what it should be. Reading them is a series of short shocks of (agreeably envious) pleasure.'
- A S Byatt, Book of the Week, *The Guardian*

'A superb collection'- *The Independent*

'This is a haunting collection filled with delicate clarity. Constantine has a sure grasp of the fear and fragility within his characters.'
- A L Kennedy